Dr. S.S. WESLEY
1810~1876

Portrait of a Victorian Musician

PAUL CHAPPELL

With a Foreword by Lionel Dakers

MAYHEW-McCRIMMON

Great Wakering

First published in Great Britain by
MAYHEW-McCRIMMON LTD
10-12 High Street
Great Wakering Essex

Cover design: Neil Summerland

Printed by Mayhew-McCrimmon Ltd.

To commemorate the 250th Anniversary of the Annual Meeting of the Three Choirs of Gloucester, Hereford and Worcester, and the Wesley Society of Great Britain

It is imperative to point to a most timely and convincing vindication of the right of the Wesleys to a prominent place in the history of the nineteenth century. Rarely have their great gifts been so wisely and justly emphasised. Musicians have too long ignored their influence upon the modern renaissance in England, of which they were as undoubtedly as they were unconsciously the forerunners. The genuinely English school, to which they gave the strongest impulse since Purcell, bears upon the face of it the impress of their incentive.

Sir Charles Stanford,
from his *Studies and Memories* (1908)

Contents

Illustrations

Foreword

This book is the first exhaustive biography of S. S. Wesley. As such, it reveals a wealth of interesting information together with not a few sidelights on a remarkably versatile family whose total significance in the Victorian scene is not in any way to be underestimated. The book also contains much incidental detail which was certainly new to me, especially in those parts concerning Exeter.

No one would deny but that Wesley was on numerous occasions a difficult person, but he did live in difficult times. His toughness, resilience and determination contributed in no small measure towards making possible much of what we accept to-day as the norm in cathedral music circles. After all, the situation he knew was a very different proposition from what prevails to-day.

S. S. Wesley was not entirely a child of his time; he was, however, something of a visionary and a prophet. This is constantly reflected in his music and, perhaps even more importantly, in his life and in what he doggedly set out to achieve. I find it interesting to reflect that many of the ideals he gave birth to and wrote of in a hopeful way have in many respects come to fruition, not least, if incidentally, in certain aspects of the work of the Royal School of Church Music.

If one wanted to quote a particularly significant passage from the book, I would readily seize on Wesley's speech at the farewell dinner given in his honour on his leaving Leeds in 1850. This seems to me a particularly significant and characteristic utterance.

We should be grateful to Paul Chappell for revealing so much to us about this more than colourful and many sided Victorian personality. To achieve a biography of this stature must have cost much in research and perseverance, but the result is here for us all to read, to applaud, and to be grateful for.

LIONEL DAKERS

Director of the Royal School
of Church Music and Organist
of Exeter Cathedral (1957-1972)

February, 1977

Acknowledgments

Living in a cathedral community one cannot be unmindful of its past history and music, especially as the contemporary scene has been moulded by them. Some eight years ago, while studying the history of the organists of Hereford Cathedral, I came across that fascinating musician and angler, Samuel Sebastian Wesley, whose centenary was observed last year.

The background material of this biography was used by the B.B.C. in a television documentary, and Chapter V was delivered in a public lecture in Leeds Parish Church by invitation of the Thoresby Society; and the book itself could never have been accomplished without the co-operation of the following librarians: F. C. Morgan, Penelope Morgan, Paul Yeats-Edwards, Peter Gwyn, Audrey Erskine, Suzanne Eward, John Dunhill and Dr Watkins Shaw. Moreover, the generosity of the Deans and Chapters of Hereford, Exeter, Winchester and Gloucester Cathedrals, has made available many unpublished documents and minutes.

And I am equally indebted to the British Library Board, the Secretary of the Associated Board (for the portrait on the back cover), the Royal School of Church Music, the Royal Academy of Music, the National Portrait Gallery in London, the Director of the Royal College of Music, the Council of the Royal College of Organists, the Warden and Fellows of Winchester College, Sir Thomas Armstrong, Sir John Dykes Bower, and the Rev. David Parkes, for allowing the publication of both correspondence and pictures in their possession, and above all, to Mr Michael Dykes Bower for showing where Wesley's grave is.

The following publishers have kindly given permission for their copyright material to be reprinted: Hinrichsen Edition & Peters Edition Limited (London), for extracts from *The Bach Letters to Benjamin Jacobs,* edited by Eliza Wesley (1875), and also *A Few Words on Cathedral Music* by Samuel Sebastian Wesley (1849); Oxford University Press, for extracts from *Walter Parratt, Master of Music* by Sir Donald Tovey and Geoffrey Parratt (1941), *A History of Music in England* by Ernest Walker (3rd edition revised by Sir Jack Westrup, 1952), and Thomas Edward Brown's poem 'The Organist in Heaven' in *The Oxford Book of Victorian Verse,* edited by Arthur Quiller-Couch (1919); and Messrs. P. & G. Wells Limited, for the quotation from Alan Rannie's *The Story of Music at Winchester College (1394-1969).*

Lastly, I must thank Mrs Hilary Coppen for transcribing crabbed handwriting into excellent typescript, and also Mr Lionel Dakers for writing the Foreword.

M.P.C.

SAMUEL WESLEY, Aged 60

From a portrait by John Jackson, R.A. (1766-1837), by permission of the National Portrait Gallery.

CHAPTER ONE

The Prelude

THE WESLEYS were a remarkable family in both Georgian and Victorian times, having made their distinctive contribution to the religious, the military and the musical life of the nation. The names 'Wesley', 'Westley', and 'Wellesley' were derived from Somerset. Nevertheless, the family later divided into two branches: one remained in the West Country and the other migrated to Ireland.

In the seventeenth century, Sir Herbert Wesley, of the Dorset branch, married a daughter of Robert Wesley of Dangan Castle, County Kildare. Their son Bartholomew, a Nonconformist minister and physician, became Rector of the Dorset villages of Catherston and Charmouth, but was deprived of his benefices under the Act of Uniformity in 1662. His wife Ann was the daughter of Sir Henry Colley of Carbery Castle, County Kildare, and a sister of Richard Colley about whom more will be said later. Their son John held the benefice of Winterbourne Whitchurch in Dorset, having been imprisoned several times for the same reason as Bartholomew. He married a daughter of Dr John White, a notable Nonconformist. And it was their son Samuel Wesley (1662-1735), who, for some forty years, was Rector of Epworth in the desolate fens of Lincolnshire. His wife was Susanna Annesley, the daughter of a prominent Nonconformist preacher in London; and their children included John and Charles Wesley, the founder and the poet of the Methodist Movement respectively.

Samuel lived a somewhat chequered life. He quarrelled with his people, who resented his Toryism and High Churchmanship and his persecution of sexual offenders in the ecclesiastical courts. Also he quarrelled with his wife, after she had declared that William of Orange was unlawfully king: 'Sukey, you and I must part, for if we have two kings, we must have two beds!'

In spite of an income of £200 a year, Samuel was unsuccessful at farming his glebe. And he wasted his money on expensive visits to London, where he attended Convocation meetings and frequented the coffee-houses. Although he was imprisoned ostensibly for debt, it was actually because of his violent attacks against Nonconformists. Thus his wife was left to preside over the daily life of an impoverished family with her natural grace and firmness.

THE WELLESLEYS

By the close of the fourteenth century, the Irish branch of the family possessed much property in County Meath. And in Charles I's reign it was confiscated, because of the Wellesleys' waywardness towards Roman Catholicism. Fortunately at the Restoration, on the pretext that he was an innocent Protestant, Gerald Wellesley (or 'Garret Wesley' as he now styled himself) managed to secure the return of the family estates. He married Elizabeth Colley. And since their son, also called Garret Wesley, had no heir, it was agreed in 1722 that his maternal cousin Richard Colley, born about 1690, should be bequeathed the family estates on the condition that he assumed the surname of Wesley. After marrying Elizabeth Sale, he was created the first Baron Mornington.

In 1760 their son Garret Colley Wellesley or Wesley (1735-81) was created the first Earl of Mornington, and four years later he was appointed Professor of Music at Trinity College, Dublin. Afterwards he moved to London, where he conducted concerts, became Chairman of the Governors of the Lock Hospital, and was the first English aristocrat to walk the streets unashamedly carrying a violin case! Of his distinguished sons, the most illustrious was undoubtedly Arthur Wesley (later changed to Wellesley), who became the first Duke of Wellington. Needless to say, the Musical Wesleys were very proud of their Irish 'cousins'.

A RAPTURE OF PRAISE

Methodism began its life as a religious movement within the Evangelical wing of the Church of England. The founder, John Wesley (1703-91) was the great uncle of Samuel Sebastian. And through his enthusiasm and organisation, John laid the foundations of a new way of life for the working masses of industrial England. He covered a quarter of a million miles on horseback, and many drop-outs were won over by his magnetic preaching — thus fulfilling his claim that the whole world was his parish. He also established watchnight services on Saturdays, so that the miners addicted to beer-drinking would be able to spend their leisure in more beneficial activities.

On the one hand he immensely valued the set forms of worship in the Church of England and said: 'There is no liturgy in the world, either in ancient or modern language, which breathes more of a solid, scriptural, rational piety, than the Common Prayer of the Church of England.'[1] And on the other, he wrote this striking defence of Methodist worship in 1757:

> Nor are their solemn addresses to God interrupted either by the formal drawl of a parish clerk, the screaming of boys who brawl out what they neither feel nor understand, or the unseasonable and unmeaningful impertinence of a voluntary on the organ. When it is seasonable to sing praise to God, they do it with the spirit and the understanding also; not in the miserable, scandalous doggerel of Hopkins and Sternhold, but in psalms and hymns which are both sense and poetry, such as would sooner provoke a critic to turn Christian than a Christian to turn critic.[2]

And with his brother Charles, he edited the Large Hymn Book (1780) which was intended to be a companion to the already existing collections of hymns and to the Book of Common Prayer, so that it served as 'a little body of experimental and practical divinity.'

CHARLES WESLEY (1707-88)

This great writer of almost seven thousand hymns has been called 'the sweet singer of Methodism'. His poetry reflects Christian beliefs in an intelligible manner to ordinary folk. Never narrow but profoundly catholic, it has both intensity of personal feeling and concern for human suffering. It seems that his Moravian experiences taught Charles to value the amazing love of God's forgiveness, so that he once declared: 'For all, for all, my Saviour died.' Moreover, his hymns are based upon the careful study of Scripture, e.g. 'Come, O Thou Traveller unknown' (*Genesis* 32), and the well-known ordination hymn, 'O Thou who camest from above' (*Leviticus* 6:13) in which his total religious 'experience might almost at any time be found in the first two verses.' Hence Charles's sentiment —

> When quiet in my house I sit,
>   Thy Book be my companion still,
> My joy thy sayings to repeat . . .

If his brother was the iron-willed commander of the Movement, Charles himself was certainly the more attractive and compassionate personality. It was significant that having left his brother with depressed feelings, Charles wrote afterwards: 'We parted as we met, without either prayer or singing.'[3]

At Westminster School, he won a King's scholarship and was appointed School Captain in 1725. He then proceeded to Christ Church, Oxford, where he was a Student and later a Tutor. A devout young man, he founded the 'Holy Club' or 'Bible Moths' as it was nicknamed, for the better use of undergraduates' time in methodical study and prayer and in pastoral visits to the local prison. And later, looking back to his Oxford days, he recalled:

I took my degrees, and only thought of spending all my days in Oxford. But my brother, who always had the ascendant over me, persuaded me to accompany him and Mr Oglethorpe to Georgia. I exceedingly dreaded entering into Holy Orders, but he over-ruled me here also, and I was ordained by the Bishop of Oxford, and the next Sunday priest by the Bishop of London.[4]

His secretaryship to General Oglethorpe, the Governor of the new colony of Georgia, was a miserable experience; for within six months he had returned to England, where his conversion took place on Whitsunday of 1736. Concerning this religious event, he declared: 'I now found myself at peace with God, and rejoiced in hope of loving Christ.'[5]

In the early days of the Movement, Charles acted as his brother's assistant. But he remained faithful to the Church of England throughout his life, though he was much displeased with the hysterical scenes at the charismatic meetings and with John's subsequent ordinations.

And in 1749 Charles was married by his brother to Sarah Gwynne, the daughter of Marmaduke Gwynne, Squire of Garth, near Builth Wells, who was himself a conscientious magistrate and devout churchman. It was a successful marriage, apart from the sadness of bereavement. Because out of their eight children, only Charles (1757), Sally (1759), and Samuel (1766) survived infancy.

Of his father's musical gifts, Samuel wrote in his *Reminiscences*:

My Father was extremely fond of Music and in the early part of Life, I believe performed a little upon the Flute. He had a most accurate Ear for Time, and in every Piece which had Repetitions, knew exactly which Part was to be played or sung twice, which when anyone failed to do, he would immediately cry out, 'You have cheated me of a Repeat!'[6]

On the other hand, the real musician was his wife Sarah, a fine singer, to whom Charles once addressed the crushing rebuke: 'Not a word of your music! That is a bad sign; a sign of idleness, I fear. When you would have me look out after a harpsichord for you, you will tell me so.' And in another letter, he instructed her 'to encourage [their son] Charles in writing, riding, and music. As to the last, he needs no spur, but attention only.'

In 1771 the Wesleys moved from Bristol into a large, well-furnished house in Great Chesterfield Street, Marylebone. Its lease had been presented to Charles by a Methodist friend who had seen that 'the cellars were well-stocked with wine and abundance of table beer.' Of greater importance, one of the rooms had been adapted for private concerts. It contained two chamber organs, a harpsichord, ten music desks, and enough space to seat an audience of some fifty-six people. Here, the children delighted the London nobility and members of the Cloth with their delightful music.

A manuscript book in Charles Wesley's handwriting, now in the possession of the Royal Academy of Music, makes fascinating reading; for it contains the lists of the subscribers, the domestic accounts, and the music programmes of the entire seven fortnightly concerts that were given annually, between 1779 and 1785.

SAMUEL WESLEY (1766-1837)

He was certainly the most gifted musician of the family, belonging very much to the eighteenth century, since he only lived to see the first four months of Queen Victoria's reign. His instrumental music exemplified that he was one of the first pioneers of the symphonic style in this country, and his variations on popular melodies revived a forgotten art form of the past. And yet, most of his extensive choral works have never been published. Concerning his childhood, he wrote:

> When my Brother [Charles] played I used to stand by, scraping a sixpenny Fiddle, and beating Time. . . . Doctor Boyce came to my Father, and said to him: 'Sir, I hear you have got an English Mozart in your House!' — I had scrambled down the Oratorio of *Ruth*; the Doctor looked over it and seemed highly pleased. He said, 'This Boy writes by Nature as good a Bass as I can by Skill and Study. There is no Man in England has two such Sons.'[7]

Samuel was essentially a scholar-musician. His letters, masterpieces in themselves, were written in a leisurely style. His excellent general knowledge was owed to a great extent to his father. And in later life, he recalled with affection his inherited abilities to learn Latin, Greek and Hebrew; and nothing was more hurtful to him than to be classed as 'a *mere* Musician':

> I have (from a Boy) been a Lover of more of the Alphabet than the seven incipient English Letters; and had I not been an idle Dog, under the Instruction of my classical Father, I might long ago have been well qualified to bandy Latin and Greek along with Parr and Porson.

Although he became a Londoner by adoption, Samuel seized every opportunity to get away from 'that vile, detestable, accursed and damnable Spot, which, the sooner it is swallowed up by an Earthquake, the better.'[8] So he gave lectures and organ recitals in East Anglia and the West Country, having also conducted the Birmingham Festival of 1811.

He possessed a keen sense of humour, for he once compared the Bachelor of Music hood at Oxford to 'a mouse on an Ox's back.'[9] And in a letter to his friend Vincent Novello, he remarked: 'So, Cocky Wellington has been serving it out to 'em again. Frenchmen are not fond of the Bayonet, which is very extraordinary you will say. Of an *Irishman* I have heard it observed that nothing puts him sooner into a bad Humour than running a red hot Poker into his — —.'[10] A true gourmet, he sent his compliments to a Norwich lady, 'for her Epicurean Treat of rich *unadulterated* Sausages — an Article unattainable in the pestilential Pork Shops of lovely London!'

In 1809, when railway transport was merely in its infancy, the stage-coach was the main means of travel. And here is Samuel's witty account of his journey from Tamworth to London:

> I must set out To-morrow morning, and I mean to Travel in the Oxford two Day Coach, to prevent over Fatigue, which I was obliged to submit to in the

First Instance, from the Necessity of going at *Night,* which constantly disagrees with me; and if you remember the Weather on Monday Night (or rather Tuesday Morning), you must know that the Situation of Coach Travellers, whether inside or out, could not be over and above eligible, especially as we were troubled with a restless Companion, who was continually jerking the Windows up and down for what he called *Air,* but which was a furious wind and pelting Rain, so that it was next to a Miracle I did not take a Cold *for the Winter.*[11]

Unfortunately, there was a touch of the Mr Micawber about him as he was ever in debt and hounded by his creditors. He suffered from long periods of nervous depression and irritability, when he was unable to fulfil his musical duties. This mental condition was due to financial worries caused by the breakdown of his marriage, but above all to an accident at night in 1787, when he fell into an unprotected building excavation. He later tried to commit suicide by hurling himself through a window. And it seemed that he sometimes alleviated his depressions by turning to the gin bottle, since in 1814 he wrote to Vincent Novello:

This used to be one of your Leisure Evenings. Will you come and take a Quartern of Gin with old rubicond-faced Sam? Perhaps you are not aware that I am cruelly in the Dumps at having missed the *certainty* of being kicked and cuffed about by the Governors of the Bawdy House.[12]

In April 1793, he was married to Charlotte Louisa Martin in Ridge Parish Church, Hertfordshire. She was an assistant teacher at the same private school in Marylebone, where Samuel used to give piano lessons to unappreciative school-girls. They had three children: Charles, who became Sub-Dean of the Chapel Royal, John William and Emma Frances. But the marriage was an unhappy one, resulting in a deed of separation which ordered Samuel to make regular payments to his wife. His apparent inability to fulfil these financial commitments eventually landed him in prison. In 1810 he was living with his housekeeper, Sarah Suter, by whom he had seven illegitimate children: Samuel Sebastian, Rosalind, Eliza, Matthias Erasmus, John, Robert Glenn and Thomasine.

Furthermore, he had already joined the Roman Catholic Church, much to his father's distress — though he later denied ever having been a convert. It was, in fact, his love of Gregorian music which had drawn him to their chapels; and Pope Pius VI's letter in acknowledgment of a Latin Mass seemed to suggest that he had indeed become one.

By the end of 1812, Samuel had discovered that his labours in the cause of Gregorian Chant had been in vain, and he therefore remonstrated with Vincent Novello:

As the Gregorian is beginning to be proscribed *by the Clergy themselves,* it is plainly an unfavourable Epoch to reckon upon its Encouragement, and had I been aware of the sudden and silly Revolution taking Place in your Choir, I should certainly have employed much of my Time otherwise. . . .

P.S. Scrape together all the Gregorian Masses and Anthems, and bundle them all up for a good Bonfire on the 5th of November.[13]

In becoming a Roman Catholic, Samuel had indeed lost all chances of ever obtaining a cathedral position in the Established Church. On the other hand, he played for several services in Norwich Cathedral; and in 1829 he visited Winchester Cathedral, having 'strummed the Cathedral Service twice in the absence of Chard,' whom he had previously seen and found 'to be much less disagreeable than Musicians in general.'[14]

Samuel was devoted to the music of the classical composers of the Church, like Palestrina and Allegri; and he declared that 'our countryman William Byrd' was a perfect model of the most pure Church Harmony,[15] not forgetting his great admiration of Henry Purcell. But his greatest love was for Bach's music then almost unknown in England, for he enjoyed playing the violin sonatas at the recitals organized by Benjamin Jacobs in the Surrey Chapel. He was well-acquainted, too, with the *B minor Mass* and endeavoured to get its *Credo* published in 1815. His masterly Motet *In exitu Israel* was inspired by Bach's *Jesu meine Freude*. And in co-operation with K. F. Horn, he also issued editions of both the Trio Sonatas (1809-10) and the Well-tempered Clavichord (1810-13) later promoting the English translation of Forkel's *Life of Bach* (1820).

His introduction to Bach's *48 Preludes and Fugues* was due to the violinist G. F. Pinto (1785-1806), who had drawn attention to one of the German editions. Undoubtedly, Samuel had read A. F. C. Kollmann's essays on Harmony and Counterpoint (1796-99), where there were printed many examples of Bach's music, including the Riddle Canons of the *Musical Offering*. Kollmann himself had come from Hanover and was the first apostle of Bach in England.[16] Yet it was Samuel's idea to form a society (humorously called 'Our Sebastian Squad') that would promote Bach's works, and he therefore wrote to Benjamin Jacobs on the subject in 1809:

> I can think of nothing more expedient than the Formation of a junto among ourselves, composed of Characters who sincerely and conscientiously admit and adhere to the superior excellence of the Great Musical High Priest; and who will bend their Minds to a Zealous Promotion of advancing the Cause of Truth and Perfection.[17]

Samuel's hero-worship of the Master was expressed in numerous epiphets, like 'Our Apollo', 'Our Idol', 'Our Demi-god', 'Saint Sebastian', or just simply 'THE MAN'. He also named one of his children 'Sebastian' and composed a three-part *Eulogium de Johanni Sebastiano Bach*. And it was fitting that his final organ recital at Christ Church, Newgate Street, in September 1837, had been given in the presence of Mendelssohn who had done so much towards the Bach Revival in Germany. No wonder, the eighteen year old Eliza Wesley had to leave the building in tears![18]

7

CHAPTER TWO

Early Childhood and
the Chapel Royal (1810-1832)

SAMUEL SEBASTIAN WESLEY was born at No. 1 Great Woodstock Street in London, on the fourteenth day of August, 1810. About this important event, Samuel Wesley later reported:

> I believe a lying-in-month was never gone through with less expense, yet it would have been otherwise in the reign of Charlotte, for then the house was full of gossips and hangers-on from morning to night.[1]

It is significant that the first child of this union, between Samuel Wesley and his acting-housekeeper Sarah Suter, was to be named after the family's great musical hero, J. S. Bach. Moreover, the following remarks prove that this little boy was very much in his father's thoughts; for in 1813 he wrote from Ipswich, imploring Mrs Wesley:

> I wish to God you could manage to have him at some *near* place, where you or I could see him almost everyday. Kiss him for me. Tell him I will come home very soon, and try if you can to fatten him a little with arrowroot.[2]

Three days later, while he was staying with a friend in Norwich, Samuel wrote:

> I hope to find my dear boy not *ill*. Mrs Linley is in a bad way. I think she will either die or destroy herself before long. She has sent Sammy a nice handkerchief with *S.W.* marked by herself.[3]

And he anxiously declared:

> I'm afraid by your way of writing about Sammy, that he is but poorly. Do hearten him up, as much as possible, and you may safely tell him now that he

is likely to see me very soon;' but belligerently adding, 'I'm in great passion with you for not packing up a pair of drawers in my trunk. I have worn the only pair almost off my arse, not to mince the matter![4]

In 1816 'Old Sam' wrote to his friend Vincent Novello, giving his reasons of absence from an organ meeting:

> Our Little Boy Blue is in so precarious a state that I much fear I must sacrifice the pleasure I anticipated of meeting you at Surrey Chapel tomorrow, at one o'clock. However should any formidable change take place I will be with you.[5]

When Sammy began to show evident signs of musical promise, his father realized that a good education in the art and craft of music would be necessary, and the best place in London was at the Chapel Royal. So negotiations were begun towards the end of 1817 with the notable William Hawes, to whom 'Old Sam' sent this note:

> Pray accept my best thanks for your extremely kind offer to my little boy. He is a very apprehensive child, and very fond of music; how far he may have talent and voice sufficient to do credit to your valuable instructions, experience will best show. His temper and disposition I believe to be good, wanting only due discretion, and I know him to be susceptible of kindness, which, with you, I am confident he will meet. My good friend Glenn[6] will doubtless confer with you fully upon points of necessary arrangement.[7]

THE CHAPEL ROYAL

Mr William Hawes (1785-1846), the Director of Music at the English Opera House, had been the official Almoner of St Paul's Cathedral since 1812. And five years later, he was asked to look after the ten Children of the Chapel Royal, so that he was now responsible for the general education and the boarding of both establishments in his large house on Adelphi Terrace, overlooking the Thames. A maid supervised the washing and the combing of the younger boys, of whom one, we are told, was subject to a verminous complaint, in spite of having his head 'constantly washed with a strong decoction of larkspur and brandy!'

The education of the Children of the Chapel Royal was very poor. A schoolmaster attended for an hour and a half's instruction, twice a week. And they were called 'slate days' because most of the time was spent in teaching Arithmetic. The rest of the time was fully occupied in learning the music of the daily services, nor must be forgotten their operatic engagements at the Lyceum Theatre.

Hawes's teaching methods were original and assured; for he would collect the boys around him, having placed a lady's hunting-whip at the side of the piano. Unfortunately the younger boys had to stand in front of the rest, and if any of the Children sang a wrong note or misbehaved, the whip was quickly used upon the nearest, unlucky victim. And even the delicious buns, supplied by their friend Miss Hackett, would fail to ameliorate the stings of the chastisements.[8] Apart from such painful interludes, Master Wesley was happily contented; and Hawes later declared him to be the best musician that he had ever taught.

It must have been an exciting experience for a twelve year old to find himself selected to sing in the special choir that had travelled down to Brighton, in order to take part in the services of the private Chapel attached to the Royal Pavilion, which the King, George IV, had built when he was the Prince Regent. And it must have been equally exciting for the Wesley family to read of their son's achievements in the Court News of *The Morning Post* (March 11, 1823):

> The harmonious part of the Service was sublime. The King's Band was on duty. Mr Attwood presided at the organ. Master Wesley, from His Majesty's Choir at the Royal Chapel, St James's, took the soprano and leading parts in the anthem, & with sweet and divine effect.

Much to the boys' disappointment, the King was unable to attend the service, owing to an attack of the gout. But the following Sunday he did attend, when he was dressed in blue and wore a small star, with his left hand resting in a black, silk sling. The service lasted for more than two hours, and 'Master Wesley was included in the new choir.'[9]

And yet, these winter visits to Brighton must have been an uninviting experience for a child in a draughty coach; for in October, Master Wesley sent this note to his mother:

> I wrote to let you know that I am going to Brighton next Saturday week, so I hope you will let me have a new coat, as I should not like to go in the same one as I did last year. Mind you send those bits of wood out of the Catherine wheels.[10]

Another reference to his singing reported that 'the soprano of Master Wesley was remarkably clear; his shake was open, his every intonation distinct and correct.'[11] On this occasion, the Dean of Hereford (Dr Robert Carr) preached the Sermon on the text: 'Boast not thyself of tomorrow, for thou knowest not what a day may bring forth,' little realising that, after his appointment to the bishopric of Worcester, Master Wesley was to become the new organist of Hereford Cathedral.

And in December, 1823, an important visitor to Brighton was the celebrated composer Rossini, who performed a duet with Wesley in one of the evening concerts. And we are informed that the King had so much enjoyed the boy's fine singing that he later presented him with a gold watch.

Wesley's youthful love of fishing is evident in this poem, copied out in his childish handwriting and now in the possession of the British Library —

One lovely morn I chanced to walk
    down by the river side,
I met a friend, and had a talk,
    he then proposed a ride.

We rode from place to place
    and then we went to fish,
And when that we had caught some plaice,
    I put them on a dish.

We then went home and ate them fast
    which made me feel great pain,
And 'ere the day away was spent,
    they were all up again.[12]

Writing to his father from the King's School, he said: 'I hope you will not forget to spend my evenings at home. I have not seen the Bandit yet. I should be glad if I should never see him again.'[13] As to the identity of this person, we have no means of knowing.

While visiting Cambridge, 'Old Sam' wrote to his fifteen year old son:

'Dear Boy,
    Buy a shilling or 18 penny penknife, and I will give you the money again when I return.
    You say nothing of the poor girls, or whether the baby has caught the meazles. I hope you "dwell together in unity", and if I find it otherwise, I shall not patiently overlook it. . . .
    Give me a *full, true, and particular* account of all things you can cram into *three pages,* for you must not leave an inch of paper unoccupied, and as with a *good* knife you *may* make a good pen, with a good pen you *may* write a good hand, which, I assure you, Master Sammy (I beg your pardon, *Doctor,* I mean), I wish you would set about to do. At all events, you ought now to be a forward *English* scholar, and I do not despair even of your becoming a Latin one, if you make good use of the most valuable article in life, which is time. . . .
    P.S. Spell *wantes* so — wants, and *knives* — knife. Make your *O's* round.[14]

Apparently, Hawes had been led to augment his boarding school fees by hiring out the boys under his care to sing at the numerous banquets and concerts in the City. Although he maintained that this was all good experience, Miss Maria Hackett (1783-1874) thought otherwise. And since 1811, she had been conducting a personal crusade against their nocturnal excursions, even 'if the sum allowed to the Almoner for their board became, through the depreciation of money, totally inadequate to their support.' Furthermore, in her statement to Bishop Randolph of London, she had said:

To remunerate their Singing Master for his trouble, the Children are hired out to Public Concerts, and are exposed, unprotected, to the contagion of any

Society they may meet with in these Nocturnal Assemblies. No one on these occasions is appointed to have an eye upon their conduct; no one to return them to their friends. After the conclusion of the Concert, these Youths are left to walk the streets alone at midnight, and to find their way home as they can. What effect this vagabond life, at so early an age, is likely to have upon their morals, in most instances, may be easily imagined.[15]

Samuel Wesley's objections to these occasions were entirely mercenary; for in several letters to Vincent Novello, he had complained of Hawes's forbidding his son to assist in their own evening concerts, and I quote:

The only *hitch* is the probability of our worthy friend Hawes's interference, who will not suffer Sam to budge from his prison on any day that he can rob him of a guinea.[16]

I shall try for Sam on Thursday evening, but you know that Mr Hawes is Mr Hawes: to say anything more of him that is *true* would be libellous![17]

With the advent of adolescence, Wesley's days at the Chapel Royal were numbered. For in a letter to Vincent Novello on 19 August, 1825, his father observed: 'Sam will be with us on Sunday, but alas! his voice betrays symptoms of anti-vellutism and, moreover, he begins to show signs that a razor must before very long form one article of his toilette.'[18]

Finally, a testimonial stated that 'Mr Samuel Sebastian Wesley was formerly a Chorister of His Majesty's Chapel, St James's, and that he has received his musical education among the Gentlemen of the establishment, and that he is fully competent to undertake the musical duties of any Cathedral.'[19]

YOUTHFUL EXPERIENCES

In his endeavour to get a suitable appointment for his son, Samuel Wesley had sought the assistance of Bishop Howley, who, as dean of the Chapel Royal, was ultimately responsible for its members' welfare. And in March, 1826, Edward Holmes replied: 'The Bishop of London is not a musical man, and His Lordship has requested me to state to Mr Ward all I know of your son. I have great pleasure in doing this, and sincerely hope your son be successful.'[20]

Bishop Howley was so unmusical that he had the audacity to appoint his wife's younger brother, the Rev. C. A. Belli, as Precentor of St Paul's in 1819. And another member of the Chapter, Canon Sydney Smith, later gave Belli the nickname of 'the Absenter'.

Wesley was fifteen years old when he became organist of St James's Chapel in Hampstead Road.[21] Meanwhile, his father was happily browsing through the manuscripts in the Fitzwilliam Museum, Cambridge, where he discovered three of Handel's hymn-tunes (*The Invitation, Desiring to Love,* and *The Resurrection*), all set to Charles Wesley's words.[22] And yet, he had the time to send a belligerent message to his son:

I hope you will not receive me on Saturday with dreadful Stories of Raw-heads and bloody Bones, and Quarrels, and Bailiffs, and Executioners, a great deal of all of which I am generally welcomed with, whenever I leave any peaceful place to return to that vile, detestable, accursed, and damnable Spot, London, which, the sooner it is swallowed up by an Earthquake, the better. . . .

P.S. Tell *Maister* Gibson, with my best compliments, that he is a right cunning Caledonian! If that was a halibut, not a turbot, halibuts have changed their form and their flavour.[23]

With no further concerts with Hawes, Wesley was now available to help in his father's musical enterprises — hence 'Old Sam' was able to inform Sarah Wesley, that the sum of fifteen pounds due to his boy would be postponed for months.[24] In 1827 the report of a morning concert held in Christ Church, Newgate Street, was printed in *The Atlas*:

The vocal pieces were accompanied on the organ by Mr S. Wesley and his son, in many places with a judicious variety and contrast in the management of the stops. . . . There was no organ *extempore* from Wesley, but a gentleman named Topliff made a noise which was dignified with that appellation.

In writing from Brighton to his wife 'Pexy', Samuel Wesley humorously declared that their son was a born conjuror; for in a letter to his parents, he had told them that the postage had cost him eightpence, having very wisely inserted the words 'Post Paid' on the envelope.[25]

And in 1828, Master Wesley informed their friend John Emett, who was organist of St Mary Magdalen's Church, Bermondsey, of the sad news of his Aunt Sarah's death in Bristol, and how his 'father together with his illness is greatly disturbed by it.'[26]

At the beginning of 1829, Wesley was elected organist of St Giles's Parish Church, Camberwell, where he was fortunate to have the celebrated organist Thomas Adams (1785-1858) at the neighbouring church of St George's. And since the services in the latter church finished later, Wesley used to deputise for him by playing the congregation out at the end of the morning service.

A VISIT TO THE WEST COUNTRY

While visiting Blagdon in September, 1829, Samuel Wesley reported to his wife: 'I have the promise of Redcliffe organ [Bristol], where an advantageous performance is pretty certain, as also three more — one of them at Wells Cathedral.'[27] And in another letter to her:

I suppose that Master Sam has acquired by this time the scale of the hurdy-gurdy and the salt-box under his learned instructor and companion in the Fisherman's Hotel. Dr Wesley's sister sent him £5, last night, and he has had an excellent offer to conduct a review which will bring in £30 a month, but say not a word to any soul about it.[28]

14

It seemed that some secrecy was essential because the family patriarch, Charles Wesley, had already expressed a note of censure in a letter to a feline friend:

> My son talks of going to Bristol (I hope not), to give a paltry five-shilling benefit concert which always hurts my feelings; *it is a low affair indeed.*[29]

Undaunted by such feelings, the Musical Wesleys travelled to Bristol as they wanted to test the new Harrison-Byfield organ in St Mary Redcliffe and to discuss the final arrangements for their concert, so that 'Old Sam' was pleased to inform his wife —

> It is all agreed that I am to have the use of the church, and that *a share* of my profit is to be applied to defraying the expenses of the late repairs and additions to that organ.... We are to dine, to-morrow, with the Churchwardens and several of the Vestry, the Organist, the Organ-builder, and I don't know how many others, who are all in hoity-toity spirits upon the occasion, and seem eager to do me all the service they can.[30]

Wesley must have been proud to see his father's name advertised on the bills as 'the celebrated Fugist and Editor of the Works of the Immortal Bach.' An enthusiastic report of their organ recital subsequently appeared in a local newspaper, and I quote:

> The great praise of Mr Wesley and his able and interesting Son, who occasionally accompanied him in a Duet, and gave also *God save the King,* with variations of his own composition, is, that to that powerful instrument the organ, they have far beyond their compeers,
> "Enlarged the former narrow bounds
> And added length to solemn sounds."[31]

Although Wesley's 'Variations on the National Anthem'[32] is a youthful piece in many styles, the reference to the playing of organ duets is of much greater interest.

Whereas the 18th-century English organ had no pedal-board, the use of duets enabled the Wesley family to play Bach's 'Trio Sonatas'. Furthermore, 'Old Sam' had himself composed 'Eight Short and Easy Duets'[33] for his talented daughter Eliza's amusement. And the duets performed in Bristol were probably his 'Grand Duet in C major' (first played with Vincent Novello) and 'Duet in C minor' (composed for the Memorial Concert to William Russell in 1812),[34] which also served as a useful introduction to Bach's 'St Anne' Fugue.

Meanwhile, a growing tension within the family is revealed in the correspondence from Samuel Wesley to his wife, which was caused by young Sam's reaching the age of adolescence and having no longer any further desire of being attached to his mother's apron-strings:

15

I hope that Master Sam does not worry you, if he cannot or will not *help* you. If ever he should have a family of his own, he will then know what his duty to them is and how much ought to be sacrificed to *their* welfare, whatever inconvenience might occasion him.[35]

Another reason was the transference of his father's affections to his younger brother Johnny, who later became a bookseller and publisher. An example of this can be seen in one of his letters home wherein 'Old Sam' described how he had 'travelled one Part of the Way with a sweet little Boy, just Johnny's Age and Size,' whom he could not help cuddling 'for Want of my *real* Calf, I so long to see.'[36]

However this tension was short-lived. If 'Old Sam' was proud of the rising career of his musical son, Samuel Sebastian was equally proud of his father's fine musicianship, so that he was able to write to his mother:

I so entirely clung to my father, or rather, still cling to him, that I do not know how I can pass my life, for not only have I to deplore the loss of a father — a sorrow which of all others from my childhood I always thought the most acute — but also that of my best and most perfect friend during the last few years, and my instructor in art and life.[37]

With the death in 1829 of Benjamin Jacobs, organist of St John's Waterloo Road, Thomas Lett (the donor of the organ in 1825) immediately wrote to the Clerk of the Vestry, in order to state that, in accordance with the request of the Vestry for him to nominate an organist, he had selected from the list of candidates Mr S. S. Wesley, 'believing him in every respect qualified for the situation.' And a small leather-bound register of attendances, labelled 'Organist', has since confirmed Wesley's appointment.

In the British Library there is a fishing licence, issued by the Director of the Commercial Docks in Rotherhithe, which admitted 'Mr Wesley to ANGLE in the TIMBER DOCKS [from June 9] until the THIRTY-FIRST DAY of DECEMBER 1830, SUNDAYS excepted.'[38] Hence Wesley's desire to obtain the post of evening organist at Hampton Parish Church in the following September, especially as the Thames was adjacent to the Church.

OPERATIC EXPERIENCES

It is not generally known that Wesley used to assist at the English Opera House in the Strand by conducting a band — hence the following playbill:

This Evening, Monday, June 29, 1829, will be presented a Comick Opera, the music from the masterly compositions of Mozart, called TIT FOR TAT or the Tables Turned! altered and adapted from COSI FAN TUTTE.[39]

Whereas the music on this occasion was arranged under the guidance of William Hawes, the choruses were conducted by Mr S. Wesley junior, who later confided that his greatest ambition in life was to compose a comic opera! And three weeks after his appointment to Hereford Cathedral, the English Opera Company performed a melodrama, called the 'Dilosk Gatherer' or 'Eagle's Nest' (libretto by Fitzball), about which performance at the Royal Olympic Theatre, the music critic of *The Theatrical Observer* stridently reported:

> Messrs Hawes and S. S. Wesley claim the honour of composing the music; but to our thinking, it is scarcely to the reputation of those gentlemen.[40]

A mordant remark, expressed in one of his father's letters home, probably referred to a similar event and is worth quoting: 'I am not sorry that Master Sam has taken his roosting perch with Atkins; he will begin before long to know the value of what he was dissatisfied with before.'[41] However, he redeemed himself to his parents by acting as the organist to the oratorio concerts under Sir Henry Bishop's conductorship; and in one of them his new *Benedictus*[42] was first performed on 30 March, 1832.

Wesley's other compositions were his choral and orchestral work, 'Young Bacchus in his lusty prime,'[43] and several piano pieces, e.g. 'Air with variations in E' (dedicated to his friend J. B. Cramer) and the 'Waltz' which he presented to *The Harmonicon* (1831). Also in the September copy of this musical journal, a criticism appeared of his first published anthem, 'O God, whose nature and property,'[44] when Wesley's attention was drawn to his use of double octaves, 'not reckoned orthodox in ecclesiastical music.'

HEREFORD CATHEDRAL NAVE, LOOKING EAST

From a drawing by Dr Carless, 1830-40, by permission of Mr F. C. Morgan.

18

CHAPTER THREE

Hereford Cathedral (1832-1835)

HEREFORD CATHEDRAL saw the arrival of Dr John Merewether as the new dean in June, 1832. A person of vibrant energy and varied interests, he was to become within three years the brother-in-law of Mr S. S. Wesley, then evening organist at Hampton Parish Church, where he had once served a curacy.

Merewether was a voluminous letter-writer, a gifted artist, and an enthusiastic, amateur archaeologist, whose *Diary of a Dean* (1851) described his scientific excavations of Silbury Hill. His eighteen years at Hereford Cathedral witnessed many improvements: the raising of the standard of choral worship, the restoration of the beautiful Lady Chapel, and the saving of the Central Tower from a state of total collapse. On the other hand, in his rejection of Canon Hampden's nomination to the bishopric in 1848, the dean was the recipient of the following curt note from Lord John Russell: 'Sir — I have had the honour to receive your letter, in which you intimate to me your intention of violating the law.'

His first Chapter Meeting passed the following resolution:

> In consequence of the long and increasing deterioration in the Choral Service of the Cathedral, proceeding as they are aware from Dr Whitfeld's infirm state of health, which has for a long period experienced the forebearance of the Chapter, the Dean and Chapter now feel it to be their indispensible duty to communicate to him their decision that the Office of Organist will be vacant at Midsummer next.[1]

The applicants for the organist's post were Messrs. Moss, Smith and Wesley. It seemed that Wesley had been attracted to Hereford, partly because of the fishing prospects of the River Wye below the Cathedral, and partly because of the triennial Three Choirs Festival Meeting that gave him an opportunity of conducting both choral and orchestral music. A minute in the Act Book, dated 10 July, 1832, recorded that 'Mr Wesley, the Organist of Hampton Church near London, was elected to succeed Dr Whitfeld as Organist of this Cathedral on a salary of fifty-two pounds (and eight pounds paid by the Custos and Vicars) and the addition of forty pounds to take place after the decease of Dr Whitfeld.'[2]

Accordingly the creation of Dr Clarke-Whitfeld's pension resulted in the deduction of £40 per annum from his successor's stipend, which was then the normal custom; but this action subsequently became a matter of contention between future organists and the capitular authorities.

The same Chapter Meeting, at the recommendation of the dean, also resolved that Mr Bishop should be requested to come as soon as it was convenient to repair and tune the Cathedral organ.[3] Such a decision must have pleased the new organist, though the work was delayed until the autumn when Mr Bishop attended another Chapter Meeting, at which it was finally decided that the organ should be repaired and tuned. And the contract named the following items:

A new Swell containing four Stops, namely Open Diapason, Principal, Trumpet, and Oboe from [Tenor] C to F in Alt.; the Choir action to be altered to form a recess of a foot deep for knee-room for action upon the Pedals	£105. 0. 0.
A spring reservoir for regulating the supply of air to bellows	£15.15. 0.
Two octaves of Pedals	£12.12. 0.
A coupler to unite the Swell to the Great Organ	£7. 7. 0.
A new Twelfth	£10.10. 0.
An octave Twelfth and a Tierce	£8. 8. 0.
Sesquialtera	£12. 0. 0.
Double G added to the Bass & D sharp, E, and F to the Treble to the Great Organ, Choir Organ and Swell with sound boards, movements, and pipes complete	£52.10. 0.
Revoicing	£21. 0. 0.
New Pedal action	£10.10. 0.
Clarabella Stop — in lieu of the present Cornet	£8. 8. 0.
Cremona Stop to F below fiddle G in place of the Vox Humana	£18.18. 0.
Entire New Ivory and Ebony Keys	£12.12. 0.
	£295.10. 0.

The same to be paid for by three yearly equal instalments, namely the sum £98.10.0.[4]

And yet, another sum of 75 guineas was to be paid to Mr Bishop for the following items: 'Fourteen pedal pipes on a large scale'; [seven] from CCC to meet the GG and seven at top making the two octaves of pedal pipes complete, with sound-board movements and a sufficient supply of wind, to be executed in the best manner.'[5]

Meanwhile the dean caused several improvements to be made in November the same year. First, painted notices were to be placed inside the Cathedral, 'prohibiting all persons from walking about the Church or talking during Divine Service.' Secondly, a tailor was to be asked to provide cloth and to undertake the making of new clothes 'of equal, if not better quality than at present' for the Choristers and Langfordian Scholars, and also to include the making of 'a square cloth cap with a loop and button on the side' for each boy.[6]

An anonymous writer, therefore, reported: 'We are delighted to find better things in store for Hereford Cathedral. The holy and venerable edifice has undergone, as our readers are aware, a very effective renovation, entirely we believe through the well-directed zeal, and pious liberality of Dean Merewether. And in the same spirit, the Dean and Chapter have just filled up five vacancies in the College of Vicars Choral.'[7]

Although his appointment was made in July, Wesley did not arrive in Hereford until the following October, since there was no need for him to be present until the official opening of the Cathedral organ at the beginning of November.

In the following letter to his father, written in the Chapter Garden and dated October, 1832, we catch a hint of the young musician's solitary existence and concern for his family in London:

> I write to inquire some intelligence respecting your proceedings at Islington. Have you got people in your house yet? I am very anxious to learn what has been done since your last letter, how *you all* are, and what prospect you have of a more comfortable life for the future?
>
> The distance between us, and the impossibility of my affording any immediate assistance, makes me request that you will not give a worse account than need be. Summers has no claim upon you until your lodgings are taken. My sending that you require is at present impossible. . . .
>
> I have taken up comfortable lodgings near the Cathedral for the present. I think it probable that soon I shall be allowed rooms in the College [of Vicars Choral] here. I should then have to get furniture.
>
> I find that much teaching may be had within fifteen miles of Hereford. I should, of course, have been better pleased to have lived quietly without this tiresome and somewhat degrading occupation. The salary at the Cathedral is, however, insufficient; and by teaching I hope shortly to be able to send you money — that is in the course of three months, probably. I must hire or keep a horse when I commence, as the pupils live many miles away and apart.
>
> I shall not do any duty at the cathedral until the sixth of November. The organ is being enlarged considerably. My payment will, however, be the same. I am therefore glad of the liberty. If I can afford it, I think of going a short distance into Wales, should the weather permit. Lately we have had rain night and day.

Hawes, Atkins, etc., have been giving a concert at which I played a pianoforte and a violin duet with Loder, of Bath. We got on tolerably well, but I hate playing the mountebank on these occasions. Nothing is to me so pleasant as to join in the performance of good music; but when a certain quantity of twaddle is to be played that some imposter may beg money, I'd rather be far off than mix in the mess. . . .

Write and let me know what you are all about. I have not been able to go and buy poultry yet. Tell me when you want it most. Five geese cost about three-and-sixpence; fowls, two-and-threepence a couple; ducks in proportion. . . .

P.S. Take care what you say to me in your letter. Being idle I am in course nervous. Tell mother to think of my knives and forks, and the other things. But be careful how you mention them in your letter, as it may miscarry and be opened.[8]

THE WILDERNESS

Wesley's idea of travelling a short distance into Wales indicated how he was occupying his leisure, while the Cathedral organ was being renovated. His subsequent enjoyment of the bubbling brooks and the magnificent scenery of the Black Mountains undoubtedly inspired his extended verse-anthem, 'The Wilderness and the Solitary Place', with its telling words from the Book of the Prophet Isaiah (Chapter 35). . . . 'The desert shall rejoice and blossom as the rose. Then shall the lame man leap as an hart, and the tongue of the dumb sing; for in the wilderness shall waters break out, and streams in the desert.'

Certainly the new additions to the Pedal Organ must have influenced the composer's registration notes; for in an autograph score,[9] dated 1834, he has carefully indicated where the Pedals were to be used — hence his directive to Mr Bishop, the organ-builder: 'The Choir Organ to be altered to form a recess of a foot deep for knee-room for action upon the Pedals.' Also notice his instructions in the organ score making full use of the new Stops, e.g. 'Swell Oboe', 'Sw. Diap.', and 'Swell Reeds'.

This fine anthem forms a landmark in English Cathedral music. Its exciting modulations in the middle section, as well as splendid organ chords, immensely impressed the Hereford citizens attending the re-opening of the Cathedral instrument on 6 November, 1832, and I quote:

> The Audit was never more fully attended on any former occasion, and never were the full powers of the beautiful instrument more successfully and skilfully developed, very much to the admiration and gratification of all present.[10]

Naturally the youthful Wesley decided to enter his new composition for the blue ribbon of cathedral music, i.e. the Gresham Prize medal — then valued at five pounds. The idea of holding a contest, however, had come from Miss Maria Hackett, who was also the donor. And every competitor was required to compose either an anthem or a service in what the main adjudicator, Dr William Crotch, had called 'the true sublime style' which was defined more fully in his *Lectures on Music* (1831):

> As long as the pure sublime style — the style peculiarly suited to the church service — was cherished, which was only to about the middle of the seventeenth century, we consider the ecclesiastical style to be in a state worthy of study and imitation — in a state of perfection. But it has been gradually, though not imperceptibly, losing its character ever since; church music is therefore sadly on the decline.[11]

With no time to lose, Wesley hastily despatched the following message to his mother on 15 December, 1832:

> 'Call on Monday morning at the Coach Office for a parcel. It is an anthem I have written for a prize in London and must be delivered on Monday, or it is too late. . . . You must keep Father at home, as he will have to write a motto in Latin. You had better mention it at once. Tell him I wish it to be — *Let justice be done,* or Weigh and consider, or anything he chooses.[12]

Mrs Wesley undertook his orders, and 'Old Sam' duly endorsed his son's letter with a characteristic flourish of 'pothooks and hangers', *Fiat Justitia.*

And ten days later, he again wrote to his mother, dealing with domestic troubles caused by an unwelcome visitor and his father's chalking up an immense bill for tea and sugar at the grocer's:

> You ought to be very careful whom you admit into your house. What does Mr Jenner want of you? Everybody you know almost has robbed you as yet, and why make a new acquaintance now there is a prospect of your being better off? Let me know in your letter, who and what he is, and what he wants?
>
> I am glad the Cottage is let. Mind you are paid for it and at the proper time. Remember your landlord won't give you credit . . .
>
> I have no teaching. The Cathedral is not open and until that is, I shall scarcely see anyone about the place. I must be patient and so must everybody . . .
>
> Saturday is market day. I will send something. It will arrive at the Coach Office in Fleet Street on Sunday morning. You must send for it: there will be some poultry and letters I want you to attend to . . .
>
> Father may order tea and sugar of Kemp now. Let him take care how he gives lessons. He can't teach the girl much, but Mrs Kemp is very particular in her way, and a great fool! Don't let your account for tea exceed that for lessons.
>
> What have they done at St Dunstan's? Who has got it? Does Glenn come much? How does 'Fish' get on, and Lizzy, and the rest? Answer these questions.

Poor Mrs Wesley must have felt quite overwhelmed with so many letters to deliver; for she was then asked 'to call and pay Mr Light, and to send a pair of white straps for trousers.' Yet her demanding son continued —

How is Father? He might write better letters to me. I want a copy of his Church Service[13] to perform at the Cathedral. How can I get Father's manuscripts — must I come to London for them? I should very much like to have a copy of Charles and John Wesley's *Letters,* Eliza made. I could return them, if you wish. Pray attend to these things, as I am getting melancholy here.

It seems that Wesley was finding the cost of living expensive; and he had to change his lodgings since he could no longer pay the weekly rent of ten shillings. Moreover, he had to find further money for the carriage of his boxes from Hampton, so that he had to inform his parents:

I must make you pay the carriage of your poultry. I am getting very poor. Don't give anything away I send, eat it all, and invite nobody. Don't let Mr Jenner come any more. You have been blessed enough. Nobody assists you, when you want assistance.

And finally some bossy advice to his favourite sister: 'Tell Ros to get a dictionary and look out any word she don't know how to spell. Her letter was imperfect, and Father did not correct all mistakes.'[14]

By the end of a frosty and damp December, Wesley was in need of some warmer clothing and therefore wrote to his mother: 'If you have got the clothes, send them immediately and whatever else you may have.' In addition there were three other matters that required her attention: first, the acquiring of the choral and orchestral parts of his father's *Confitebor* (1799); secondly, the result of the recently held Gresham Prize Competition for which he had entered; and thirdly, the purchase of a new pair of shoes:

Go to Afflecks, the boot-shop, and order a pair of dress shoes. The pair I have has lasted me all my life as yet. Let them be *very long in the quarter.* Perhaps he has a pair by him; if so, you can send them with the parcel. The postage here is dreadfully expensive. Don't let them be *pumps,* but *shoes,* very thin as possible. . . .

How is Father? He shall come here to conduct his music. I don't say anything about coming to town for the expense, at present, would ruin me. I suppose you can live without seeing me yet. I very much wish I could come though. *Burn my letters!*[15]

Although Wesley's entry for the competition was too late, he was more than anxious to publish 'The Wilderness'; for in writing to a possible publisher in March, 1833, he said:

The Dean [of Hereford] offers to have it performed at Windsor before the Queen, and to take me to accompany it. If I choose to go, which would be expensive, I should dedicate it to the Dean.[16]

However, the journey was never made, nor was his anthem dedicated to his future father-in-law owing to personal reasons; but it was dedicated to the Dean of Winchester in 1853.

Wesley unhappily lost the next competition to John Goss, because he had not fully realised that it was only necessary to write a dull, scholarly work to win the Prize. Hence Dr Crotch's significant remarks to Miss Hackett, and I quote: 'The introduction of novelty, variety, contrast, expression, originality, etc., is the very cause of the decay so long apparent in our Church music.' And it appears that he had Wesley's anthem in mind, since Bumpus later maintained that the Professor had 'expressed his dislike of the whole design of that immortal composition by drawing on the copy the portrait of a chorister boy with his face distorted with agony in the effort to reach the high note in the concluding verse.'[17]

Another examiner was the Gresham Professor of Music, Richard Stevens, who, having found that one copy had been written so closely that he could hardly understand it, then decided to add insult to injury by declaring: 'It is a clever thing, but not Cathedral music!'[18]

Wesley took these criticisms to heart and later wrote in the Preface to his Service in E:

> The few who have already done so, especially those who have *gained the Prize,* are sufficiently punished by the fact of one of the two umpires to select the best candidate having declared that the awards hitherto made have ever been in opposition to *his* judgement; for that this colleague would always have *his own way,* and so, he would have nothing to do with the matter.[19]

AN EASTER ANTHEM

Wesley's most popular anthem is undoubtedly 'Blessed be the God and Father,' having been composed at the request of the Dean of Hereford for performance in his Cathedral on Easter Day 1833 or 1834. However, the state of the choir was, on that occasion, so lamentable that only trebles and a single bass voice were available — tradition maintaining that this solitary gentleman was none other than the dean's butler! According to Kendrick Pyne, one of Wesley's pupils, 'An epidemic of sickness had so reduced the choir that only *two* men and several boys were available for the service.'[20]

The Cathedral choir consisted, when complete, of twelve singers who were all in holy orders: four were Minor Canons, and the rest were Vicars Choral. Because they held benefices and were responsible for the duties, hardly any of them attended the Sunday services in the Cathedral: one at eight o'clock in the morning, and two at five o'clock in the evening. This fact explains the existence of three unpublished settings of the Communion Service for boys and a single bass voice, that Dr Clarke-Whitfeld had written to meet a similar situation.[21]

In a letter to his friend, Alderman Dyson, of Windsor, which was written from Winchester in 1865, Wesley made this modest statement concerning his Easter Anthem:

I assure you I view it merely as a sort of showy sketch, or little thing just made to stop a gap, and never meant for publication. It may be something new in its style, and certainly is effective, but it does not satisfy me as to being true church music. However, people *all* seem to like it, and perhaps it may lead people to look at better things of mine.

I felt much obliged to you for getting it noticed at Windsor. I viewed Windsor as a place that would never do anything for me.[22]

Meanwhile the dean was anxious to enhance the standard of the Choral Service in the Cathedral. He had previously ordered new Prayer Books for the use of the choristers.[23] And in 1833 he wrote to the deputy Succentor because he wanted to explain certain alterations in the next bills of the Cathedral Service:

It is not for mere personal gratification that I propose this measure, but from an anxiety to restore the Service to its former course and to leave, if possible, no points in which those who have evil will at Zion may found just Chance.[24]

And even sixteen years later, the same dean reported that the Cathedral choir was then reduced to such disgraceful inefficiency that it was utterly impossible to perform a Choral Service, since the state of its members was as follows:

Robert Pearce (aged 78) — exempt.
Christopher Jones, asthmatic (67) — resident 7 miles off.
Edward Howells, in bad health (62) — never attends.
Henry Pearce, in very bad health (53) — uncertain.
William Munsey, not efficient (65) — resident 6 miles off.
Edward Bulmer, not efficient (55) — resides out of the city.
Thomas Gretton, subject to bad health (50).
Albert Jones, subject to bad health (49) — resident 6 miles off.[25]

In September, 1833, Wesley made his first appearance at the Three Choirs Meeting — acting as the official pianist, or accompanist, for the Worcester Festival. Some anxiety was caused beforehand by someone declaring the Cathedral building to be unsafe, but it was dismissed as groundless by two distinguished architects.

DOMESTIC MATTERS

Inasmuch as there had been no news from home, Wesley wrote to his mother in April, the following year:

I am surprised at not having heard from you, and cannot help thinking that something very unpleasant must have occurred! Perhaps *good fortune* has made you careless of me; but I cannot hope the *latter,* when I think of its improbability. Whatever may be the cause, I will trust you will not withhold it from me.

I suppose I am not expected on the occasion of my sister's wedding. My presence could effect no good object; and just now I am not able to afford the journey's expense for what is mere amusement. I trust she will be happy, and I think she must be.

You complain of Father's misconduct again. I had hoped that every bad effect of his dreadful [mental] illness had passed away. I grieve to hear that it has not. Perhaps he is better now. I have not heard from you for a long time . . .

What will you think when I tell you I have a very excellent opportunity of settling in this *county*. I have the permission to *marry* the daughter of one of the most respectable clergymen in the neighbourhood. At present, she will have but little money, but at the death of her parents will have something *useful*. This would, of course, give me great reason to be thankful as I should not only have a *companion* (and the misery of living *alone* I have borne till I am quite tired thereof), but it would so establish me in my profession here that, I think, I might look to the future with a reasonable hope of prosperity. I should have mentioned this sooner, but I scarcely hoped it could ever happen . . .

There is no music master within 50 miles of Hereford that a respectable person would learn of. I intend advertising in all the papers my intention to teach. It appears people are afraid to apply to me because I visit *the dean*.[26]

Whose lucky daughter was in love with the Cathedral organist? A clue to her identity can be found in Wesley's cryptic remark, namely that people were afraid of asking him for music lessons because of his visitations to the deanery, where he had made the acquaintance of the dean's musical sister Marianne Merewether, whom biographers have sometimes mistaken for his daughter. Whether or not Wesley had been in love with a respectable daughter of the Cloth, his sister Rosalind was very jealous of the affair, which is evident in the following letter to his mother:

I have received another letter from Ros, which was of the same one as the first as regards *my* affairs. It mentioned you, respecting my letters lately which I ought not to have written and would not have, had I thought it was impious, however, to have done what was wanted. I can't write secrets in this letter, but is it not a little hard upon me not to have one friend in the world living away from everyone who knows me, which I suppose it is all for the best?

I hope Father is well? I received the books safely. How is Eliza? If she has got any good clothes, I would invite her to come and see me. Does she behave like a lady? Has she got that horrid wriggle in her walk, she used to have? Suppose I invite her, can she come? What would I give to get rid of the frightful melancholy which besets me at all turnings![27]

THREE CHOIRS FESTIVAL 1834

Wesley made his first appearance in his capacity as the Festival Conductor at Hereford. The following account of the opening service appeared in the *Hereford Times*:

The scene during the performance was one of uncommon splendour . . . for it was impossible to listen to the pealing of the organ, the harmonizing tones of the instruments, and the thrilling sounds of the voices, without feeling that we were in the midst of grandeur. We confess that we had our doubts as to the effect of removing the site of the performances from the Choir to the Nave; we feared that there would be a reverberation of sound almost totally destructive to harmony; we were, however, delighted to find that our fears had been groundless.[28]

The music included Spohr's Overture to his oratorio, 'The Last Judgement' (1825), Handel's *Dettingen Te Deum* (1743), and Attwood's Coronation anthem 'I was glad' (1820); and the service finished with Boyce's instrumental anthem, 'Lord, Thou hast been our refuge', an impressive work, which had been composed for the Festival of the Sons of the Clergy in St Paul's Cathedral.

On the Tuesday evening, an audience distinguished for rank and fashion attended the first secular concert that began with an overture, and finished with Beethoven's 'Pastoral' Symphony (1826). Afterwards, Mr Edward Jones's dance band played quadrilles in which everybdy danced with much spirit.

In spite of torrential rain on the Wednesday morning, more than 700 people heard Spohr's 'Last Judgement', Part I of Haydn's 'Creation' (1798), selections from Handel's 'Judas Maccabaeus' (1747) and his 'Ode to St Cecilia's Day' (1739), as well as Samuel Wesley's *Antiphona* (1827). And the conductor also contributed 'a well-written *Sanctus*', now in the possession of the British Library.[29] At the next evening concert the music consisted of Mozart's Overture to *Don Giovanni* (1787), an Aria from Spohr's opera 'Azor and Zemira' (1819), and the conductor's 'Manuscript Overture' that indicated considerable talent. (It can be seen in the Parry Room of the Royal College of Music and was first broadcast from Winchester Cathedral in 1976.) Finally, the dance band again kept 'the light fantastic toe' actively employed until the early hours of the following morning.

On the Thursday, every seat was occupied for Mozart's *Requiem* (1791). It was followed by the Aria 'Let the bright seraphim' from Handel's 'Samson' (1742), Samuel Wesley's brilliant five-part *Exultate Deo,* and the conductor's Sacred Song, 'Abraham's Offering' with an orchestral accompaniment.[30] The celebrated baritone, Mr Henry Phillips was the soloist, but it was 'performed in a manner that seemed as if none of the parties engaged quite understood the composer's meaning.'[31] The programme ended with selections from the *Messiah,* resulting in the following mordant comment: 'This departure from all precedent has never been repeated, and it is hoped never will be.'[32]

The music of the final concert included the Overtures to Spohr's 'Jessonda' (1823) and Mendelssohn's 'A Midsummer Night's Dream' (1826). Moreover, 'the silvery notes' of Mr Nicholas Mori's violin playing very much delighted the audience.

Wesley's next letter to his mother, dated 3 October, 1834, was concerned with his father's improving health, the best way of keeping tea and sugar, and his wish to obtain a newspaper report on the recent Hereford Festival:

> I am delighted to hear on all sides that Father is much better. I trust he finds some proper amusement somewhere. I should think he might have a great deal of a pleasant time at Mr Glenn's, if he is careful with that most dangerous thing, *the tongue*. . . .
>
> I am endeavouring to live cheaply, for I find I shall not receive money for sometime, and the expense of a horse is great indeed. . . .
>
> Did I tell you I got a prize for a glee lately?
>
> I should like to get a copy of *The True Sun* newspaper, which contains the criticism of the Hereford Musical Festival. If you get it me, get it yourself. Don't employ anybody else to buy it, or let them know I wish to see it.
>
> What is a good way of buying tea and sugar and of keeping it? Can you send me any kind of box which would hold it safely, and could you send it to me regularly?
>
> I received the fish which was not *very good*. Who bought it? You did, did you not? Market better next time! However, I was generally pleased and obliged.[33]

PRIZES FOR GLEES

Glee Clubs were very popular in our English cities between 1750 and 1830, and even members of the Royal Family patronized them. The Manchester Glee Club, for instance, had a membership of 50 male singers, who used to meet from September to April. Singing began at seven-thirty and continued until mid-night, with an interval for supper at ten o'clock. No refreshments of any kind were allowed to be brought into the Club-room before supper was served. And fines were imposed on all latecomers and absentees.

Wesley himself won two prizes for glees. The first was awarded in 1832 for his dull setting of one of William Linley's poems, 'At that dread hour.' (The Linleys of Bath were a celebrated family of musicians, and William became a distinguished poet and novelist.) And the second prize, referred to in the preceding letter, was awarded by the Gentlemen's Glee Club of Manchester in 1833. It was a setting of Lord Byron's poem, 'I wish to tune my quiv'ring lyre' and has unusual discords in the section 'Or Tyrian Cadmus roved afar.'

While he was in Hereford, Wesley also wrote several songs, like 'Wert thou like me in life's low vale', 'There breathes a living fragrance' and 'The bruised reed.'

In writing to his mother in October, 1834, he described a visit to another Festival:

> I have been away from Hereford to the Birmingham Music Meeting, and have been spoken very highly of in the newspaper. It has been a very gay

one: immense numbers of people there. Did not Father once conduct those meetings?[34] How came he to let that slip out of his hands?

Poultry just now is intolerably dear. The people where I live say it will be cheap next week, and I assure you I am obliged to think twice, or thrice, before I spend a shilling. I dread Xmas. Something I must do to get *ready* money.

Poor Lizzy! I *will* have her here shortly, but at the present my whole time is taken up in thinking how I shall get money. This great people are so fanciful and whimsical that I have more trouble in getting an opportunity to give a lesson than in giving it!

Hereford is very dull. Our dean is made a canon of Windsor, which adds about fourteen hundred a year to his income!! I wish I was a dean![35]

HIS MARRIAGE

In 1835 Wesley was unsuccessful in his application for the organist's post at St George's Chapel, Windsor, which was given to the youthful (later Sir) George Elvey, a lay clerk of Christ Church, Oxford. But his disappointment was quickly forgotten, since the marriage registers of Ewyas Harold Church, in Herefordshire, recorded:

> Samuel Sebastian Wesley, of this parish, Bachelor, and Mary Anne Merewether, Spinster, of the [Cathedral] parish of St John in the City of Hereford, were married in this Church by Licence this fourth day, May 1835. William Bowen, Vicar. In the presence of William Bowen, Junior, [and] John Parry.

It was certainly a case of a runaway marriage between the Cathedral organist and his dean's sister. Marianne was the fourth child and only daughter of John Merewether whose country residence was at Blackland, Wiltshire.[36] And in the Parry Room of the Royal College of Music there can be seen a manuscript volume of miscellaneous music in her handwriting. Its contents include piano pieces and songs by composers, like Arne, Balfe, Donizetti, Haydn, Horn, Mendelssohn, Mozart, Schubert, Spohr and Samuel Wesley.[37] Another volume has the 48 hymn-tunes that she had collected in 1879 and dedicated 'to the loved memory of One, whose preferences have chiefly guided this selection from his Father's hymn tunes.'[38]

During the Gloucester Festival of 1835, Wesley presided at the piano and his new vocal quartet, 'Millions of spiritual creatures' (now in the Parry Room), received its first performance. Also in September, the Hereford Chapter accepted his letter, informing them of his resignation from all Cathedral offices at the end of that quarter, though they had to state the matter of Wesley's stipend would have to wait for the return of his brother-in-law.

The dean finally decided that the organist was not entitled to any payment beyond that which he had been receiving[39]; hence Wesley's postscript to his mother's letter: 'I grieve to think I can't send the money, yet.' On the other hand, the dean later baptised Wesley's third son, Francis Gwynne, at Exeter in 1841, so there were no unfriendly feelings between them.

S. S. WESLEY, Aged about 25

From a portrait by an unknown artist, by permission of the Royal College of Music.

CHAPTER FOUR
Exeter Cathedral (1835-1842)

SHORTLY BEFORE Wesley's appointment to Exeter Cathedral was made official on the 15th of August, 1835, William Landon, Vicar of Braunton, Devonshire, wrote a confidential report to the Dean of Exeter, Dr Whittington Landon:

> Everything I can learn confirms me in the opinion of Mr Wesley's personal respectability. Dr Clutton, one of the Canons [at Hereford], particularly mentioned the great improvement of the Boys in the Choir since Mr Wesley became their Organist. . . .
>
> Mr Dixon's name is new to me — and of his Merits I have no right to doubt: but the Choir at Norwich is a very different establishment from that at Exeter. The Vicars Choral are the Minor Canons, and the Boys in my time were by no means as well qualified to take the leading parts of Anthems and Services, and to fill *Choruses,* as our Boys at Exeter; indeed I do not think that any of Handel's Choruses were ever attempted in the ordinary Service of the Choir. As far as my information goes, I am not disposed to alter my opinion in favour of Mr Wesley; and if the Chapter are at all divided in their judgement between him and Mr Dixon, I must be considered as decidedly favourable to Mr Wesley.[1]

Also in the Cathedral Library there is another testimonial from the musician and solicitor (later Dr) Henry Gauntlett (1805-1876), written while he was organist of St Olave's, Southwark:

> 79 Queen Street, Cheapside,
> 10 July, 1835.
>
> Sir,
>   At the desire of Mr Samuel Sebastian Wesley of the Cathedral, Hereford, I beg to forward you as Clerk to the Dean and Chapter of Exeter my testimonial as to his character and abilities. I have known him for about ten

years and consider him to be one of the brightest ornaments of the profession.

As an Organ Performer, although there may be one who possibly exceeds him in brilliancy, clearness, and rapidity of execution, yet in the sublimity of the Ecclesiastical School ... and his perfect command over the subtle intricacies of fugue writing, I know of none who excel him. In his extemporary performances he displays great concentration of mind, and a ready flow of imagination exemplified in his varied melodies and profound modulations. His performance on the Pedals is truly extraordinary, and he exhibits a perfect command over all the mere mechanical difficulties connected with a just use of the King of intruments. I have heard most of the celebrated continental organists, and am well acquainted with those of this country, and I have no hesitation in saying that I consider him in some respects superior to them all. . . .

That Mr Wesley is one of these characters and qualified to advance our Church music to a state of perfection, which it has not reached, I have no doubt. Educated in the Chapel Royal, from his childhood he has been intimately versed in the writings of Purcell and the long train of illustrious composers for the Church who succeed him. To this Mr Wesley has added an unlimited acquaintance with works of the German writers in the Organ School of which Sebastian Bach is the great head; and his extraordinary combinations to be met with in the modern Opera places him as a deeply read musician far above his contemporaries.

I am happy to add that I believe his character as a man and a gentleman to be perfectly unimpeachable.[2]

One can almost picture the faces of the Dean and Chapter as this grandiloquent letter was read out. In December, Wesley received half of the organist's salary that was due for the period June 21 to September 29; and the remaining half was divided between the late organist's apprentices, who had played for the Cathedral services since James Paddon's death in August of 1835.[3]

Wesley was very interested in the art of organ construction. On 6 January, 1838, he wrote to the Cathedral authorities because his name was being used in the correspondence column of the *Western Luminary*:

The Reverend Mr Vicary in his remarks on the Cathedral Organ has made an observation which is very disagreeable to myself and has left the public to infer from what he states that I require the opinion of an Organ Builder to assist me in the judging of an organ.

I intend to offer no remarks on Mr Vicary's statements. excepting that when he suggests that Organ pipes are improved by age, he cannot be aware of the immense improvements which have occurred in the *voicing* of those pipes, and that three times the power and brilliancy of tone is now produced from pipes voiced at the period in which John Loosemore flourished, I may first observe, that these improvements in the voicing can be applied to pipes as old as those of the Cathedral Organ.

I cannot but regret that Mr Vicary has written at all on this subject, excepting his allusions to the previous liberality of the Chapter, which I had wished to bear testimony myself only I thought the subject better passed unnoticed altogether, as he is manifestly uninformed on the subject of Organ Building, and I must observe to you, that the unfavourable opinion which has been expressed of the Organ in its present state did not originate with myself, but with the professional musicians visiting Exeter.[4]

Nonetheless this adverse newspaper publicity had the desired effect of the sum of £240 being spent on improvements to the organ, when the compass of the Swell Organ was extended and the Pedal Pipes were also added to the instrument. Mr Gray, of London, undertook the work under the watchful eye of Wesley, and a further sum of £12 was spent in order to give additional support to the organ case.[5]

THE OXFORD DOCTORATE

Wesley held decided views on the subject of musical degrees: 'An ordinary academical degree is not to my fancy. I would have it only conferred upon men of position. I was a candidate for the Chair of Music at Edinburgh. It was then considered advisable for the candidate to be doctored, and consequently I applied for the degree at Oxford.' Moreover Mrs Wesley later told one of his pupils that for many years Dr Wesley had refused to use the title, but to prevent confusion between his father's initials and his own, he had eventually adopted it.[6] When did Wesley, therefore, decide to work for his doctorate? The answer lies in the following letter, written by his father to Dr William Crotch, the Professor of Music at Oxford:

8 King's Row,
Pentonville,
Wednesday, March 30, 1836.

My dear Sir,

My Son requests me to forward to you a Copy of a few of his Compositions and a Manuscript which he submits to you as an Exercise for the Degree of Bachelor in Music. He has some fear that it is not precisely the Kind of Exercise which the Statutes require, but if it can be accepted he would feel himself greatly indebted, as the Distance at which he resides from London (being Organist and Sub Chanter of Exeter Cathedral) makes every Communication between us rather lengthy and expensive Matter.

You have heard no Doubt that his Abilities (from a Child) were extraordinary, having been Organist at Camberwell, Waterloo and Hereford Cathedral, and now at Exeter; and I rely on your great Kindness that if you can serve him in any Way, you will. . . .[7]

It must have been very tedious to settle down and write 'the kind of Exercise' that the Oxford Statutes required. And it was certainly ironic to find Wesley coercing his father to correspond with Crotch, particularly after the unforgettable experience in the Gresham Prize Competition. Three years were to elapse, however, before any further action was taken.

35

In 1839 Wesley wrote to the University Registrar, Dr Bliss, enquiring whether he would be allowed to accumulate two degrees at the same time.[8] Having received a satisfactory reply, another letter was posted from Taunton on May 20:

> I beg to express my best thanks for the kindness of your letter. I have not yet addressed Dr Macbride on the subject of my entering my name at Magdalen Hall, as it occurred to me that if my name would be admitted at Magdalen College, I might perhaps be allowed to perform my exercise in the Chapel, which would be very desirable as the exercise consists of a cathedral anthem and would be more effective when performed in a place where anthems are usually sung. . . .[9]

Anxious to avoid the expense of having to hire professional singers from London or elsewhere, Wesley pursued the idea of making use of the talent available at the Oxford Musical Festival. And in another letter, he wrote:

> I am really ashamed to intrude my affairs again on your notice, after the great trouble you have kindly taken, but being intimately unacquainted with the manner in which it might be proper for me to address the Vice Chancellor to his appointing a day for the performance of my exercise, and being rather anxious to obtain leave to make use of the Festival days of June, and the First if possible, I have feared to make any communication to the Vice Chancellor lest an unwelcome one might be rather an obstacle than otherwise to my wishes. . . .[10]

Wesley received an adequate answer and matriculated at Magdalen College on the 17th of June, 1839. But he had an anxious time when the old fox Crotch refused to accept his exercise, an extended anthem, 'O Lord, Thou art my God', unless certain passages were immediately altered to comply with the more traditional laws of harmony as practised by the classical composers. But the composer stuck to his manuals, so that the Professor had to back down. Meanwhile Wesley was duly capped on June 21, and the following candid account of the proceedings appeared in a local newspaper:

> On the morning of Thursday last, S. S. Wesley, Esq. of Magdalen College, and organist of Exeter Cathedral, performed his exercise for the Degrees of Bachelor and Doctor of Music, by commutation, in the beautiful chapel of Magdalen College. The ante-chapel was filled with company, and at half-past twelve, on the arrival of the Vice Chancellor and Proctors, Mr Wesley commenced his performance. The introduction on the organ was exceedingly good, and did great credit to the author, both as a composition and performance. Of the remainder of the piece, as regards the instrumental department, we may say the same; but of the vocal line we could not fairly judge, the singers, in many parts, being both out of time and out of tune.[11]

The poor standard of singing is understandable considering the lamentable state of church music in the Oxford Colleges at this time. Although Walter Vicary had been organist at Magdalen since 1797, the instruction of the Choristers was nominally in the hands of an elderly don who allowed them to run wild.

In July, Dr Crotch wrote to congratulate Wesley upon his success, but also reminded him, 'My fee for the degrees accumulated is 3 guineas, which, as I am going out of town and also to remove my residence a few doors off, I will trouble you to pay at your perfect convenience.[12] The Professor was moving to Camden Villas, Bedford Place, Kensington.

THE CORRESPONDENCE WITH VINCENT NOVELLO

In 1839 Eliza Wesley was anxious to get a list of subscribers so that her father's *Confitebor* might be published. One of them was Mr Vincent Novello, who wrote to Dr Wesley in order to ascertain what progress had been made. And in November, he replied:

> Of my Father's work, I regret to say, I know not of their being any chance of its immediate publication. Its publication was undertaken, I fear, by a gentleman [Mr Draganott] whose view was quite as much to introduce his own name to the musical world by such means as to bring out the work ...
>
> I hope to be able to comply with your desire respecting the Voluntary. I have now several engagements to fulfil with Publishers in London, but the dreadful nature of an organist's, I mean a country Cathedral organist's occupation, that of giving lessons all over the country from morning to night makes composition a pleasure hardly to be indulged in. How much should musicians strive that the offices connected with the art in Cathedrals are not of a nature to make them independent respecting money, so that they might give their attention to the improvement of the decaying, much degraded musical state of the Church ... the Clergy will never move in the matter. They know nothing of their real interests, and consequently the Establishment is going to ruin.'[13]

This letter, however, remained on Wesley's desk for several days for the following postscript was added:

> I have just received you letter of the 16th. I open my letter to say to you that it would have been finished much sooner, but that I preferred waiting until I had an opportunity of addressing you free of postage.

Wesley's next letter to Novello, dated 29 January, 1840, mentioned the possible publication of his anthems, as well as to the voluntary promised in the previous correspondence:

> Allow me to inquire whether it would be agreeable to you to publish two little Anthems and a Creed. They are chiefly for treble voices and I set no store by them as they are fitter for the drawing-room than the church, although this may be in their favour in one respect. I publish them for the opportunity it will afford me of offering a few remarks on the sadly fallen state of our Cathedral Service. ...

But I beseech your indulgence for the music. They are written for country folk, and the requirements of such people is, I trust, beyond your inception. I am preparing some, I think, better things for publication and wish the present things produced separately.

I felt obliged by your sending me Mr Walmisley's new fugue, not that I thought anything of the new composition, but because it made me acquainted with the nature of the work for which you desire my contribution, which shall be sent to you as soon as possible.

Miss [Clara] Novello[14] has very much delighted everybody here. I always endeavour to send my pupils to a good performance, but on this occasion their minds were made up to *go* before I offered an opinion. I have been striving hard to get a Festival in our fine, roomy Cathedral but our Clergy are at present unfavourable to it.[15]

Can any of the above music be identified? The Creed is derived from Wesley's Communion Service for Trebles that was later modified for his Cathedral Service in E. And the Voluntary is certainly the *Introduction and Fugue in C sharp minor* (dedicated to Vincent Novello in 1836 and published by Mr J. Dean, who became Station Master at Winchester, while Wesley was organist there). This austere, demanding music was first advertised as 'The Studio for the organ, exemplified in a series of exercises in the strict and free styles,' and may be compared with Mendelssohn's *Organ Sonata No. 3* (1839-45). Wesley's bold *Introduction* was later extended from 26 to 44 bars; and the *Fugue* has a finely constructed subject related to the preceding themes in the *Introduction*. Yet a contemporary music critic declared:

Here is a tough, weather-beaten Fugue. They who desire to tackle it, and the Lord be with them that do, will meet in the course of their progress, the characteristics of real fugue-blood breeding. Before attacking it, a course of gymnastics is recommended.[16]

According to William Spark, 'Old Sam Wesley was not a great pedal player whilst his son was a skilled pedaller, and had written and often played a fugue in C sharp minor that bothered many a hard-working organ student.'[17]

In 1838 Wesley published *A Selection of Psalm Tunes*, 'adapted expressly to the English organ with pedals.'[18] And a second edition, issued four years later, has an interesting Preface stating that the composer's object had been 'to assist the young church organist in his accompaniment of congregational psalmody, and to furnish him with a work to which he may refer to his endeavours to make use of the Pedals, and acquire an independent command of the left hand.'[19]

A SAD EVENT

The sudden death of their nine month old infant Mary on the 13th of February, 1840, caused great grief to the Wesley family. She was buried in the Old Cemetery just outside the City Walls. And on the day of her passing, Wesley himself bravely wrote to his mother in a very shaky hand:

> I have the sad intelligence to give you, our dear baby is no more. It left us last night, at almost twelve o'clock.
>
> I cannot tell you how we loved it, and what a dear infant it was. We are suffering the loss most acutely, and I am too weak as yet to desire any consolation, only that we hope and pray to have it again with us, hereafter . . .
>
> I felt more fond of the dear child because it was very much like myself. I cannot write more.[20]

Whether this loss eventually caused Wesley's angular relationship with the Cathedral Chapter, we have no means of knowing. However, in May the Chapter Clerk informed him that he was no longer to give lessons on the Cathedral organ, though his apprentices would be allowed to practise for services.[21] This directive displeased Wesley immensely, because the Cathedral organist had been allowed ever since 1808, 'to use the organ for the instruction of his apprentices on Tuesdays and Saturdays from nine to ten o'clock, and from after Morning Service to one o'clock in the afternoon.'[22] And yet, if he had been giving private tuition to Lady Acland, of Killerton Park, near Exeter, no doubt the Chapter would have been afraid of a public scandal, or more likely, a little jealous of his hob-nobbing with the County!

Lady Lydia Acland was the only daughter of the famous London banker Henry Hoare, who had devoted his life to the revival of both Convocation and the Lay Synods of the Church of England. At the age of twenty-one, she married Sir Thomas Dyke Acland (1787-1871), a keen supporter of Catholic Emancipation and a future head of the religious party in the House of Commons, in succession to Wilberforce.[23] Further, his friendship with the Hoare family introduced him to the Evangelical circle as well as to the Irish divines, Alexander Knox and Bishop Jebb, whose nephew Wesley would later meet in Leeds. It seems that the Aclands had promised to subscribe to the concerts that Wesley was arranging in Exeter,[24] but nothing came of the enterprise; for in replying to William Hawes's request for a similar event, he had to inform him regretfully:

> The success of such undertakings as the one you propose is very uncertain. I once endeavoured to give concerts here by subscription, but could not get enough subscribers. Another professor made the attempt and certainly gave excellent concerts, but lost much money. I do not think I should like to engage your party.[25]

Lady Acland was an accomplished musician, and to his pupil Wesley respectfully dedicated two sets of *Three Pieces for a Chamber Organ* (1838). She died in London on 23 June, 1856, and was afterwards buried in the family chapel of Columbjohn, near Broad Clyst.

SONG SCHOOL TROUBLES

In June, 1840, the Chapter Clerk was instructed to inform Wesley that his private engagements should not interfere with his attendances at the Chapter Meeting on Saturday morning,[26] when the following week's music was fully discussed and then entered on a printed sheet by the organist.[27] Unfortunately, more serious trouble occurred after the Choristers had attended the local Glee Club without the organist's permission. Hence the following letter, which Wesley had despatched to the Dean of Exeter:

> I beg to mention for your consideration the circumstances under which the application to you was made for the attendance of the Choristers at the Glee Club. . . . That request not having been made to me, I have prevented their attendance at the practice meetings of the singers; and in consequence, Mr Cole has waited on yourself to give leave for them as he believes in opposition to my wishes.
>
> I trust you will not think me to entertain any intrusive or disrespectful feeling if I suggest that the organist of the Cathedral has always been here and is in every other Cathedral town, the authority conferred with on matters connected with the musical services of his pupils, the Choristers, and that he will be placed very often in unpleasant situations if the public are allowed the use of the boys' services without the sanction of their music master, for they may often be called upon to perform things of which they know nothing. . . .
>
> If, however, the Chapter intend to depart from custom on this subject, I shall be happy to acquiesce in their determination; but believing that they have no such wish, I take the liberty of making these observations in reference to the irregular interference of Mr Cole. . . .
>
> I beg to add an apology for this hurried communication, being in the midst of preparation for a long journey.[28]

But this civil letter failed to mention the serious incident that had happened on the day it was written. For in the presence of both Canon Bartholomew and Mr Ralph Barnes (Chapter Clerk and Legal Secretary to the Bishop), two Choristers described what had actually occurred in the Song School:

> John Homeyard stated that on the previous Sunday before the Morning Service, Mr Chamberlain (Dr Wesley's apprentice), Robert Kitt and himself had been practising a glee without the organ, when Dr Wesley had come in late, and, having heard them, asked if they had been practising for the Glee Club concert with Mr Risdon and Mr Cole, the night before. They said that

they had. Wesley then inquired who had given them orders to go. They replied that the men had asked the dean, who had given leave for them. Dr Wesley declared that the dean was not their master and that he was their master. And he went over to the window, turned round and ran over to the Choristers, and said that they should not have gone without his leave. He next struck Homeyard, several times, hard blows with his fist on the back. By that time, Homeyard was holding down his head in order to avoid the blows; and he then received another blow on the point of his chin by a kick from Dr Wesley, a hard blow, and subsequently there had been a mark on his chin for several days.

Kitt, next, took up his side of the story by reporting how, as he quitted Homeyard, Dr Wesley had struck him, too, a blow on the side of his face and had knocked him down with another blow; and how, when he was on the floor, Dr Wesley had kicked him.[29]

In the absence of the organist, the Chapter Clerk then noted that the whole attack upon the boys had been equally infamous. And he sent copies of their complaints to Dean Lowe and to other members of the Chapter, who desired Dr Wesley's presence in the Chapter House after Matins, the following Tuesday.[30]

At the Meeting Wesley was asked whether he had anything further to say concerning his treatment of the Choristers. Although he admitted that their statements were substantially true, he maintained that he was entitled to punish them because they had failed to obtain his permission to attend the concert and to inform him of the dean's previous approval. The Chapter, nevertheless, declared unanimously that 'he was unjustified in inflicting any punishment, much less of making the attack, which was an indignity unworthy of his situation and degrading to the boys.' And besides, they took exception to Wesley's uncontrollable temper and inability to apologise, so that they felt that he must be suspended from the duties and the emoluments of his office until the next Chapter Meeting at the Christmas audit.[31]

Then Wesley foolishly rushed out of the Chapter House in a state of rage. After coming to his senses through his wife's becalming influence, he wrote to the Chapter Clerk:

> I was not surprised to find by your note that the Chapter were much offended by the expressions used by me at the Meeting, and immediately became sensible of the extreme impropriety of my conduct, and, if it can be received as an apology, I have no hesitation in expressing my regret that my remarks should have induced me to show more warmth of manner than was becoming in me.[32]

A bundle of letters, relating to the unhappy incident, was later enclosed in a paper wrapper but endorsed by the Chapter Clerk: 'The most to be avoided man I ever met with!'

In December, the same year, Dr Crotch answered Wesley's inquiry concerning the prickly subject of whose right it was to choose the hymn-tunes for church services, and I quote:

> I am very happy to give you my opinion on the subject, you propose, but must add that it can be of no weight being a mere opinion of a private individual whereas you want that of a bishop or a lawyer at least.
>
> I consider an organist bound to play the tunes appointed by the clergyman though I regret that the latter should have anything to do with the music, though he ought to choose the words. I consider the tunes you mention as very objectionable but probably if that were respectfully submitted to your curate he would not appoint them again, even if he still continued to like them. At all events we cannot *compel* any one to have a musical taste or to *see that we have,* when they have not.
>
> I expressed my opinion very freely in the preface to my Psalmody; but the duty of an organist must, I fear, be to perform what *they* please who appoint him to that office.[33]

Crotch's sound advice was later reiterated by Sir Robert Phillimore's judgement in the case of *Wyndham v. Cole* (1875), namely: 'It would seem that in the absence of custom or agreement to the contrary the organist must obey the minister's directives even as to a choice of music.'[34]

In June, 1841, Wesley was reprimanded because of absence without leave, having left the organ-playing to an inexperienced pupil.[35] And it seems that this person was the eighteen year old William Spark, whose fascinating *Musical Memories* (1888) has this description of Wesley at Exeter:

> He looked much older than he was, being then slightly bald; in after years he was denuded of all his black hair and always wore a wig. The Choir had been greatly improved, and this, with Wesley's playing, and the introduction of better anthems and services, attracted large congregations to the Cathedral. . . .
>
> I became his articled pupil for five years, and I made such progress in playing the Cathedral services, that he often left me for two or three days, and would go off to one of the numerous rivers in Devonshire to exercise his favourite pastime of fly-fishing.[36]

Sadly for Wesley, his relationship had deteriorated with the new dean, Thomas Hill Lowe (elevated from the precentorship in 1839), so that he was more than anxious to escape from the restrictive life of a provincial cathedral to the more enervating one of a university city. The first opportunity came at Edinburgh with the death of the Reid Professor of Music, John Thomson. And in May, 1841, he collected an impressive number of testimonials from his musical friends, like Thomas Adams, Charles Clarke, William Crotch, William Knyvett, Vincent Novello and Henry Smart.[37]

Meanwhile, in September, the new parish church of St Peter's, Leeds, was consecrated by the Bishop of Ripon. An influential member of the congregation, Mr Martin Cawood, later suggested to the Vicar Dr Walter Hook, that the organist of Exeter Cathedral might be invited to give the inaugural recital on their new organ, which had been built by a local firm at the cost of £1,241. And its distinctive case with no visible pipework can be seen to-day.

Wesley's recital was given on Monday, October 18, and there was a favourable report in the columns of *The Leeds Intelligencer,* with a special mention given to his accompaniment of the selections from both the *Messiah* and the *Creation*:

> Of Dr Wesley's style of performance we may speak with equal confidence; there is a chasteness and delicacy of feeling in his accompaniment of the vocal parts rarely to be met with, whilst in bolder and more prominent performances, his mighty and Herculean grasp of all the varied powers of the instrument displays the great vigour and power of his mind. The voluntaries which he played were really admirable, particularly one of his own compositions, and J. Sebastian Bach's celebrated Fugue in E flat major.[38]

On the other hand the same critic had noticed that the organ was a little out of tune, owing to the excessive heat of an overcrowded church.

The warm welcome by the Yorkshire people gave Wesley a new lease of life. 'He was so much impressed with the wealth of Leeds, and delighted to be asked by two rich merchants to select grand Broadwood pianos for them, that bearing in mind his disagreement with Dean Lowe of Exeter, he forthwith accepted from the Vicar and Churchwardens the offer of organist at £200 per annum, guaranteed for ten years.'[39] And in a letter to a friend, the Vicar reported: 'Dr Wesley says that our service is most sublime, beyond anything he ever heard in any cathedral.'[40]

But Wesley was in no hurry to accept the Vicar's kind offer, although he had informed the Chapter Clerk on November 20 of his intention to resign from his offices.[41] Because, on that same date, he had collected three testimonials from local people,[42] thus showing his desire of delaying his departure from Exeter in case he might be offered the Chair of Music at Edinburgh. Here is Professor Walmisley's testimonial to the Principal of the University:

Trinity College, Cambridge, Nov. 22, 1841.

> Sir,
>
> I have much pleasure in writing this, though my opinion can add but little weight to the universal consent of all musicians in England, that Dr Wesley is the first among us, both for extraordinary talent and for unwearied diligence in improving that talent to the utmost. He is not only the finest organ-player that we have, but also a most accomplished musician. I am sure that his

appointment would give entire saitisfaction to the body over which you preside, as it would be hailed with delight by all who know his worth and can truly estimate his abilities.[43]

In spite of this glowing praise, the University elected the composer of the popular lyric 'Home, sweet home,' Mr Henry Bishop (1735-1855). The Presbyterian electors, ever suspicious of Episcopalians, were naturally a little daunted by the idea of appointing a young cathedral organist from the Church of England.

HIS RESIGNATION

On New Year's Day, 1842, Wesley finally informed the Chapter Clerk that he would be giving up all his duties at the end of March,[44] but he had already left for the busy, hubbub of industrial Leeds. And he wrote to thank the Cathedral authorities for having confirmed that they would be taking over his house in the Close. As to their request that his articled pupil, William Spark, might be allowed to remain until the end of the next quarter, he remonstrated:

> I do deeply regret that at the present moment the Chapter should ask a favour of me, as it is only with the most extreme pain that I have been led to move myself and family from a place and neighbourhood to which I was so much attached as Exeter. I have written to say that I am unable to do without Mr Spark's aid here as soon as my quarter expires. I am obliged to go from Leeds as soon as I can have him here.[45]

In another letter Wesley had requested that the Chapter Clerk should attend to his little account, waspishly adding, 'I have no doubt it has escaped your memory, being occupied of course with more profitable things!'[46] And he had also sent a belligerent note to the dean, who directed that it must be read out in the next Chapter Meeting, resulting in the following reply from the Chapter Clerk:

> The insolence of the note is so surpassing that you can expect no other answer than that announcement. No future communication, addressed to the Dean, will receive any reply whatever. If you have any to make to the Dean and Chapter, I beg it may be made to me in terms fit to be communicated.[47]

Wesley's walking stick, with its serpentlike stem and eel-shaped handle, can still be seen in the Song School — a true symbol of his stormy times there.

Dr S. S. WESLEY, Aged 39

From a portrait by William Keighley Briggs, by permission of the Royal College of Music.

46

CHAPTER FIVE

Leeds Parish Church (1842-1849)

IN VICTORIAN England, Leeds was a typical town of the West Riding. 'The ordinary people were rough, uncouth, headstrong, and independent in a degree calculated to daunt and repel a stranger, until he discovered that below this rugged surface there often glowed warm hearts, generous feelings, and strong earnestness of purpose.'[1]

In 1837 Dr Theodore Farquhar Hook, the thirty-nine year old Vicar of St Peter's Parish Church, moved into Park Place. It was, and still is, a pleasant residential district within a few minutes' walk from the town centre, and 'yet not so near as to be overwhelmed by the smoke of its multitudinous factories and mills.' And here he planned his great ideal for the people of Leeds, and I quote: 'We must never rest until we have provided for every poor man a pastor, and for every poor child a school.'[2] Within twenty years or so, Hook had built twenty-one churches, twenty-three vicarages, and twenty-seven schools.

Disregarding the apathy of the churchwardens, the congregations became so large that scarcely standing room was available at the Sunday services. Furthermore, six hundred and forty parishioners signed an address asking for better seating arrangements, which resulted in the building of a new church in the Gothic style, designed by the celebrated architect Robert Dennis Chantrell.

Its interior plan exemplified the main principles of the Camden Society, containing three units of Nave, Chancel, and Sanctuary. But the last two units were separated by a considerable flight of steps, so that there was enough space for every communicant to kneel on the wide steps below the altar-rails. The choir also had a special place in the Chancel. And the full effect of their singing was now felt in the most distant parts of the church.

This innovation was due to the Vicar's liturgical and musical consultant, Prebendary Jebb, of Limerick Cathedral, who maintained:

> In the constitution of her choirs, the Church of England has made the nearest possible approach to a primitive and heavenly pattern. Her white-robed companies of men and boys, stationed at each side of her chancels, midway between the porch and the altar, stand daily ministering the service of prayer and thanksgiving.

The above statement was made in one of the *Three Lectures on the Cathedral Service of the Church of England* that had been given in the Leeds Church Institute, Albion Place, by invitation of the Vicar in 1841, and afterwards published by Rivingtons. Moreover, we are told that they eventually removed all local prejudice against the newly-styled 'Decorated Parochial' Service, and that several gentlemen had joined the choir as honorary members, believing 'it a privilege to be permitted to be robed in the vestments of the Church.'[3]

It seemed that a robed choir of both men and boys had existed in Leeds Parish Church since 1818. (The custom of wearing surplices was certainly unusual for parish churches, though not for cathedrals or college chapels.) Another instance of this practice was at St John's Church, Donaghmore, in Northern Ireland, during the dedicated incumbency of Prebendary Fitzgibbon (1830-32), of which Jebb has this to say:

> In the midst of an extensive and impoverished parish, in the heart of the city of Limerick, where the small endowment of the benefice rendered the employment of a curate impossible, though oppressed with toilsome duties, and afflicted with a broken constitution, he kept up the services of the Church: he instituted a small choir of men and boys, who were habited and arranged according to the best choral precedent.[4]

THE CHORAL SERVICE

Dr Hook was a liberal broad churchman, whose beliefs came between Tractarianism and Evangelicalism. His views on the Choral Service are stated in a letter addressed to Miss Harcourt, who was a sister of the Archbishop of York:

> Our service, especially when sung, is so essentially Catholic that I only wonder how it has been tolerated by Protestants; I suppose it can only be accounted for by the fact that Protestants cannot reflect. . . .
> Now it is the essence of Protestantism to refer everything to self; it is of the essence of Catholicism to refer everything to God. A Protestant goes to church to get good to his soul, a Catholic to glorify God; a Protestant to have his own mind impressed, a Catholic to do God service; a Protestant desires to have a service addressed to himself, a Catholic to offer a sacrifice to God; a Protestant desires to have his ecstatic feelings excited, since he judges of the state of his religion by the state of his blood; a Catholic desires to have

everything so done that he may be solemnly reminded at every point of the service, that he is engaged with saints and angels in an unearthly work. He confesses his sins, but it is with the Church; he praises God but with the Church; he prays but with the Church, in the Church's own peculiar language and peculiar tone. According, then, as your feelings are more Catholic or more Protestant, you will like or dislike Cathedral Service. A Protestant must hate Choral Service, though, if he likes music, he may commit the sin of going to Church unworthily to hear the anthem; a Catholic though he knows nothing of music, will go far to attend regularly the Choral Service, because it accords with his feeling of performing a service. During the last century the mind of England became thoroughly Protestantised, therefore Choral Service fell into disuse; it is now becoming again Catholicised, and Choral Service is coming in.[5]

In writing to his life-long friend and fellow Wykehamist, William Page Wood (later Lord Hatherley), the Vicar said:

I am now fully occupied in preparing to form a choir, a subject on which I am profoundly ignorant; but John Jebb has kindly assisted me. I have secured a man named Hill and his nephew from Westminster Abbey. I am to pay them £120 a year. How I shall raise the money I know not; but this I know, a good choir must be formed, if I go to prison for it. . . . My whole heart is set on the business.[6]

This sympathy towards choirs was indeed remarkable, considering that he had once mistaken the melody of the Old 100th Psalm-tune for the National Anthem.[7] Most important of all, many parishioners had expressed a strong desire that a daily choral service should be held in their new Parish Church. And the Vicar willingly agreed, but on the condition that no expense would be spared in order 'to ensure that the music should be in every respect absolutely first-rate.'[8]

In writing again to Wood on the subject of the Choral Service that involved an expenditure of six or seven hundred pounds a year on a professional choir, the Vicar wrote: 'I feel oppressed with the weight of the whole concern — so much so, that even now alluding to the circumstances makes my head to throb, and to feel quite wild.'[9]

II.

Wesley commenced his duties at Leeds Parish Church in February of 1842. His salary of £200 a year had been generously guaranteed by Dr Hook for ten years. Looking back on his *régime*, his articled pupil William Spark later reported:

It is therefore not to be wondered at that under his direction the services speedily attained to a comparatively high state of perfection, although it may be admitted that the occasional eccentricities of the Doctor militated, now and then, against the perfect rendering of the music so much desired by the vicar and his devoted curates. Organists, and lovers of music generally, flocked from all parts to hear the services.[10]

And so it was very difficult for a non-pewholder to find a seat at the Sunday services, because of the Vicar's eloquent preaching and the well-performed choral services.[11]

What is meant by the term, 'the Choral Service'? According to *The Parish Choir* (1846), it was 'that mode of celebrating the public service by both priest and people, in which they sing all portions allotted to each respectively, so as to make it one continued psalm of praise, confession, and intercession from beginning to end.'[12] Hence the choir's task was to lead the congregational singing — a view also supported by *The Ecclesiologist* (1846), and I quote: 'No music of the common parts of our offices is admissible, which cannot be easily sung by all.'[13] On the other hand, both Jebb and Wesley maintained that it was the duty of the parish choir to sing to a *listening* congregation, since they believed that the Cathedral form of the Choral Service was the ideal — even if the Leeds congregation were allowed to sing the Psalms to Anglican Chant on Sundays, with the assistance of their own professional singers.

Just before Wesley left for Winchester Cathedral in 1849, an anonymous report on the state of the music at Leeds Parish Church appeared in *The Parish Choir*, and is worth quoting:

> The choir now numbers on Sundays twelve, frequently fourteen, men, and twelve boys. The Canticles are sung to Services by Tallis, Gibbons, Aldrich, Purcell, Rogers, Croft, Kelway, Cooke, Russell, Boyce, S. Wesley, Attwood, Mendelssohn, and S. S. Wesley; the Anthems are chiefly by the same composers, with the addition of Byrd, Tye, Farrant, Creyghton, Weldon, Greene, Crotch, and, I regret to say, some few adaptations from the oratorios of Handel, Spohr, and Mendelssohn. Though there is nothing in the slightest degree objectionable, either in the music or the words of these adaptations, yet, with the treasury which our Church possesses of genuinely ecclesiastical music, no performances should be heard within the sanctuary which may distract the devotions of the congregation by recalling the idle associations of the concert-room. A fault prevails here, though not to the extent which is heard in some cathedrals and churches, that is to say, of playing as a voluntary, at the conclusion of Evensong, a rattling fugue, brilliant chorus, or semi-sacred overture, instead of such solemn music, whether jubilant or penitential, as might deepen the impression which the services of the day have tended to produce on the minds of the congregation.[14]

ORGAN COMPOSITIONS

In 1842 Wesley was undoubtedly at the height of his musical powers, both as an organist and church composer, when he published his two sets of *Three Pieces for a Chamber Organ*. This collection contains the *Andante in*

E flat, *Andante in F*, *Choral Song* (and Fugue), and the *Larghetto in F sharp minor* (with Variations) — thus forming Wesley's main contribution to the organ repertoire of the nineteenth century. He also published a second edition of *A Selection of Psalm Tunes*.

Meanwhile the Vicar of Leeds had baptised Wesley's fourth son, Charles Alexander, on 26 June, 1843. And in the register of the Baptisms (Entry No. 799), Dr Wesley has styled himself as a 'Professor of Music, domiciled in Albion Street.'

With several public engagements to fulfil, Wesley played the organ for the Birmingham Festival. And the newspapers reported that 'one great feature relieved the morning performance from dullness — the unequalled organ-playing of Dr Wesley, decidedly without disparagement to other men of genious, and before all to Dr Mendelssohn — the greatest organist now living.' On this occasion, he had demonstrated a new ophicleide stop, having made 'a most wonderful effect, truly Polyphemuslike!'[15]

THE LEEDS POINTED PSALTER

The introduction of systematic pointing cannot be precisely dated in the worship of the Church of England. But the antiphonal singing of the Psalms, set to harmonized single chants, was certainly an established practice in our cathedrals by the beginning of the nineteenth century, since Prebendary Jebb writes:

> Of late years, many guides have appeared in the shape of Psalters with the words contained in each bar appropriately marked. I may specially notice a beautiful one by Dr Wesley, the organist of Leeds.[16]

The first edition of Dr Wesley's *Psalter with Chants arranged for the Daily Morning and Evening Service* was published by the Leeds firm of T. W. Green in 1843[17], who, in conjunction with Messrs. Rivington, Hamilton, and Adams, issued a second edition three years later, but with the *Venite* pasted inside the front cover.[18]

Wesley had taken the trouble of pointing not only the Canticles and the Psalms for the Greater Festivals, but also the Athanasian Creed and Proper Psalms for Ash Wednesday, Good Friday, King Charles the Martyr, the Restoration of the Monarchy and the Gun Powder Anniversaries. Furthermore, in writing to a friend, he declared:

> The pointing of my Psalter will not please those persons who like Monk and Ouseley's. My pointing is founded on the Chant-singing of the best master of vocal utterance this country ever had, probably one Tom Welsh. He was the bosom-friend of the great *Kembles*. (Mrs Siddons was a Kemble.)
> Welsh was a Chapel Royal man when I was a boy there. I used to listen and admire his chanting, and it was at that time I resolved to do a pointed Psalter 'when I was a man'.

51

I do not for an instant believe that either Monk or Ouseley have had *anything like a vocal education,* but nowadays who knows the truth in such matters?[19]

Nonetheless, Monk and Ouseley's *Psalter and Canticles Pointed for Chanting* (1862) was authorised by the Archbishop of York for use in his Province.

THE EDINBURGH PROFESSORSHIP

In December, 1843, the University authorities requested Sir Henry Bishop's resignation from the Reid Professorship because he had regarded it as a sinecure, having in fact given no lectures! And besides, he had no intention of leaving his more lucrative directorships at the Covent Garden and Drury Lane Theatres for the dour atmosphere of a Scottish university. So he resigned gracefully; and Wesley again applied for the post with another collection of testimonials from his musical friends:

> Cassel,
> 30th January, 1844.
>
> By the compositions which Mr Samuel Sebastian Wesley, of Leeds, has sent me for examination, they show, without exception, that he is master of the style and the form of these species, keeping himself closely to the boundaries which the kind of composition demands, not only in sacred things, but also in glees, and music for the piano. They point also out that the Artist has devoted earnest studies to harmony and counterpoint, and that he is well-acquainted with rhythmical forms. The sacred music is chiefly distinguished by a noble, often even an antique style, and by richly chosen harmonies, as well as by surprisingly beautiful modulations. Along with this, they possess the advantage to be easily sung.
>
> Respecting the abilities of Mr Wesley as a practitioner, I heard him called, when I was last in England, the first of all (at present there) living performers on the organ.
>
> That is what I have to state about the abilities of Mr Wesley, to judge by the music in hand, and as an artist; and testify the same by my signature and seal.
>
> Dr Louis Spohr.[20]

This celebrated German composer and violinist made his first successful visit to this country in 1820, when he played in the Philharmonic concerts. He conducted his oratorio 'Calvary' at the Norwich Festival of 1839, for which event, three years later, he composed 'The Fall of Babylon'. Wesley was an ardent admirer of his music, particularly of the opera 'Jessonda' (1823), whose Overture he frequently included in his organ recital programmes. Even Stanford recalled a period when many musicians had regarded Louis Spohr (1784-1859) as a greater composer than Beethoven!

My dear Wesley,

What testimonial of mine can you possibly need? Or how can I do more than echo the general opinion of your character and attainments as a performer and a composer?

If I say that I regard you as the greatest master of your instrument (Foreign or English) that it has ever been my fortune to hear, and that, as a composer, you have proved yourself not only worthy to inherit the honoured name of Samuel Wesley, but to be ranked with the greatest masters of sacred composition, I do but echo the opinion of those who have had the best means, and who are the most competent to judge of your talents and attainments.

It is, perhaps, more to the purpose, as you are a candidate for a situation in which you are a comparative stranger, to add that I have enjoyed the privilege of long and uninterrupted friendship with you, and this enables me to speak with the means of knowledge as well as the sincerest pleasure of the integrity of your character, the love of honour and truth which has marked your course through life, and the distinguished zeal with which you have pursued the highest interests and objects of our art.

I am rejoiced to hear that you are about to lecture at the Collegiate Institution at Liverpool, and I shall hope that the time may be not distant when I may have the pleasure and advantage of having you in this place.

Edward Taylor,
Professor of Music, Gresham College.[21]

Dr Taylor (1784-1863) began his life as an ironmonger in his native city of Norwich, where he subsequently was made a sheriff. He developed a fine bass voice. And between 1829 and 1843, he was the music critic of *The Spectator,* having been elected to the Gresham Professorship in 1837.

The Reid Professorship went this time to Mr Henry Pearson (1815-73), whose father was afterwards nominated to the deanery at Salisbury. But his love of Germany resulted in his resignation from the Chair and changing his name to Heinrich Hugo Pierson!

THE LIVERPOOL LECTURES

Wesley gave a course of lectures on the subject of Church Music at the Liverpool Collegiate Institution, for which he was thanked in the following letter, dated 17 August, 1844:

My dear Sir,

The great delight which your lectures and performances occasioned to all with whom I have communicated, I cannot describe to you. Everyone is loud in their praise, and I have not heard a *single* objection of *any* kind. Indeed it is the only instance within my recollection of any public event of a like nature that has given universal satisfaction. Will you consent to reappear amongst us at the commencement of the year with a short course, say of four lectures upon the organ and organ music? If you do consent, it will be doing much service to the organists of the town. One of them, of no mean reputation, told me, that your last performance did him more good than years of previous study.

Pray don't refuse to come — for my part, I shall not think our Lecture season is complete unless our Syllabuses announce your coming at least twice a year. . . .

J. Gregory Jones, Secretary.[22]

In spite of such generous remarks, Wesley was unable to repeat his lectures until two years later, as he had undertaken a similar course at Manchester in 1845. According to William Spark, 'lecturing was certainly not his *forte*,' since he had apparently wasted nearly four months of his assistant's time, 'in copying out separate parts for the singers who were to illustrate the lectures, from old manuscripts which had belonged to his father, as well as from Burney and Hawkins' *History of Music*.'[23]

III.

Wesley's Morning, Communion and Evening Cathedral Service in E (*Te Deum, Jubilate, Kyries, Nicene Creed, Sanctus, Magnificat* and *Nunc Dimittis*) was published in instalments between 1844 and 1845,[24] and it was important for two reasons:

(i) It contained a Preface (dated 'Leeds, February 1845), forming a remarkable statement of Wesley's views on the subject of Cathedral Music — that is to say, his views already embryonic at Exeter, since, in writing to Vincent Novello concerning the possible publication of his two anthems and a creed, he had said:

> I publish them for the opportunity it will afford me of offering a few remarks on the sadly fallen state of our Cathedral Service.[25]

Hence Wesley began the Preface with some belligerent remarks on the Service music of our early Tudor composers, although he admired Gibbons's 'Short Service' for its 'beautifully subdued tone of pathos and solemnity.'[26]

Wesley particularly disliked the use of similar motifs for texts that expressed opposite emotions: 'The same jog-trot emphasis appears from the first word to the last, let sentiment be what it may.'[27] In his jaundiced opinion, the composers of the 'Golden Age' might have been more usefully employed in writing short anthems and madrigals than in producing monotonous settings of the *Te Deum*. Having observed some of the good features in Tallis, Tye, Farrant, and Gibbons, he stated that such examples were rare:

> A few sheets of paper, less than twelve perhaps, might contain all the really unexceptionable specimens in this school available for common use, which have descended to present times in connection with the musical worship of the Church of England. . . . It may, perhaps, be allowed that the epigram-

matic was within their reach: they could fill a page, without disobeying the claims of contrast, keeping analogy, or losing sight of the general effect: but not so the Epic: their Te Deums were failures: A volume was beyond their powers; but 'little' as there may be 'in a name,' the Kings, the Scrogginses, Joneses, Porters, and Smiths, of Cathedrals! — what have they been known to do *well*?[28]

Wesley next added some observations on the subject of Church Music Reform. In his opinion, the present malaise in Cathedral worship was due to a host of inferior organists and choirmen, the complete absence of self-criticism, and to the appalling fact of Church Music being subject to the irresponsible control of those who were not only quite ignorant of the subject, but who openly professed to regard it as a matter of secondary importance. He held that the Church musician was reduced to a level of a mere machine, having realised that the real position of his Art was scarcely in advance of that of Astronomy in the time of Galileo. And he felt that Cathedral organists needed encouragement 'to do their duty in that state of life in which it has pleased God to call them.'

Finally, he offered some positive suggestions that would assist in the reform of Church Music in England. He considered it was insufficient for a Cathedral organist to have been a chorister or a deputy organist, because he ought to have acquired some knowledge of 'the higher departments of musical science.' Lay clerks needed to give more attention to self-culture (an Act of Parliament might be needed to enforce their compulsory attendance at Choir practice); and the musical taste of the clergy required improvement, if they were to act with absolute wisdom in musical matters. University Professors should have some voice in the election of Cathedral organists, and the organists themselves should be consulted in the appointment of singers. As for the musical profession as a whole, it could scarcely be said to have had any voice in the matter of Choral Worship because its management had been completely in the wrong hands.

Both the Preface and the music of Wesley's Service became the subject of a belligerent review, published in the *Morning Post* (26 February, 1845):

S. S. Wesley is a grumbler and a Radical Reformer, a rater of the clergy, and particularly of the dignitaries of the Church, but like most Radical Reformers has no reason that we can see for his discontent. Whatever in this composition is new is not good, and whatever is good has been heard before in a better form and in better company. We rather think the composition was originally written in E *flat*, and transposed into E *natural*, which makes the harmonies look somewhat fresher and more novel.

(ii) Its publication was important because a certain gentleman, Mr Martin Cawood had proposed to Wesley that he should be allowed 'to remunerate him for his work, and incur the sole risk and responsibility of its publication.' As Wesley judiciously observed:

The good intentions of Mr Cawood surely deserve notice, in times when an act of such liberality is entirely without parallel; and when it is remembered that Cathedral bodies rarely encourage (even by the purchasing of a few copies for the use of their Choirs) such undertakings.

What is known about this benevolent individual, who had been instrumental in getting Wesley appointed to Leeds Parish Church?

Cawood flourished in the eighteen thirties and forties. His father, John Cawood was a brass-founder and the head of an engineering firm in Leeds, who was presented in 1809 with 'a pair of silver cups as a compliment to him for his services on the organ, during the time we were without an organist.'[29] In the town, Martin was recognised as one of the most enthusiastic patrons of the arts, though he was not wealthy according to contemporary standards. He was an amateur composer, too, and several local firms published his music, including his setting of the popular ballad 'True Love' (J. Sykes, 30 Boar Lane), that was popularized by military bands and reached a tenth edition.[30]

On one occasion, Wesley was invited to dine with the Cawoods in North Street. And during the meal one of the guests said he could not understand the Doctor's erudite compositions, nor the music that was sung at the Parish Church, requesting at the same time that he might compose something lighter which they could all appreciate. Wesley, for once, accepted the challenge by writing a book of piano duets; and he used to play them with his charming hostess, Mrs Cawood. They were called *Jeux d'esprit: Quadrilles à la Herz* (Chappell, 1846).[31]

When the Wesleys first came to Leeds they lived for a few months at No. 43 Park Square, a fine Georgian terrace of houses where both the legal and medical professions now have their offices and consulting rooms. Leeds is full of fashionable Squares, originally protected by wrought-iron gates which were closed at dusk. St Paul's Church, where Dr Edward Naylor's grandfather was a former Clerk to the Vestry, was also in Park Square. Their next address was No. 25 Albion Street, which was a few doors above the former sight of *The Yorkshire Post* Offices (now the new Austin Reed block).

In 1847 they moved to No. 11 Grove Terrace, in order to be nearer the Cawoods who had just moved into Brunswick Place. Its celebrated Methodist Chapel was the religious mecca of the middle classes; and Samuel Wesley had opened its new organ in the summer of 1828. Finally, the Wesleys settled in Hanover Square, a select neighbourhood which included Denison Hall, built by a family of merchant bankers.[32] By this time Mrs Wesley must have been very tired of frequently changing houses, or was she possibly wanting to keep up with the Cawoods?

In 1846 Tavistock Parish Church was the scene of great activity; for John Rundle had carved new oak pews and Messrs. J. W. Walker and Sons, of London, were pulling out all stops in order to get the organ completed in time. The Church Committee were, therefore, anxious to find a suitable organist, and, realising Wesley's partiality for fishing in Devon, they wished to obtain his services as quickly as possible, so that *The Plymouth, Devonport and Stonehouse Herald* had prematurely announced in April:

> Negotiations having been closed with Dr Wesley, his services have been secured. The Parish of Tavistock may now be proud of its church, one of the best in the West of England, and of its future organist, whose predilection for Devonshire is the cause of his again coming to reside in this County, preferring its salubrity to the dingy atmosphere of Leeds.

Wesley reached Tavistock on the Monday night of June 22, and all available hands were called in to get the organ finshed for his opening recital on the following Thursday. The organ specifications had been drawn up by a notable Exeter musician, Mr K. J. Pye.[33] Admission would be by tickets only: two shillings for one and three shillings for both the morning and the evening performances, since the Committee were faced with a considerable organ debt.

Unfortunately, the Bishop of Exeter Henry Phillpotts (1778-1869) had been invited to preach; and, having been informed of the above charges, he immediately ordered that no money whatever was to be received for admission. And to appease the Committee, the 'good Bishop' made no objection to a collection being taken after the performances! He also objected to one of the organ pieces that had been advertised in the programme, but it was later omitted.[34] Was this Wesley's transcription for the organ of Spohr's Overture to his opera 'Jessonda'? However, the following report appeared in *The Plymouth Weekly Journal*:

> Of the Doctor's performance it would be quite superfluous to add our meed of praise to talents that have long been acknowledged to be unequalled, and to those who could fully appreciate the extraordinary development of his powers in the execution of the difficult Pedal Fugues by Bach, the treat was of no ordinary kind. We were much struck with the delicious effects produced in the 'Harmonious Blacksmith' Air by Handel, which was performed in an admirable manner.
>
> On the whole we may safely assert that such a musical treat in the way of an organ performance has never before been enjoyed in the West of England, and the inhabitants of Tavistock ought to congratulate themselves on their good fortune in having so talented a musician as Dr Wesley for their organist.[35]

That Wesley seriously thought of giving up his organistship at Leeds Parish Church in 1846 is proved by a comparatively unknown court case at the York Assizes.

WESLEY *versus* BURTON

It appears that Dr Wesley's legal action was to recover the balance of £158 1s. 9d. from Mr Robert Burton, who had succeeded Mr James Hill as the choirmaster of Leeds Parish Church, and also Dr Wesley as organist in 1849.[36] The court proceedings took place before Lord Chief Justice Campbell on Wednesday, 14 July, 1852. And this report later appeared in a London newspaper:

> This was an·action on agreement for £500. In the year 1846 the plaintiff, Dr Wesley, was organist of Leeds Parish Church and a teacher of music in that Town. The plaintiff having resolved to give up his employment and teaching in Leeds, the defendant agreed to give him £500 on consideration of his resigning his post and recommending him as his successor. This agreement was dated August, 1846; but the plaintiff did not leave Leeds until 1849, when he obtained the appointment of organist to Winchester Cathedral and left Leeds. The defendant, however, then agreed to adhere to his original agreement, and to pay the £500 by instalments. All these had been paid except £150, for which the present action was brought. The defendant refused to pay the sum under the impression that £50 a year was to be deducted for the three years from 1846 to 1849, when the plaintiff left Leeds.
>
> It was agreed that a verdict should be taken for the plaintiff — Damages, £100.[37]

THE NOTORIOUS GAUNTLETT

Wesley seems to have cross-swords with his former friend, Dr Henry Gauntlett, who was an advocate of a reform in organ construction by the adoption of the C compass, instead of the old F and G compass instruments, and who was also an advocate of Gregorian music. Wesley, on the other hand, was in favour of the G compass organ and detested Gregorian chanting. Both musicians were anxious to advise churches and civic authorities on organ construction, for which they no doubt received the occasional payment. So we find Wesley writing to Mendelssohn because he believed that he had supported Gauntlett in a dispute concerning the design of an organ for Leeds Town Hall. And on 15 January, 1846, Mendelssohn replied:

> When I found that you had written to me I was at first very happy to have a letter from you, for whose name and talents I always entertained the most sincere respect and for whom I have heard my English friends speak only in terms of the highest praise and admiration.

But I cannot sufficiently express to you how sorry I was when I found out the cause of your letter. The whole thing of which you speak is entirely new and unexpected to me, and the more I read it the more I regret it and the more I wish never to have heard of it. When Dr Gauntlett wrote to me he did not make the *slightest* allusion to any dispute or dissension, of course still less that I was to become *a party* in it, and a party *against* you! Had he done so, I would have answered at once the same words to him which I must now answer to you, which I always answer in such cases: Pray do not let me interfere and let me remain a stranger to things to which I really am a stranger.

Besides I am no judge in such matters. Dr Gauntlett did not send me the plan of which you tell me, and if he had I would not have been able to give anything like a decisive opinion, for I know too little of the technical part of the instrument, and little experienced in the art of organ building, and it is only when the organ is finished and when I may play on it that I can form an opinion of my own. I recollect having said so to Dr Gauntlett, and much repeat this also to you, while I beg to return the plan which you enclosed.

Accordingly, if my name has been used in order to injure your well-deserved reputation and to disparage your merits, I need hardly say that it has been done against my will, and that anything of the kind is contrary to my views and wishes. If such a thing has been done I would be the only loser by it, and it could only serve to do *me* harm; it would be of little consequence to you, for true merits will always be much more powerful in such cases than my name or any name whatever.[38]

Gauntlett was a frustrated revolutionary and certainly the most eccentric of all church musicians in Victorian times. He delighted in wearing the cassock and in calling himself: 'Henry John Gauntlett, Doctor of Music, Organist to His Majesty the King of Hanover, Lay-Minister of the Great Organ of St Olave's, Southwark, and the Great Metropolitan Organ of Christ Church, London.' A contemporary writer has referred to 'Gauntlett's confidence in his own power and in his capacity of improving on anything and anybody!'[39]

Again, Wesley's intense aversion to 'this Lay-minister of the Great Organ' is evident in a letter to his friend Miss Emett, in which he remonstrated:

I have my own troubles. That worst of all wicked men, the notorious Gauntlett has set himself at work to damage my reputation and deprive me of an engagement which I have received on most honourable and lucrative terms.

And he added:

I trust your good father has little intercourse with that person. I mention this thinking it possible that he really has. You will pardon me, I trust, in these remarks.[40]

Her father, Mr John George Emett was organist at St Mary Magdalen's, Bermondsey. And with Samuel Wesley he was instrumental in the publication of the English translation of Forkel's *Life of J. S. Bach* (1820). The Emetts lived in Ebury Terrace, Pimlico, and more will be said about them below.

IV.

In 1846 Wesley delivered a second course of lectures at the Liverpool Collegiate Union, which received a favourable report from the Secretary, Mr J. Gregory Jones:

> The matter of the lectures was exceedingly good and displayed both research and original conception. He treated his subject as an artist possessed of genuine feeling for the dignity of his lofty theme, and spirit of Church Music, rather as to what it ought to be than as to what it is[!] In manner, too, Dr Wesley was felicitous — more so in the second course than the first. Possessing a sweetly toned voice, he has the art of commanding the attention of his audiences and rivetting it upon his subject from the beginning to the close.[41]

Wesley was always ready to help a friend in trouble. And in March of 1847, he wrote to the Churchwardens of St Mary Magdalen's, Bermondsey, because they wished to terminate Mr Emett's services as their organist, after seventeen devoted years in the post:

> To most professional men an act of this nature would be absolutely ruinous. . . . I cannot believe that any gentleman in your position will commit a serious breach of that brotherly love and charity which belongs to the Christian, merely for the useless object of possessing at your church an organist who, inferior to Mr Emett in the many essential points, may be just able to display more rapid execution with his fingers or his feet, and perhaps by that very means lead to disorder in your musical services, against the possibility of which the sound taste of Mr Emett may be viewed as a perfect guarantee.[42]

This support of his fellow organist unfortunately ended in a sad finale, as the following letter of condolence was sent from Leeds to Miss Emett, within five months of the preceding one:

> I will not trouble you with my own feelings at having lost the only friend I had to whom I might be willing *to say anything* in confidence. But I must express my hope that the friends you possess near you will take care to remind you that it is in many respects a duty not to be overcome by afflictions, and that you will *at once* try some change of scene by going a distance.[43]

AN ACCIDENT

In the late evening of Thursday, 23 December, 1847, Wesley was alone fishing in the River Rye, near Duncombe Park, in the North Riding, when

60

he met with a serious accident. Since on New Year's Day, *The Leeds Intelligencer* reported:

> In leaping across a small brook [Dr Wesley] fell, and received a compound fracture of the right leg below the knee. Unfortunately there was no person with him at the time, and he lay for four hours before any assistance was rendered. Eventually he was discovered by some boys; and other aid having been quickly procured, he was promptly conveyed to Helmsley.

On the other hand, William Spark's account maintained that Wesley's accident was caused by his unsuccessful attempt at climbing over a stile with a heavy creel, so that he fell headlong on the deeper side, resulting in 'a compound fracture of the left leg, from which he never entirely recovered.' He was afterwards laid up for almost six months at The Black Swan — a fine Georgian inn beside the Market Place in Helmsley, 'unable to do anything but occasionally compose an anthem.'

And in January, Mrs Wesley informed her sister-in-law, Eliza Wesley, of the essential facts:

> I have much wished to write and tell you of your brother's progress, but he did not seem to like the idea, and he questions me so narrowly it is scarcely possible to do anything without his knowledge. . . .
>
> Intelligence was sent to us by telegraph and I immediately came to him, bringing with me Mr Teale, the very eminent surgeon. *We* were detained *four hours* by an accident on the Mail [train] but arrived in time for Mr Teale to do all that was necessary. He did not conceal from me that *his* danger was *imminent,* and for five days I was *sick with apprehension.* Since then all bad symptoms have gradually disappeared, and for the last week there has been no fever, no swelling, no inflammation, and the wound becoming every day more healthy. . . .
>
> I have no nurse, nor came anyone to sit up with me. I have a little bed in the same room, and thus your brother has every comfort and advantages, but it is a miserable life to him. I scarcely can leave his room.
>
> The people in the neighbourhood are extremely attentive in cooking, sending game, and offering any service in their power — and several of my own friends have offered to come if I wish. But he cannot bear the thought of anyone being near him but myself. I can only wonder that I am able to go through what I do. It is a sad grief to me to be away from home, with all five of the children at home; but I have an excellent person as nurse who has lived five years with me and whom I can trust implicitly. She or Johnny writes to me almost every day and they all remain quite well.[44]

Mr Thomas Pridgin Teale (1801-67), the celebrated surgeon of Leeds Infirmary, was the inventor of a new technique in leg amputation — a traumatic experience Wesley was fortunate enough to escape from. And he was one of the subscribers to his patient's *Twelve Anthems* (1853).

Another letter to Eliza mentions the forthcoming election of the Professor of Music at Oxford:

I will take care that your brother sees all your letters, as soon as I think it safe. But, though many friends are corresponding with me about this professorship, I tell him nothing at present. And I think he is so far aware that he has had a relapse, so that he does not insist on seeing letters. . . .

You would be surprised at the little absolute pain in the leg that he has suffered, but his *sufferings* have been, and are, great notwithstanding. You may imagine it must be a dreadful thing to be, day after day, and night after night, in the same position, besides the constant fear of moving the leg and so doing mischief; for the *wound* has hitherto been too large to allow any stay being applied to the carbuncle. But the worst trouble is dreadful starts, so violent that they shake his whole frame whenever he becomes at all drowsy, so that, poor fellow, he is afraid to sleep. . .

Thank you for offering to send anything, but we get everything from York with great ease. Port wine and all sorts of nourishment are ordered. A friend at Leeds sent a hamper of remarkably fine Old Port as a present. I make blancmange and calves-foot jelly, which the poor invalid takes at all odd times in the day when he can. Although he is much reduced, I do not much fear keeping up his strength.

You will imagine him to be a *difficult* patient to manage, but no one unless they saw him could think *how difficult!*[45]

However, at the end of January, Wesley was able to write a short note to his mother: 'I am going on well as the doctor informs me; you will excuse my writing more.'[46] And Marianne wrote to thank Eliza for her kind idea of sending some oysters, but also adding: 'They would be very good for our poor invalid, but the conveyance here is so roundabout, I doubt if we could get them safely.'[47] Four days later, however, Marianne announced their arrival in excellent condition:

Your brother enjoyed a dozen of them which I opened for him by his bedside, and he will take more to-day.

Yet she was very sorry to tell Eliza that he had not been quite so well, owing to some anxiety over business matters.[48]

THE OXFORD PROFESSORSHIP

At the beginning of February, 1848, Wesley sent many testimonials to the University because he was then well enough to enter the contest for the Chair of Music. The Precentor of Carlisle expressed his opinion that Wesley had no equal in England as a cathedral organist.[49] The Chairman of the Directors of the Liverpool Collegiate Institution maintained with pleasure that Wesley's lectures had been delivered with great success.[50] And the final one, from a singing teacher in Cheltenham, John Barnett (1802-90), declared:

It only remains to state that which may not be so universally known, but which I know from personal observation, *viz.* his ability as Conductor of the

Chorus, having had frequent opportunities of witnessing the able and masterly manner in which he conducted the Chorus at the English Opera House.[51]

In March, Wesley wrote a longer letter to his mother:

> I am going on well. I have been on my back three months — you may guess the trouble. Perhaps, another month may enable me to be got up but we cannot judge. The wounds heal very slowly.
>
> I hope you are pretty well. You may suppose my anxieties. Mrs Wesley constantly ill for the last two years.
>
> I may have to write to you again on a matter of great consequence, but do not allude to it in any way. If I *do* write, I hope you will be kind to me in my trouble and do the best you can. Do not allude to this if you write to me.
>
> Rosalind is very kind and a most excellent nurse. I should like to see you and all the young ones — remember me to them.[52]

The patient was now able to enjoy the occasional game of chess with his sister Rosalind, though he was a bad loser. If the game went in her favour, he would craftily pull at the bed-clothes, groan about his sore leg, and contrive simultaneously to upset the chess-men!

Sadly for Wesley, news came of Sir Henry Bishop's election at Oxford — the musician who had defeated him at Edinburgh seven years before. Bishop's interests were in the wider field of the opera house and concert hall; and above all, he was socially more acceptable to the academic world. Thus the cause for musical reforms within both universities was delayed until the appointments of Sir Henry Oakeley and Sir Frederick Gore Ouseley to Edinburgh and Oxford, respectively.

Meanwhile Wesley wrote to thank one of his friends for kindly deputising at Leeds Parish Church, during his convalescence:

> April 14.
> Helmsley, York.
>
> My dear Mr Bower,
>
> I cannot longer delay expressing to you my sincere thanks for your most obliging attention to my Sunday duty at Church.
>
> I will not use many words at this moment as I hope soon to see you, and then I shall possess the advantage of a better opportunity of acknowledging the obligation.
>
> I ought to add that your playing has given *general* satisfaction, and this it could not have done under such difficult circumstances as attend a performance of the Choral Service at Leeds, without your exerting talent of a most decided kind. But this I always knew you to possess. Not exactly as an organist, however, until now, but as a pianist and a philosopher, musically speaking.
>
> I have, in the newspapers, seen the announcement of very difficult music for the Sunday. Should it occur again, during the time your kindness and conscience may allow of your continuing to serve me, I hope you will have it altered, as I am sure it *can* be altered.[53]

Mr William Bower (1820-93) was organist of the fine Georgian Church of Holy Trinity, in Boar Lane, Leeds. He lived in Park Square and later married Mary Ann Dykes, a first cousin of the celebrated Victorian hymn-tune writer, Dr John Bacchus Dykes (1823-76), who was precentor of Durham Cathedral and afterwards vicar of the neighbouring parish of St Oswald's. One of his grandsons, Sir John Dykes Bower later became organist of St Paul's Cathedral.

V.

Wesley's convalescence at Helmsley gave him an opportunity for writing and composition, in particular one of his masterpieces, the miniature anthem 'Cast me not away' with its telling discords at the end, describing his painful experience — 'That the bones which Thou hast broken may rejoice'! And here he embarked upon a treatise on Cathedral Reform, resulting in the publication of a remarkable, half a crown pamphlet on 24 may, 1849:

> A FEW WORDS on CATHEDRAL MUSIC
> AND THE MUSICAL SYSTEM OF THE
> CHURCH with A PLAN OF REFORM by
> SAMUEL SEBASTIAN WESLEY, Mus.Doc.[54]
> The following pages have their origin in considerable experience in the practical working of the Church-musical system, and are submitted to public notice under the belief that circumstances call loudly for the intervention of professionally educated and practical musicians. For the reprobatory tone occasionally adopted by the writer no apology is offered; the necessity for it forming, in fact, the justification of the present pamphlet.

What were these circumstances? In 1832 Dr Thomas Arnold, head-master of Rugby, had stated in a letter that 'the Church, as it now stands, no human power can save.'[55] And seventeen years later, Wesley had also expressed a similar sentiment, namely that 'the Music as it is now performed in our Cathedrals, when compared with well-regulated performances elsewhere, bears to them about the proportion of life and order which an expiring rush-light does to a summer's sun.'[56] And another reformer, Pre-bendary John Jebb castigated Westminster Abbey as follows:

> The Choir, till of late years, wretchedly few in number, were permitted to perform their duties by deputy; and these were discharged in a manner which at best was barely tolerable, without life or energy. The lessons were commonly read with the same degree of solemnity as the most ordinary document by a clerk in a Court of Law. The service was opened in a manner the most careless: no decent procession was made; and the striking of a wretched clock was the signal for beginning the race through the Office: there was a squalid neglect in all the accessories of divine worship; the books were torn and soiled, and the custom of the place apparently enjoined on the Choirboys the use of surplices more black than white. The whole aspect of the Church plainly indicated the mechanical performance of a bothersome duty.[57]

St Paul's Cathedral was no better. Did not the businesslike diocesan, Bishop Blomfield, once stand on Ludgate Hill and say: 'I look at that great Cathedral and think of its large revenues and great responsibilities, and ask myself what good it is doing to this great city; and I feel compelled to answer, not any to a single soul in it.' And in his report on the efficiency of the Cathedral choir, submitted to the Chapter in 1835, Canon Sydney Smith had advised that the singing boys should be pensioned off as soon as they were no longer serviceable.[58] And yet, without superannuation and with the existence of freeholds, it was impossible to get rid of useless lay singers unless they had committed a serious offence; for the following minute was recorded in the St Paul's Act Book (1901):

> News was received of the death of Mr Charles Lockey who was admitted to the Vicars Choral in 1844, but owing to the loss of his voice has been represented by deputy since 1859.[59]

'In my boyhood, neglect and indifference as to the state of sacred buildings was universal,' an observer wrote of Hereford Cathedral, where 'there were to be seen broken pavements, monuments uncared for, and the grand Norman pillars buried in coats of whitewash.'[60] The Cathedral staff were certainly characters: Meepy Davis, the organ-blower was 'an inveterate chewer of tobacco,' and Charles James Dare, the organist (1805-18) was so unsatisfactory that he had to be given notice:

> His bibulous propensities earned him rheumatic gout; his gout made him indolent and unlocomotive, consequently it now and then happened that he was behind his time. I think I hear him now crawling upstairs into the organ loft, which was perched between the nave and the choir, while the Psalms were being chanted; gradually and stealthily he manipulated the keys, till all at once he broke into the note of the chant. It was something wonderful, and doubtless often saved him a wigging from the residentiary.[61]

On the whole Cathedrals were beginning to initiate reforms, and their Deans and Chapters were certainly not heartless. In 1847, for instance, Durham granted a fortnight's leave of absence and the sum of £20 to Mr Matthew Brown, an excellent lay clerk, in order 'to defray the expense of a set of teeth and of his journey to London for that purpose.'[62]

Since the so-called 'Cathedral Crushing' Act of 1840, inflation was the sinister enemy. The spiral cost of fabric maintenance and the reduced income from capitular estates caused by the agricultural depression, all these factors had produced a radical reduction of lay and musical staff; and for that reason the Dean of Winchester had actually considered closing his Cathedral to visitors in 1880. Hence Wesley's *cri de coeur* was activated by a Parliamentary Bill which would have reduced provincial choirs to the least possible efficiency — the Cathedral Commissioners having left some places with only one voice to a part:

Now this is in itself a thing ridiculous enough, we must confess,' Wesley wrote. 'What, for instance, can anyone who has visited the Opera Houses, the Theatres, Exeter Hall, or any well conducted musical performances, think of a chorus of *one* to a part? Ask the men working the mills of Yorkshire and Lancashire what they would think of it?[63]

Wesley next attacked the musical indifference of Cathedral Chapters, in general:

Various attempts to bring capitular bodies to a right understanding with respect to Cathedral music have been made, but always with one result, *i.e.* evasive politeness at first; then abrupt rudeness; and ultimately, total neglect.[64]

Such abrasive statements would not have won Wesley many friends among those with whom he had to work. No wonder his relationship with the religious authorities lacked warmth! He particularly disliked precentors, having classed them as amateur musicians, and above all else, 'the irresponsible directors of Cathedral music,' so that he felt that it was his duty to warn enthusiastic musicians against applying for Cathedral posts:

Painful and dangerous is the position of a young musician who, after acquiring great knowledge of his art in the Metropolis, joins a country Cathedral. At first he can scarcely believe that the mass of error and inferiority in which he has to participate is habitual and irremediable. He thinks he will reform matters gently, and without giving of offence; but he soon discovers that it is his approbation and not his advice that is needed. . . .

The painter and the sculptor can choose their tools and the material on which they work, and great is the care they devote to the selection: but the musician of the Church has no power of this kind; nay more, he is compelled to work with tools which he knows to be inefficient and unworthy — incompetent singers and a wretched organ! He must learn to tolerate error, to sacrifice principle, and yet to indicate by his outward demeanour the most perfect satisfaction in his office. . . .

If he resigns his situation a hundred less scrupulous candidates soon appear, not one of whom feels it a shame to accept office on the terms. . . . His position, in fact, is that of a clergyman compelled by a dominant power to preach the principles of the Koran instead of the Bible. This censure may not apply to *all* Cathedrals, it is allowed: to *some* it assuredly may and does.[65]

Wesley disliked the Puritan emphasis upon the preaching of God's Word, and especially the tenet maintaining that the 'said' service was more devotional than the 'choral' one. He equally disliked 'the mixture of the choral and parochial modes.' And he questioned the congregation's right to participate in what he called 'the ceremonial of religion' because he thought the Choral Service was an act of contemplation by the individual worshipper, who must never be coerced into uttering anything that would interrupt 'the prostration of the mind.'[66]

This view was later supported by the Rev. Thomas Helmore, Precentor of St Mark's Teacher Training College, in Chelsea, who had said in the course of an address to the Church Congress in 1867, and I quote:

> I fear many persons may not have fully realized the fact that it is possible to stand before the altar in worship silently, while a choir is raising some solemn or joyous strain to the praise of Almighty God, as it is to stand while the Scripture Lesson or Epistle is read.[67]

And yet, unlike Helmore, he depreciated the revival of plainsong in Anglican churches, since it is significant that Wesley's pamphlet was published the same year as Thomas Helmore had issued his *Psalter Noted* (1849), for the purpose of introducing the Gregorian tones to his students. Wesley disparaged the advocates of plainsong because he thought their musical culture belonged to a by-gone age of absolute barbarism. In fact, he wrote: 'All is "Gregorian" that is in the black diamond note! These men would look a Michael Angelo in the face and tell him that Stonehenge was the perfection of architecture!'[68]

Concerning the unfair relativity of payments for creative work between the Church musician and the Professional artist, Wesley has this observation to make:

> The work of a few days produces for the artist a sum of money greater than the work of a life would to the Church musician. Mr Landseer, it is said, has in eight days painted the picture of a horse for which he has received a thousand guineas.
>
> Turn we to Cathedrals. Were the musician, who should produce a work of the highest merit in eight days, to ask not a thousand guineas, but a thousand shillings, pence, farthings, the reply would be invariably, 'NO!' Let him study hard in his art, from the age of eight to thirty-five, sacrificing every interest to this one sole pursuit, let him offer his work as a present to *some* Cathedrals, and *they would not go to the expense of copying out the parts for the Choir!*[69]

Wesley also observed in a footnote, that the multiplication of uninteresting churches in the outskirts of large towns with a preacher as the sole attraction, however good in intention, had not been a successful experiment. But one magnificent cathedral, if placed in a manufacturing town, with its services *properly* performed, would undoubtedly attract many people.[70]

A PLAN OF REFORM

1. Every Choral Foundation must number at least twelve Lay Clerks, with a minimum salary of £85 a year. Yet, 'the constant vibration of a Lay Clerk between his shop and his cathedral' would make him 'a tradesman among singers, and a singer among tradesmen.'
2. The election of a Lay Clerk to be in the hands of a committee, composed of three cathedral organists and the clergy of the appointing capitular body, who would judge 'the religious fitness of the candidate.'

3. At least three supernumeraries to be appointed at a retaining fee of £52 a year, to meet all cases of absence owing to illness or outside engagements.
4. The Cathedral Organist to be a professor of the highest ability, a master in the craft of composition, and a competent choirmaster.
5. The Musical Directors of Cathedrals to have a salary between £500 and £800 a year, because they were 'the *bishops* of their calling.'
6. A College of Music to be founded for the education of all composers, choirmasters, organists, and lay singers.
7. A Commission to be established to exercise authority in the musical matters of the Church, and to administer a Common Fund for the training of choristers, the provision of music, and the restoration of organs.
8. A Copyist for every Choral Foundation.

Nonetheless Wesley concluded his treatise, by declaring his belief in a brighter future for English Church Music:

> Among the dignitaries of the Church are several distinguished persons who are fully alive to the high interests of music, and who do not forget that whatever is offered to God should be as faultless as man can make it.

VI.

In September, 1849, Wesley was again invited to give an organ recital in Birmingham Town Hall, when he played both a Fantasia (the first performance of his *Andante Cantabile in G major*) and an extemporisation, in the form of a fugue, about which performance *The Musical World* wrote:

> Dr Wesley's performance was greeted with uproarious applause, and while he was playing, it was interesting to observe the members of the orchestra and chorus crowding round the organ, anxious to obtain a view of his fingers or his feet, with which he manages the ponderous pedals with such wonderful dexterity.[71]

He also took an active part in the concerts organized by the Leeds Musical and Philharmonic societies, that were held in the Mechanics' Institute and the old Music Hall in Albion Street. Moreover, he once conducted a performance of Haydn's 'Seasons', when there was such a small audience that *The Musical Times* reported that the Leeds Choral Society might have to be dissolved. In fact, on practice nights, Wesley appeared to suffer from nervous excitement, so that ultimately he had to resign from his conductorship.

Wesley was undoubtedly happy and successful at Leeds, and he could have made more money had he not been so unpredictable in his professional dealings. As William Spark says, 'His fame and talents were in the mouths of all Yorkshire musicians; they flocked in scores to hear his extempore fugues after the evening service — performances which were often of the grandest, most beautiful, and elaborate in character. These were always best after one of his fishing excursions; he seemed to have returned like a musical giant refreshed with nature's glories and invigorating air.'[72]

FISHING EXPEDITIONS

With his friend Mr Greenwood, the retired organ-builder who had renovated the instrument in Leeds Parish Church, Wesley would venture forth like another Izaak Walton to fish the trout streams near Bolton Abbey and Kilnsey, or other rivers, like the Wharfe and the Aire at Skipton. His favourite place was on the Rye near Helmsley. And it so happened that William Spark once, and only once, accompanied the Doctor to 'The Nunneries' where the following incident took place:

> It was a lovely summer's day in June. We adjusted our rods and flies, and then the Doctor took a general survey of the river, which at that spot was very low just then, and quite wadeable.
>
> 'Dear me, look! They are rising well on the other side of the river. Do you mind, Spark, as I'm not allowed to wade just now, taking off your shoes and stockings, tucking up your trousers, and carrying me across?'
>
> 'Doctor,' I said, 'I fear you'll be too heavy; but I'll do my best.'
>
> 'Oh!' he added quickly, '*that* will be all right, as I'll carry the rods and all!'
>
> He got on my back; I noticed that he was getting his right arm free with the rod and flies in his hand; and just as I was suffering from the sharpness of the stones on my bare feet in the middle of the river, I said I feared that I should fall with him.
>
> 'Now stand quite still!' he exclaimed, 'there's a fine trout rising just below there, and I can get at him nicely with a good throw.'
>
> 'Doctor, doctor!' I shouted, as well as my nearly exhausted state would allow, 'if I don't try to reach the bank at once, we *must* both tumble into the river.'
>
> I managed just to get through and fall on the bank breathless, and the Doctor went clean over my head like a shuttlecock. He got up, and then stood for a moment regarding me with considerable contempt.
>
> 'I'm disgusted with you! Surely you could have stood with me for a few minutes, while I got that trout. I never behaved so to my master [William Hawes], and often as a boy carried him across the river when he went fishing.'
>
> 'Indeed!' I said, 'what! across the Thames?'[73]

Wesley's relationship to his articled pupil was similar to that of Don Quixote to his squire, Sancho Panza! Here is another amusing incident related by Spark:

It was on a Friday evening, after Dr Hook had been preaching an eloquent sermon in the Parish Church, that I walked home with Wesley as usual; he deviated towards Duncan Street, and suddenly went into an oyster shop.

'Will you be good enough,' he said to me, 'to stand at the door while I get a few oysters, and if you see Dr Hook coming, let me know, and I'll slip into the little back room until he has passed by?'

'All right, doctor; I'll watch.'

But when he had partaken of two or three fine bivalves, without inviting me to indulge also, a sudden mischievous idea occurred to me, and at the moment he was putting another to his mouth, I shouted out, 'Dr Hook, Dr Hook!'

In an instant the unshelled oyster fell on the sandy floor with a flop, and I heard Wesley slam the door of the little room. Of course I bolted, and took care to be out of the great master's way for some days afterwards.[74]

FAREWELL TO LEEDS

In writing to Henry Ford, organist of Carlisle Cathedral, in September of 1858, Wesley declared that he had earned a fine income at Exeter and had loved the County of Devon, but that he had sacrificed everything in order to go to Leeds, where, 'attached as I am to *nature,* to scenery, fine Air, & all the advantages of the County, & disappointed as I was with Dr Hook & his powers to either aid his Church Music or me, I soon bitterly repented of leaving Exeter & when this place [Winchester] was vacant I offered for it & was elected.'[75]

Notwithstanding such unfair remarks about the Vicar of Leeds, whose personal generosity had guaranteed his organist's salary for ten years, a farewell dinner in Wesley's honour was held at the Scarborough Hotel, on the Tuesday evening of 11 February, 1850. It was truly *recherché* and admirably served under the watchful supervision of the manager Mr Fleischmann. But Wesley's successor, Mr Robert Burton, was noticeably absent owing to an unavoidable engagement!

During the dinner, the Choir Committee presented Wesley with his portrait, painted in oils by a local artist and singer, Mr William Keighley Briggs, which is now in the possession of the Royal College of Music. It was accompanied by a formal address,[76] beautifully illuminated on vellum by the architect Mr W. R. Corson, and was signed by the following gentlemen:

W. F. Hook, D.D.	Thomas Brookes	George Shaw
Thomas Tennant	Thomas Eagland	William Holt
R. L. Rooke	R. Slocombe	John Hudson, M.D.
Joseph Holt	Henry M. Sykes	R. S. Burton
John Wm. Atkinson	William Bower	William Barmby
George Brookes	Wm. J. Raynar	

Wesley, who had apparently come from Winchester on the previous Friday to open the new organ in St George's Church, then rose to acknowledge their warm applause:

> Gentlemen, it is now my duty to express my thanks for the very kind compliment which has been paid to me, and I assure you that the kindness shown to me in Leeds has been, and through life will be, a source of high gratification. No one could be insensible to the good opinions of his fellow-men; I am not, and I receive with great satisfaction and pleasure the present to my family so kindly bestowed.
>
> I belong to a profession which confers, perhaps, no real and substantial benefits on society. I am not like the surgeon, the engineer, or the divine. At the same time it must not be thought that my profession needs no encouragement, or that encouragement would be of no use. Although the profession of music may confer no solid advantages, a mastery in musical art is not attained with less natural ability and less industry than are essential in other walks of life, and so long as music is connected with our acts of public worship, you will, I am sure, agree that what is done should be done well. But it is not from private individuals that the necessary encouragement should be expected, but from the highest authorities in the Church. Perhaps, at the present time, church music is not appreciated in this country. . . .
>
> In Leeds, you have made a noble effort. I do not know where church music has made such progress as in this town. The expense of the Parish Church Choir is as large as any unendowed choir I know of, if not larger. It originated with the Vicar, who has often incurred great responsibility connected with it. But the way in which it has been supported is such as I know not to be unequalled in any other town. I do not mean to say that it was prompted by my labours — (*Yes, yes*), but I did my best in the situation I occupied.
>
> I beg to assure you that my coming to Leeds has been the source of great gratification, and I feel deeply the kindness which I always met with from the Choir Committee. I beg to offer my sincere thanks for the handsome present — handsome on account of the cost, and not on account of the subject — (*Laughter and applause*).[77]

WINCHESTER COLLEGE CHAPEL, LOOKING EAST

From a watercolour by James Cave, 1802, by permission of the Warden and Fellows.

CHAPTER SIX

Winchester Cathedral and the College (1849-1865)

CHARLES KNYVETT (1773-1852), who was one of Wesley's friends and the organist of St George's, Hanover Square, describes the Winchester scene as follows:

Hey Cottage,
Shaw,
Near Oldham,
June 22, 1849.

My dear Wesley,

I have written *this post* to the Bishop and Dean of Winchester ... having taken every possible shape in *abusing* your detestable talent and your unaccountable presumption in offering yourself as a Candidate. I now wish you, my dear friend, all success, but I much fear the result proving as I could wish; for there is a person named *Long,* not only so named, but measuring 6 ft. without his night-cap, who has served as Dr Chard's Deputy for many years, and therefore may stand in your way.

I had not heard of the vacancy till your letter came, which I judge has taken place by the death of Chard unless by his usual and universally condemned neglect, he has perfected the situation. Although possessing a very nice feeling for music, he was much more attached to fly-fishing and hunting; for frequently, when on his journeys to scholars, of which he had as many as time could occupy, if perchance he heard the hounds, 'Tally ho!' 'tis the merry toned horn, says he. 'Have at ye, go it my Pippins, over hill and dale into the adjoining County,' and with, or without, the brush of the Fox, would brush into the first Public house handy for brandy, pipes and backie, till sometimes breakfast was next morning waiting his return, besides the many pupils that had been *hard* practising (during his absence) the *Battle of Prague.*

I have now to scold you for not having for so long given me one line in regard to the progress of your leg and also general health, with that of your excellent and better half, for you owe me at least two letters which, with compound interest, will shortly amount to four!

Of all Cathedral stations in England I should prefer Winchester, not only on account of its matchless locality, but for teaching, which is of the first class, with also no mean appendage in the neighbourhood — Trout fishing *very good. ...*

The Birmingham Festival takes place this year under the management of Costa; last Festival under Moscheles' baton proved a failure in performance and receipts, which together with the *Harmonious Blacksmith* for an organ performance by Mr Gauntlett, left nothing to wish for![1]

Although Wesley had applied for the organist's post in July, the Cathedral authorities were in no hurry to elect a successor to Dr George Chard, whose long innings ended with his death at the age of eighty-four. On the other hand, the College immediately appointed Mr Benjamin Long as their organist; for he had already been assisting in the singing lessons of the Quiristers, *i.e.* the College choirboys.

At a private Chapter Meeting in August, the rules in the Statutes,[2] relating to the duties and the conduct of the Cathedral organist, were read over and carefully explained to Wesley. His salary was fixed at £150 a year, and he was also free to employ an assistant, towards whose remuneration the Chapter were prepared to grant a further sum of £20. Although having been elected organist, he was not formally admitted into his offices until the 5th of October.[3]

The Wesleys first lived in a large house in Kingsgate Street, now No. 8 and No. 9a, a few minutes walk from Winchester College, where three of their sons (John, Francis and William) became Commoners. Meanwhile their father, anxious to acquire more private pupils, had advertised in *The Musical Times* his intention of giving organ lessons in London, for which a course of twenty lessons would cost 10 guineas.[4]

THE ROYAL ACADEMY PROFESSORSHIP

In March 1850, Sir Henry Bishop suggested to the Committee of Management of the above Institution, that Dr Wesley might be appointed a professor for the Organ. A letter of appointment was sent to him, declaring that they had placed him on the staff-list. And Wesley immediately wrote to the Committee, requesting his desire to discuss with them the financial side of the post. But they replied that there were no organ pupils as' yet, and that they would tell him when such a class had been formed. Meanwhile Wesley wrote to his friend Miss Emett, who was then staying in the Little Cloisters of Westminster Abbey:

I am not surprised that the books are not lent to a stranger. Few people return borrowed books in a fairly straightforward manner, as I know to my cost. I often come to town now and shall hope to see you. I am appointed a Professor at the Royal Academy, and am attempting to make a teaching connection in town.[5]

Wesley's patience was happily rewarded. In May 1851, the Minute-book stated: 'Mr Cazalet has arranged for an organ class for Dr Wesley, at seven shillings per hour.' And in January, two years later, it was recorded that cheques amounting to the sum of £22 8s. 0d. had been made out to Dr Wesley for tuition until July 1852. However, nothing is certain regarding the termination of his contract apart from a letter, dated 8 September 1866, appointing Charles Steggall as a professor for the Organ.[6] Since that date also coincided with Wesley's appointment to Gloucester Cathedral, it seemed he had resigned from his professorship.

WINCHESTER COLLEGE

Sadly for the musical life of the College, Benjamin Long died at the early age of forty-eight. And in December 1850, his post was offered to Wesley, who was able to procure a salary of £80 a year and also the rights to fish the water meadows next to the College. Mr Alan Rannie has made the following observation concerning Wesley's tenure:

> It would be pleasant to be able record that this eminent composer and organist . . . achieved some notable advance in the musical life of the School. But the truth is that he did nothing of the kind, nor indeed did he attempt it. It may be that he improved the singing in the Chapel to the extent of insisting that all three lay clerks should come from the Cathedral, but in the main he was just another Kent or Chard as far as College was concerned, though he did not linger on the scene so long.[7]

In all fairness, Wesley had endeavoured to get the Chapel organ enlarged. (It had been rebuilt by Samuel Green in 1780.) But architects and musicians seldom agree, and Wesley's plan resulted in the following abrasive note from the School architect, Sir William Butterfield, to the Governing Body:

> I do trust that Dr Wesley will not be listened to about the organ; it is a pity that he is the organist. A building of that size requires only a moderate organ. If the boys would sing and respond one might almost say it requires no organ.[8]

Furthermore, during this period, music was the Cinderella of public school education. Both the Head Master Dr George Moberly (later to become Bishop of Salisbury) and the Second Master, Frederick Wickham, regarded music as an undesirable distraction; so that, on one particular occasion, when a boy had brought back a violin at the beginning of term, the instrument was immediately confiscated. Nevertheless, the College organist's duties were 'to teach the choristers chanting and singing, to assist the clerks in learning new choir music, to provide that the organ shall be played on all occasions of choir service throughout the year, without exception of the vacations if choir service is ordered in such vacations, to attend personally on all Saturday evenings and Sunday evenings of choir service, to assist at the performance of solemn Grace in the Hall, and to employ as deputy nobody but such as shall be sanctioned by the Warden for the time being.'[9]

In his fascinating book, *The Passing of Old Winchester* (1924), Dr W. A. Fearon describes both Cathedral and Chapel life in Wesley's day, and how on Sundays, after Morning Chapel at 9 o'clock, the College also attended Litany, Ante-Communion and Sermon in the Cathedral at 10.30:

> There was the enlargement of outlook. We could study the glory of the building. I knew all the inscriptions on the sepulchral chests by heart. And there was the beauty of the music.... Dr Wesley, the organist, was in the habit before the sermon of extemporizing a voluntary on the organ to a greater length than the Canons sometimes approved. This was, to any of us who had music in our souls, a special delight. Sunday after Sunday I was in the habit of discussing this voluntary with my socius....
>
> All my contemporaries must well remember how Dr Wesley, with his 'gim' leg, used to stump up Chapel after the sermon, for the only entrance then to organ-loft was through Chapel.[10]

On the other hand Wesley received more encouragement in the Head Master's house, for his daughter Miss C. A. E. Moberly later wrote:

> Dr Samuel Sebastian Wesley came regularly twice a week for ten years and taught each one of us when old enough to join the singing class. We were all musical, and had good voices, and were so many that we possessed not only a first and a second quartet, but a chorus as well, and reading music became no difficulty to any of us. Dr Wesley could be fierce occasionally, and charming at other times, and would come of an evening to accompany our home singing. He once made us sing all through Rossini's opera of the *Cenerentola* at sight, and sometimes brought his own compositions to try over....[11]

Miss Moberly also included a family letter, relating this amusing incident:

> Dr Wesley came unexpectedly this morning, and Kitty [one of my sisters] was in a dreadful fright because she had not practised her fugues; but Mary sang with them, and they went on with that much longer than usual. Arthur came up in the middle with the news of the taking of Lucknow, upon which Dr Wesley remarked that he did not see why the English should want to take Lucknow at all! 'How should *we* like an enemy to come and take one of our towns in that way?' — showing that he had heard nothing at all about the circumstances![12]

During Wesley's time, the Winchester Cathedral authorities undertook several improvements. In 1850 they authorized the alteration of the choir-stalls and the restoration of the organ-staircase to its former position.[13] And as the lay vicars were in the habit of leaving the choir during services, they were ordered to be fined half-a-crown, if such an act of ill-discipline should occur again.[14] In November, 1851, the Treasurer was requested to provide 15 copies of Dr Wesley's *Psalter*,[15] and the sum of £20 was also donated towards the Choir Benevolent Fund.[16]

Writing to Miss Emett in May, the same year, Wesley said:

> I have heard that Dr Wordsworth is very desirous to put the Abbey music on as good footing as may be. I have produced a book to enable choirs to 'speak their words together,' as we say, in chanting the daily Psalms. My book attempts no innovation upon the present mode and gives all the best Chants, as well as *excludes the bad ones,* thereby affording unprecedented facilities to choirs in this part of the Service.
>
> Of course, as a London Chorister myself, formerly, I should like to have the work used in London; but I know too well the little prejudices and jealousies of musicians to venture to ask the organists of St Paul's and the Abbey to recommend it. . . .
>
> If I could obtain the sanction of Dr Wordsworth to its admission at Westminster, I should esteem it a great compliment.[17]

Dr Christopher Wordsworth (1807-85), a former Wykehamist and nephew of the poet, had been Archdeacon and Canon of Westminster since 1844. He later published a notable Bible Commentary and *The Holy Year* (1862) that contained his popular hymns: 'Gracious Spirit, Holy Ghost,' 'Hark! the sound of holy voices,' 'See the Conqueror mounts in triumph,' and 'Songs of thankfulness and praise.' And his musical brother Charles (1806-92) was the Second Master at Winchester, where he pioneered singing classes for the School, having enlisted the help of John Hullah in 1842. He was later appointed the first Warden of Trinity College, Glenalmond, where he initiated the building of an impressive Chapel and welcomed the itinerant singing teacher of the Choral Revival, Frederick Helmore, who, in 1850, had come to train a choir for the new Episcopalian Cathedral in Perth.

In May 1851, Queen Victoria opened the Great Exhibition in Hyde Park, which was staged in a new style of building dubbed 'the Crystal Palace'. It was intended to be the showcase of the industrial world, having united both artistic and mechanical skills. And it was also the first organized attempt at getting together all industrial representatives into one massive international fair.

In the British Library, there is a ticket from Sir George Smart to the organist of Winchester Cathedral, admitting him to a special 'Musical Performance' at the opening ceremony; for Wesley had been commissioned to compose music for M. F. Tupper's *Hymn for all Nations,* published by T. Hatchard (London, 1851); but his brother Charles later admitted that 'we all thought it very poor.'

AN ORGAN COMPETITION

Henry Willis (1821-1901), or 'Father Willis' as he was called, was a famous organ-builder in London and a person of some cunning. It appeared that a deputation from the Law Courts Committee of Liverpool had made an early visit to the Exhibition, in order to hear the powers of the numerous organs that had been erected in the building, as they had to find a firm to build a concert instrument for St George's Hall, Liverpool — 'a temple for the merchant princes', which was designed by an architect of great genius, Harvey Lonsdale Elmes. Here is Willis's account of how his firm gained that important contract:

> The Town Clerk of Liverpool wrote to me to the effect that a committee of the Corporation would visit the Exhibition on a certain day at 6 a.m., their object being to test the various organs with a view to selecting a builder for the proposed new instrument in St George's Hall. He asked me if I could be there. I was there — *all* there!
>
> The other two competing builders, in anticipation of the visit tuned their organs in the afternoon of the previous day, with the result that, owing to the abnormal heat of the sun through the glass roof, the reeds were not fit to be heard! I said nothing. At five o'clock on the following morning, my men and I were there to tune the reeds of my organ in the cool of the morning of that lovely summer's day.
>
> At six o'clock, the Liverpool Committee, which included the Mayor and the Town Clerk, in addition to S. S. Wesley and T. A. Walmisley, their musical advisers, duly appeared. The other organ builders had especially engaged two eminent organists to play for them. I retained nobody. But I had previously said to Best, who had given several recitals on my organ at the Exhibition, 'It would not be half a bad plan if you would attend tomorrow morning at six o'clock, as you usually do for practice.' Best was there.
>
> After the two other organs had been tried, the Town Clerk — William Shuttleworth, a good friend to me — came up and said: 'We have come to hear your organ, Mr Willis. Are you going to play it yourself?' 'Do you expect an organ builder to play his own instrument?' I replied. 'If I had known that the other builders had specially engaged two organists to play their instruments, I might have done the same. Why don't you ask Wesley and Walmisley? They should be made to play, unless one is afraid of the other!' As Wesley and Walmisley declined to perform, I said to Mr Shuttleworth, 'There's one of your own townsmen standing there (that was Best), ask him.' He did ask him. 'Mr Best has no objection to play,' said the Town Clerk, 'but he wants *five* guineas!' 'Well, give it to him, the Corporation can well afford it.'
>
> The matter was arranged and I said to Best: 'Now in order that everything shall be quite fair and square, would you mind playing the same piece on all three organs?' 'What shall it be?' asked W.T.B. 'The Overture to *Jessonda*' (I was always a great Spohr man).
>
> While Best was playing the Overture on the two other instruments, the specially engaged organists stood on each side of him to manipulate the

stops, etc. Meanwhile, my brother, who was a clever, quick tuner, again went over the trebles of the reeds, and everything was as trim as could be.

When Best came to play on my organ, he politely declined the similar kind help the two organists had rendered him at the other instruments, as he was perfectly familiar with my pistons, stop arrangements, etc. It was a splendid performance, and I was told that the organ was quite a revelation to those Liverpudlians.

The Committee retired to deliberate in private, but only for twenty minutes, when Wesley came up to me and said: 'I am very happy to tell you that the delegates of the Corporation have decided to recommend you to build their organ.' I was perfectly cool and collected, and, feeling very hungry, I went to get some breakfast with Henry Smart, who was also present.[18]

Willis always maintained that Wesley was the inventor of the radiating and concave pedal board, and he later describes how this invention happened:

One day, when Wesley and I were walking arm-in-arm along the Exhibition Gallery where Schulze's organ was placed, I called his attention to the fact which I had not noticed before, that Schulze's pedal-board was concave. Wesley immediately replied: 'It is a pity he did not go further, and make his pedals spread out.'[19]

On 26 June 1852, Wesley played the following programme on the new Willis instrument in St George's-in-the-East Church, London:

PART I

Fugue in E flat [the 'St Anne']	Sebastian Bach
Song, 'Holy, holy'	Handel
Chorus, 'Hallelujah'	Handel
Andante [from 'Fantasie in F minor']	Mozart
Chorus, 'The arm of the Lord'	Haydn
Variations on an Air by L. A. Kozeluch	S. S. Wesley[20]
Instrumental Piece [Overture to 'Jessonda']	Spohr

PART II

Larghetto in F sharp minor with Variations	S. S. Wesley[21]
Prelude and Fugue [probably from the '48']	Bach
Air	Mendelssohn
Andante in E flat	S. S. Wesley[22]
Extemporaneous	

Grand Chorus

CRITICISM OF 'THE WILDERNESS'

For the Birmingham Festival of 1852, Wesley had scored for full orchestra and chorus his extended anthem[23] that he had composed for the re-opening of the Hereford Cathedral organ, twenty years before. According to William Spark, 'there was a want of spirit and decision in the Doctor's conducting, occasioned by extreme nervousness which militated against its success.'[24] And so this performance produced many waspish comments from the critics. In *The Times*, for example, James Davison maintained that the score was 'deficient in melody, confused in harmony and part-writing, full of intricate combinations and *modulations run mad*; it by no means gives a true expression to the text.' Also in the columns of the *Athenaeum*, Henry Chorley's review was no better: 'It is weak, tiresome, and pedantic exercise, not likely to be again heard of.' On the other hand, within a year, Chorley himself had changed his tune by saying that the anthem was both brilliant and vigorous.

By this time, Wesley had suffered too much from the belligerent criticism of Davison's pen and therefore wrote to *The Hampshire Chronicle*:

> His criticism has been a scandal amongst us for years, and may be described as an unintelligible jargon hashed up in a plausible clap-trap fashion for the edification of persons, whom anything like serious discussion and research would weary.

And he also said of Davison in *Aris's Birmingham Gazette*:

> His criticism is as objectionable from its mongrel phraseology as from the intrinsic worthlessness of the subject-matter; and it may be likened to a glass of very bad porter, the larger and better portion of which is the undrinkable froth!

If only Wesley had heeded the sound advice of Mr Thomas Tripp, of Gloucester, who, having become exhausted with similar correspondence in *The Musical World*, wrote:

> I congratulate Dr Wesley upon having attained such a position as to be looked upon with envy, offering him this consolation, that aspersions from an unknown 'A Subscriber' go for but little — something like the Burton Ales, more *bitter* than *strong!*[25]

II.

The important publication of Wesley's first and only volume of *Twelve Anthems* (1853) involved him in much correspondence with the Subscribers. And in January, he wrote to the Chapter Clerk of Exeter concerning the Cathedral's agreement to purchase copies at the raised price of £1 11s. 6d. each:

> I dare say one or two members of the Chapter would wish to *discourage* my work — judging from the line of conduct which I experienced from them when resident in Exeter. But I did not feel inclined to notice anything of this kind, indeed I could not do so; but to avoid an altercation as to the right of a

80

claim of my publishers for the Chapter's subscription, I ventured on troubling yourself on the point, and I am still desiring to hear about it.[26]

The apparent delay in publication had arisen from the difficulty that the composer had felt in giving his complete attention to the higher department of the art of composition, 'for the Church Musician is not so much an Artist as a Mill-horse, I regret to have found.' Another reason was the loss that Wesley had experienced in the destruction of music plates by a fire some years back, which 'made the subject of again sinking an expensive speculation not a welcome one.'[26] Hence the following note was added to an autograph copy of his anthem 'To my request and earnest cry' — *'from Proofs from Plates destroyed by fire at the Engravers. S.S.W.'*

In another letter to the Chapter Clerk, a week later, Wesley said:

If all my Subscribers pay for their copies (which is very seldom done, I learn) a profit would accrue in this case, but it would not have done so had the enlarged work been issued at the original terms. . . . Many of the Subscribers, you will observe, have long ceased to feel interested in earthly music.[27]

And in answer to the Chapter Clerk's further enquiries, he wrote:

The addition made to the work is that of four, or perhaps five, Anthems extending to about 70 plates more than the number named in the Exeter advertisement last enclosed. . . . The Book will now extend to about 270, pages for which it is intended to charge two guineas.[28]

In spite of this price, the Chapter Clerk placed an order for ten copies; and further copies were ordered by the Bishop of Exeter, the Cathedral organist, and Canon Bartholomew, before whom Wesley had once appeared to account for his disgraceful conduct in the Song School.

In May, 1853, he wrote to a London friend because he wanted an advertisement to be printed in *The Times*:

I have little doubt *The Times* Office does nothing without due *remuneration,* and I think you might make up your friend at Court a little parcel of four nice Spices, Mustard, etc. which might be useful to him! I would go to half a guinea or just what you thought next.

I must try and get you a basket of *trout,* as I heard you liked them.

My leg wouldn't go a fishing at all this Season, yet. My right leg would not — the other would; but, if I knew about when you would wish them, I would make my leg do what I wished it for the occasion.

Something depends on weather, and at the Weather Office I have not the same interest which you profess at that of *The Times. All* depends on the weathercock at both.

I would not lose an hour in the appearance of the advertisement as my work is now printing and the Subscribers' list has to be printed with it.[29]

The extensive list of subscribers is certainly a *Who's Who* of Victorian musicians, *e.g.* Professor Walmisley (Cambridge), Thomas Adams (St George's, Camberwell), Sir George Smart (Chapel Royal), William Best (later of St George's Hall, Liverpool), William Spark (St George's, Leeds), Edward Hopkins (Temple Church), Sir George Elvey (St George's Chapel, Windsor); the following Cathedral organists — Robert Atkins (St Asaph), John Corfe (Bristol), Henry Ford (Carlisle), Henry Bennett (Chichester), William Henshaw (Durham), Robert Janes (Ely), Alfred Angel (Exeter), John Amott (Gloucester), John Young (Lincoln), Zechariah Buck (Norwich), Charles Corfe (Oxford) and John Hopkins (Rochester); several precentors — including the Rev. J. B. Dykes (Durham) and E. G. Monk (Radley College), and organ-builders (Bishop, Hill and Willis); numerous music publishers and choral societies, like the Sacred Harmonic Society (London), the Ancient Concert Society (Dublin), and the Rochester Cathedral Choral Society; the celebrated composer 'Monsieur F. Liszt' and the youngest of them all, Master G. Freemantle.

Other interesting subscribers were Dr George Moberly (Head Master of Winchester), Dr Walter Hook, Miss Maria Hackett, Mr Martin Cawood, Mr Thomas Teale (the notable surgeon), Mr William Bower, the Duke of Buccleuch (a fishing friend), Sir Andrew Barnard (Chelsea Hospital), Sir Thomas Acland and Sir J. G. B. Bullen (M.P.s for Devon), and two Americans, including Dr Samuel Tuckerman (St Paul's Church, Boston). The title page ran as follows:

Anthems
by
SAMUEL SEBASTIAN WESLEY
VOL. I
London, Addison & Hollier, 210 Regent Street.
Novello, Dean Street, Soho,
& Broadway, New York.
Engraved by C. Chabot, 9A Skinner Street.[30]

And on the next Page,

To
The Very Reverend
THOMAS GARNIER, LL.D.
Dean of Winchester
This Volume Is Dedicated
With Great Respect
By
The AUTHOR
1853

Dean Garnier (1776-1874) was educated at both Winchester and Oxford, where he was elected a Fellow of All Souls'. A true Whig in politics and supporter of Lord Palmerston, he had the privilege of meeting the Emperor

Napoleon, who was smiling and looking very gracious in 1802. Five years later, he was presented to the Hampshire living of Bishopstoke, where his interest in the rectory garden resulted in the planting of many rare shrubs during his sixty years there. He was appointed a Prebendary of Winchester Cathedral, and in 1840 Lord Melbourne nominated him to succeed Dean Rennell. He occupied his decanal office for some thirty-two years, and died at the magnificent age of ninety-eight. According to Kendrick Pyne, Dean Garnier loved holding services which were understood to intimate his retirement from all public duties, though not from emoluments of the office:

> 'I was present on one of these occasions,' he wrote. 'It was indeed a dismal affair — a mournful service, and an anthem by Capel Bond arranged by Handel, in which the "Dead March" figured as a movement. Dr Garnier, during the reading of one of the lessons, broke down in the middle and wept copiously. I, too, was much affected; but finding these proceedings were received with great equanimity by the congregation, and enquiring the cause, I was informed that these services had occurred before, and had lost their effect.'[31]

Nonetheless Wesley was truly grateful to the friendly dean for having bought five copies of his *Twelve Anthems,* as well as to the Secretary of the Choir Committee at Leeds Parish Church for 'the sum of Sixteen Guineas for Eight Copies of my Collection of Anthems just published.' And in writing to Mr Freemantle, of Sheffield, whose son was the youngest subscriber and a chorister of Durham, he declared:

> My 12 anthems will be good and not a mere catchpenny publication. But I cannot *puff* and go on as some do. I must let my character have its due weight, whatever it may be.[32]

And in another letter to his sister Eliza a few months before his death, he reflected:

> My published 12 anthems is my most important work. I think the style of my anthems may claim notice for the manner in which the words are expressed and for the new use made of broad massive harmony combined with serious devotional effects. What is called the Church style, in these later days, is merely a series of monotonous concords suited to the abilities of uneducated country choirs. My Church music never descends to this.[33]

The volume contains the following anthems, and the music will be discussed later:

Ascribe unto the Lord
Blessed be the God and Father
Cast me not away from Thy Presence
Let us lift up our heart
Man that is born of a woman
O give thanks unto the Lord

WINCHESTER CATHEDRAL CHOIR, LOOKING EAST

From a watercolour by James Cave, 1808, by permission of the Dean and Chapter.

O Lord, my God
O Lord, Thou art my God
The Face of the Lord
The Wilderness and the Solitary Place
Thou wilt keep him in perfect peace
Wash me throughly from my wickedness

A NEW CATHEDRAL ORGAN

In November 1853, the Dean and Chapter of Winchester made available the sum of £500 towards the purchase of the fine concert organ that 'Father' Willis had previously built for the Great Exhibition.[34] The dean had given £200 to the Organ Fund, and both the Queen and Prince Albert had promised another £150. Other donations, amounting to £850, raised the Fund to £1,700; and with Willis's payment of £800 for the former instrument, the total cost of the ambitious scheme came to the sum of £2,500.

Meanwhile, the dean had ordered that the fine woodwork of the choir-stalls was not to be altered in any circumstance.[35] And yet, Wesley's acrobatics in crawling on his hands and knees to the organ-loft in order that he might not be seen by either the clergy or the congregation, was causing much concern in the Close. (His lameness no doubt accounted for the clatter of falling hymn books and kneelers.) And to avoid any further distracting scenes, the dean authorized the building of a private staircase, resulting not only in the defacement of the thirteenth-century Chapel of the Holy Sepulchre, but in the postponement of the opening of the new organ from Easter to Whitsun Eve. Also in March, the Norwich organ-builder Mr James Corps was requested 'to inspect the organ from time to time, and to see that the work [in progress] correspond with the specifications to his satisfaction.'[36]

On the 3rd of June, 1854, an immense congregation had assembled in the Cathedral for the official opening; but as far as the organ was concerned *The Hampshire Advertiser* reported:

> The ceremony realised the old joke of the performance of the play *Hamlet* with the part of Hamlet omitted. The day was propitious, the city full of visitors, the arrangements in the Cathedral excellent, the choir full and efficient, and the Grand Organ (*i.e.* the Great Organ) *was not half-finished!* Who was to blame for this *contre-temps* does not appear, but that great blame attaches to someone is most certain.

The music for the occasion featured Wesley's Short Chant Service in F and his three anthems, 'Ascribe unto the Lord,' 'The Wilderness,' and a new work 'By the word of the Lord,' which was sung after the General Thanksgiving. Purcell's anthem, 'O give thanks unto the Lord' was also performed by the visiting singers from Durham, Ely, St Paul's, Westminster Abbey, St George's Chapel Windsor, Chichester and Salisbury, 'who kindly gave their aid from a love of church music and a desire to serve in its cause.' The singing of the basses, we are told, was particularly fine in the anthems; and the bass solo in 'The Wilderness' was most tastefully sung by Mr Marshall, of Brighton. Furthermore John Stainer, a thirteen year old chorister from St Paul's Cathedral, afterwards recalled this incident during the rehearsal of 'Ascribe unto the Lord':

> Wesley could not get the combined choirs to take the movement, 'As for the gods of the heathen' rapidly enough. So he came down into the body of the church, leaving one of his assistants to play, and beat time with a stick on the side of a choir book, a device which left no doubt as to the position of the down beats! We all thought it a great scramble at the pace he took it; but of course he was right.[37]

The Collection amounted to almost 80 guineas, and here is part of a more favourable report which appeared in *The Hampshire Chronicle*:

> Too much praise cannot be given to Dr Wesley for the admirable way in which he performed the Service upon the occasion, surrounded as he must have been by difficulties in the unfinished instrument of no ordinary character. Undoubtedly Winchester may be proud of its new Organ, and acknowledge the deep debt it owes to the dean for his indefatigable exertions in placing it in our noble Cathedral.

At the end of November, Wesley was able to display the full effect of the Organ 'before the Dean and Chapter, many of the subscribers and numerous other visitors, who were gratified with a performance which lasted two hours, in the course of which selections from Mozart, Mendelssohn, Beethoven, Wesley, Bach, Handel and Spohr, were played by the talented organist.'

III.

In July 1853, the Rev. Richard Jones, Secretary of the Royal Commission on Cathedrals in Whitehall, wrote to every precentor and organist of the Cathedral and Collegiate churches in both England and Wales, requesting that they should consider the following questions and then reply to the Commissioners, who would be meeting to consider their findings in 1854:

I   Are you of opinion that it is desirable to give greater musical power to the Choir of the Church with which you are connected, for the more effective performance of Divine Service?

II Are you of opinion that Laymen of approved piety and zeal for the worship of Almighty God, and with adequate qualifications for taking part in its celebration, might be found in your Cathedral city, and would be desirous of being connected with the Cathedral, and who would offer their services (particularly on Sundays), gratuitously, as Honorary Lay Clerks, or Vicars Choral, in addition to the present body of Singing Men and Choristers?

III If such a plan appears to you to be practicable, would you oblige the Commissioners with a statement of your opinion, as to the mode of carrying it into effect?

1. In ascertaining the qualification of such additional Members of the Choir.
2. In securing regularity of attendance.

And with any other suggestions that you may think desirable, on this subject?[38]

Just imagine Dr Wesley's surprise at being the recipient of such an important questionnaire amidst the morning mail on his study table! Of all the Cathedral organists in England, he would take such a document seriously; and a year later, he published a *Reply to the Inquiries of the Cathedral Commissioners, relative to improvement in the Music of Divine Worship in Cathedrals* (London: Piper, Stephenson and Spence, 1854).[38]

Wesley began by affirming that the musical arrangements and discipline of a Cathedral were less ordered than they had been in former times. For the singing of choirs and the playing of organists, however good, could no longer camouflage bad composition. And if Cathedrals had in some degree benefited by the progress of musical art, this was almost entirely due to the voluntary efforts of their organists.[39]

In referring to the first question, Wesley pointed out that a musician might be led into believing that the phrase 'greater musical power' meant additional vocal strength, whereas there was another and more important kind of power, namely 'the power of just expression or accuracy of style.'[40]

He maintained that twelve voices were indeed but a small compliment for a vast Cathedral, although it might be questionable as to whether any Cathedral then possessed twelve singers for the daily services — since they were being paid the same rate as inferior mechanics and ordinary labourers. Thus inflation had resulted in their undertaking a trade to supplement their lay clerk's salary. Hence Wesley declared:

> A good tradesman is almost sure to be a bad singer, and *vice versa*. Besides, a tradesman cannot devote the necessary time to his church-duty: the two pursuits are incompatible, no doubt. On enquiry, it will probably be found that at least half the number of choirmen engaged in trade had once been bankrupt, or compounded with their creditors — a result of their divided attention.[41]

Concerning the second question of honorary supernumeraries, Wesley observed:

> I would not assert that one could entirely rely on their efficiency or regularity of attendance. Far from it. Their utility, however, would mainly depend upon the mode of their superintendence. To a well-trained choir such additions should be made only with great watchfulness, or they would do more harm than good. As substitutes for an official choir, their use may be judged by the

fact that correct musical performance requires much careful and industrious preparation, and an education for the purpose which must commence during childhood; and I see not but that mercantile, clerical, governmental, or other business, can be safely confided to untutored volunteers as musical business; still, additional aid, and of some utility, may be obtained, especially in the cities of London, Manchester, Bristol, Norwich, Exeter and York; and it would be of progressive efficiency, for if church music were done justice to, it might become one of the chief and most pleasurable relaxations of the people, as the subject seems to possess an enduring vitality of interest.[42]

Under the third question as to how the Commissioners' plan was to be carried out, Wesley submitted the following Scheme:

The Choir

At least twelve lay singers, and ten or twelve boys, for daily service, sufficiently paid; with volunteer additions, where practicable, for Sundays. The twelve lay singers to have proceeded from the Church School of Vocal Music on the nomination of the Principal of that School. . . .

The Precentor

To superintend the daily services as regards the appointment of the daily music and the decorum of Choristers, and to have a deputy, a Minor Canon, as was formerly the case. . . .

The Organist

He is to be responsible for the daily organ accompaniment and for the vocal training of the Chorister boys; but as the highest requisites of Choral Service depend upon him in respect to *composition,* he should be allowed a deputy for these departments. . . . He should select boys to fill the office of Choristers, and furnish the testimonial necessary to admit boys to enter the Church Music School on leaving their Cathedrals, and also make choice of the lay singers, subject to the approval of the Dean and Chapter.

The Choristers

The boys should be provided with a comfortable home and proper tuition. In some instances, at present, boys of the lowest grade are preferred to this office, which renders all delicacy of utterance an impossibility. They catch cold, too, by playing about the streets in wet weather, and during the winter are unfit to sing.

The Organs

The bad Cathedral Organs should be replaced by good ones. It seems also very desirable to restore the Organ in all cases to the centre of the Choir: the antiphonal form of choral music renders the placing of the instrument at the side of the Choir a most serious error. In cases in which, for architectural reasons, it is undesirable to place it over the screen, the Organ might stand on the ground and constitute the Choir-screen itself.[43]

THE LIVERPOOL AND LEEDS CONCERT ORGANS

His partnership with Henry Willis in the design of the Winchester Cathedral organ led to their planning a concert instrument for St George's Hall, Liverpool. Yet Wesley's only contribution to the scheme was his insistence on the extension of the keyboard compass down to GG and the 'unequal temperament' system of tuning, which he justified in a letter to Mr William Bower in November of 1856; and in the same letter, he was obviously trying to get himself appointed as the organ consultant to the Leeds Corporation concerning the planning of a new instrument in their Town Hall:

It will be a pity that William Spark's activity in the Organ subject should interfere with the engagement of a suitable person to advise the authorities both on account of the success of the instrument and credit of the profession. No costly or even cheap musical instrument can be safely purchased without sound professional advice. The organ builders try to dispense with our services, of course. I have no doubt that in a short time one single suggestion of mine at Liverpool, that of blowing the organ by steam, which I was the first to introduce, will save the amount of my commission. That great work — for it is a great work, the Liverpool Organ — must of course open one's views extensively for the future, and wonders might be done at Leeds for £500.

[Mr William Lyndon] Smith's letter in *The Mercury*[44] is most unjust to me. *I* did not suggest the few things which he objects to. I mean the wood tubes for the bass reeds. They are always made of wood in England. Willis is now making more. The equal temperament both Willis and I are of opinion will not do for organs.... We must be content to have some good keys and others bad, and avoid the bad writing and playing as much as possible. The Liverpool Organ is to be used in a variety of ways, and I did not choose to plan a mere imitation of a Military Band, for *that* is what they now try to make an organ.

I will not sacrifice the great features of the Instrument. An organ should be *an* organ. By all means have the finest solo stops possible but don't sacrifice your organ to them. At Liverpool I was greatly interfered with through the jealousy and opposition of musicians and people who wanted to ruin the organ for the sake of the architecture.... I laboured hard to get that organ for England and think I deserve well of the musical world for my efforts — never having taken one solitary step to bring the nature of my services under public notice. Nothing seems to be known on the subject and, as yet, I have seen no justice done by the Press. But as a volume may be written on this head, I will stop short or I shall bore you unmercifully.

If I have anything to do with the Leeds Organ, rely on it there shall be a noble thing in your Hall. But *I* have made no attempt to bring myself forward with the Council. Nor shall I do so. If my friends in Leeds think proper to do it for me they need not fear the result. Do you know the names of the Organ Committee? The *Council*, however, will have to vote at any decision of affairs.[45]

Wesley's suggestion that the organ-blowing by steam-power was his original idea, and also that 'Father' Willis was in agreement against the equal temperament method of organ-tuning, are fanciful to say the least! And it seems that his advocacy of the GG manual compass became a neurosis until our friend Lyndon Smith fired his parting shot: 'I have the authority of the builder who had the management of the Leeds Parish Church organ at the time Dr Wesley officiated there, to state that the dust on the half-dozen lowest keys on the GG manuals remained undisturbed for months, clearly proving that those parts of the keyboards were almost altogether in disuse as regards the fingers.'[46]

Although both Willis and Wesley were satisfied with a typically English compromise of having the manual compass to G and the pedal-board to C, the authorities acceded to Best's request for equal temperament to be adopted in 1867, since many orchestral works were unable to be played in the original keys.

The formal opening of the magnificent organ in St George's Hall, Liverpool, took place on 29 and 30 May, 1855, when Wesley was invited to give two recitals and played his Fantasia 'Andante Cantabile' in G Major.[47] The instrument had cost £10,000, having four manuals, a hundred speaking stops, and numerous pistons of a type which Willis had invented for the Great Exhibition organ. Sadly for Wesley, he was unsuccessful in his application for the organist's appointment. It went to Mr W. T. Best, who occupied the position with great distinction for almost forty years.

IV.

Wesley's relationship with Cathedral dignitaries was ambivalent. His changeable moods kept them at a distance, although his great genius and musical reputation gained their respect. And his unfriendly dealings with that race, called Precentors, certainly arose from his inborn belief that they were nothing less than meddlesome, amateur musicians.

In June 1854, he undertook a belligerent correspondence with his own Precentor, the Rev. W. N. Hooper, so that the authorities had to step in and resolve their differences.[48] And in the following November, they directed that Wesley's pupils, whenever engaged in playing the organ, must always remain in the Cathedral until the end of the services, and that seats were to be placed in the gallery next to the organ for the benefit of the organ-blowers![49] Finally, his application for an increase of salary was flatly refused, whereas the Precentor was later given the sum of £25, 'in considera-tion of the additional duties in superintending the publication of the new Anthem Book.'[50]

Wesley received a friendly letter from a young student, called Gibbs, seeking professional advice how he might prepare himself for a Cathedral organistship without having to interrupt his other pursuits. Wesley advised

him 'to borrow Boyce's Cathedral Volumes and play the *things* from Score.'
And yet, more mercenary minded than ever, he continued:

> A little practical work at a Cathedral you should have. Could you come to me at Christmas? You would have a claim on the score of ability as well, I hope, as on the ability of your Score. Excuse a joke![51]

In November 1855, Wesley sent a holograph circular to the Dean of Windsor, 'inquiring whether in return for my producing twelve new pieces yearly, *viz*. Anthems, etc., yourself and the Chapter might deem it reasonable to award me £20 or £25 per annum.' Needless to say, their answer was a negative one.[52] And it is interesting, too, to find a similar request in the Minute-book of the Dean and Chapter of Durham: 'An application having been received from Dr Wesley for an annual stipend in order to enable him to devote the whole of his time to the composition of church music was declined.'[53]

Whether Wesley would have really retired from his Cathedral work if the opportunity had been given him is another matter. On the other hand he did undertake a lengthy correspondence on the subject with the Precentor of Ely, the Rev. W. E. Dickson, between 1860 and 1862, of which the following passages are worth quoting:

> I would give up every professional engagement, Cathedral and all, to write for the Church.[54]

> I think a man must have acquired the experience long service in a Cathedral alone gives, to write successfully. Few, therefore, will ever be able to write for a Cathedral. It is out of the question that great writers will take office in a Cathedral, at present terms![55]

> And what are the things bought? I know that Novello has raked up from its hiding-place all the discarded trash of former times and published it as novelty, and choirs have spent their money thus — Sir F. Ouseley's Services, etc. The money all goes into Novello's pocket.[56]

THE CAMBRIDGE PROFESSORSHIP

With Walmisley's death in January of 1856, the Chair of Music became vacant, and it so happened that Wesley had shown some interest in the post. Meanwhile Mrs Mary Bennett, whose husband was one of the candidates, wrote immediately to their mutual friend Miss Emett:

> I hear that Dr Wesley has never declared himself officially a candidate for the Professorship of Music, and that his name is now withdrawn from the list. Therefore I cannot help thinking how valuable his interest would be to Mr Bennett. Could you suggest in any way how we might solicit his favour in my husband's behalf?
>
> Dr Wesley has many friends at Cambridge who would value his opinion greatly, and I once heard indirectly that he spoke very highly of Mr Bennett,

but still my husband would not like to write to him not knowing him personally as it might appear very intrusive.[57]

Miss Emett, therefore, wrote to Wesley for his support in the matter, and having received no reply, she sent another letter that produced several missiles from his pen:

> I did not, I confess, feel disposed to aid Mr Bennett, for I do not think his proceedings creditable in this matter. He has taken more pains to obtain the office than becomes a man who is content that his opportunities should have justice done them. Mr Bennett, at a former competition [in Edinburgh], wrote me a very unceremonious letter, and I have not forgotten it.
>
> I dare say that, within an hour of your reading this, you will see his name in *The Times* as Professor. I could take no trouble about it. I went to Cambridge on Saturday and withdrew my name. The election was one depending on the exertions of candidates chiefly, I think. *The electors knew nothing of the office.*[58]

Although Sterndale Bennett himself was never anxious to press his claims, his wife left nothing to chance having spent a month in incessant correspondence. And the Vice-Chancellor Dr Whewell, of Trinity College, had also written to her:

> We are here growing more and more eager about the election of a Professor of Music. I have fixed Tuesday the 4th for the election. Mrs Frere [the eighty year old widow of a former Master of Downing College] is very zealous for Mr Sterndale Bennett; and, by the way of falling in with her humour, I have asked her to come and stay with me here, and canvass the College and the University to her heart's content.

But Mrs Bennett, on the day of the election, remained in London in a deadly silence, until the telegram arrived from a Cambridge music-seller: 'Professor of Music, March 4th, 3 p.m. — Close of the poll: Bennett 174, Elvey 24, Horsley 21.' Meanwhile her husband was presented with another card: 'The Company of Great St Mary's Ringers respectfully wait upon Mr S. Bennett Esquire, for ringing when elected Professor.'[59]

Is there any decisive evidence to prove that Wesley had eventually changed his mind by supporting Bennett's candidature? In the British Library there is a visiting card with his wife's regards and thanks to Wesley, having written herself in pencil the election results on the back.[60]

In May, the same year, Queen Victoria laid the foundation stone of the new Military Hospital at Netley, near Southampton. And the Winchester Cathedral Choir was also invited to sing on this occasion, when they performed Wesley's arrangement of *The Hundredth Psalm* (Novello).

And in November, Wesley informed a friend: 'I am busy getting into a new house or rather an old one. Planting fruit-trees, laying on gas, and various things of the sort absorb my spare time.'[61] It seems that the Wesleys were in the throes of moving from Kingsgate Street into No. 5 The Close, although they continued to rent their former house, thus involving them-selves in unnecessary expense which they could ill-afford.

In 1857 Wesley expressed his gladness at Miss Emett's living so near the family, and he continued:

> The spot — Hamble — is to my taste, being so fond of water one of the most agreeably possible. I was never at the Rectory, but I have also put in at Hamble, once, with two of my boys in *The Little Vessel* with the object of sleeping at one of the Inns. But they seemed very shy of strangers and gave me the idea of being rather deep in the smuggling line, and I have little doubt that such is the CASE!
>
> This is a very quiet place. Not *one* person here have I had to speak to on musical matters for many, many years. Very often have I thought of your kind, dear Father and felt his loss. All of the very few friends of my youth are gone. The last, I fear, died lately, William Knyvett.[62]

A MERCENARY MUSICIAN

Sir Frederick Ouseley wrote to Wesley in 1858, requesting a contribution from him to his *Collection of Anthems for Certain Seasons and Festivals* (1861-66). Yet in another letter, addressed to the Rev. J. B. Dykes, he had already expressed his misgivings: 'I will make an attempt on Wesley, but he is such a mercenary fellow that I fear for the result!'[63]

At last, Wesley replied but in an aloof tone:

> I regret to have to submit to you that I feel opposed to taking any part in your prospected work.... I fear the publication will do some harm. Your specimens ought all to be *great*. If they were so their Anthems, of course, would remain unpaid. Unpaid, that is, if the works of the kind are to be viewed in the same light as other works of art. Where are you to get a *single* specimen of the finest church music? I don't know. There have been only two men in my time who could publish such a thing: my Father and Mendelssohn.... It vexes me to resist your bidding thus.[64]

In November 1858, the Cathedral authorities had considered it was necessary for the organist to undertake the singing instruction of the Choristers, personally, or else to find an assistant teacher for that purpose, towards whose remuneration they were prepared to find half of the cost. Furthermore, they desired both the organist and the precentor to introduce supplementary Chants and new Service-settings, and above all, to publish the Anthem Book.[65]

Meanwhile, Wesley was owing two years rent for his house in the Close; and he was therefore informed by the Chapter Clerk that, unless his arrears were paid before next February, his salary would be withheld.[66] It appeared that he was still occupying his accommodation in Kingsgate Street. And a month before the ultimatum was due, his claim for a remission of the first quarter's rent was amicably settled, 'in consideration of the fact that Dr Wesley continued to pay rent for another house at the same time.'[67]

Writing to Mrs Merest,[68] the daughter of William Hawes and a notable contralto, who was then living in Ryde on the Isle of Wight, Wesley humorously observed:

> The want of rain is said to be the cause of illness of late. The learned say we are, or were, ten inches below the right mark in England. They evidently don't sing the Hallelujah Chorus, often enough, as there is *rain for ever and ever* here![69]

And in June 1859, he mournfully wrote to her:

> I have had a sadly monotonous, secluded life here, and for health's sake ever require a little change. I may possibly be able to get a fortnight in Scotland, as I am anxious to get permission of Lord Dudley to fish his waters in Ross-shire. He rarely uses them for himself, and, being a truly musical man, it is possible he might not take it amiss if I submitted the request to be allowed to throw a fly on his river and the lakes in that locality.... I have all sorts of permissions to fish, but I wanted a decided change of air. It is an immense way to go, more than 600 miles.[70]

A REPRIMAND

Unfortunately, the appointment of an over-zealous Precentor to Winchester Cathedral, the Rev. Henry Wray,[71] resulted in a magnificent display of pyrotechnics; for the Chapter had instructed that, unless Wesley was prepared to introduce a selection of new Chants as requested, the Precentor would be asked to carry out their orders!

Wesley was again admonished for neglecting his duties, because he had attended only 397 choral services out of a possible 780, having left the organ-playing to a fourteen year old school-boy. He had also failed to give adequate instruction in both music and singing to the choirboys. And more serious still, his threat to place a note from a member of the Chapter into the solicitor's hands had been utterly at variance with its contents and the spirit of his contract.[72] But they later conceded that the Song School had been in an unsatisfactory state — though reminding him that some personal attention might have improved matters.[73]

On 10 September, 1861, he opened the new organ in Holy Trinity Parish Church, Winchester. The fine instrument, originally built by Henry Willis for the Prince Consort, had been since 1850 in Whippingham Church on the Isle of Wight. It seems that Wesley was assisted by the Cathedral Choir, who chanted the service and sang two of his anthems, 'Blessed be the God and Father' and 'Praise the Lord, my soul.'[74] This latter work had been specially composed for the occasion, but was first published by private subscription.[75]

One of Wesley's hobbies was the collecting of bric-à-brac, and he loved a bargain. As William Spark writes:

> Vainly did we all hide auction announcements from him — he smelt them out as an African witch-doctor does the king's enemies. Consequently the house was full from top to bottom with old furniture, curiosities, etc. In the garrets could be found almost any known article of commerce, from an orrery to a tobacco chopping-machine.[76]

And in writing to Miss Emett, then staying at Tring Park, Hertfordshire, Wesley described one sale as follows:

> Things went low as they always do, and I should have bought a few things; but I could not get near to see them before the sale began. And when it once gets going, it goes so very fast that poor, country folk can hardly see their way.
>
> I only bought 3 little books, all of which have your father's name in them: a thorough-bass book with Lord Stanhope's tuning-book, and another. I wanted the Stanhope as my copy was lent to *Willis* and not returned.
>
> I should certainly have bought the Bach Manuscripts, could there have been a certainty they were Bach's writing; and where there is *the remotest doubt,* good-bye to all value in my mind. (The largeness of the notes made me think it could not be his writing: a man who writes much never makes large notes.) As Bennett believes in the writing, I cannot understand his large order for 2 things. *I* should have been inclined to sell my bedstead to buy them all. I always thought him one of the worldly-wise *snobs!*[77]

During his Winchester days, Wesley had several articled pupils and assistant organists, who became notable musicians in their own right, like G. B. Arnold (1832-1902), G. M. Garrett (1834-97), T. E. Aylward (1844-1933), F. E. Gladstone (1845-1928), J. K. Pyne (1852-1938), and C. Lee Williams (1851-1935).

Mrs Wesley was always interested in the welfare of her husband's pupils, particularly if they were ill. For example, David Parkes (the Sheffield-born music teacher and organist) had been articled to Dr Wesley between 1862 and 1865. And in writing to his sister Miss Marie Parkes, she inquired after her brother's health, also informing her that Dr Wesley had managed to trace the missing luggage thereupon she continued:

> When I saw you, I was in great anxiety about one of my sons [Samuel], who has left us to join his brother [John] in Australia, some months back, and whose arrival we had not heard of. I am thankful to say, I have just received tidings of his having safely reached his destination, and I must now let the rest of the family know — so please excuse this hurried note.[78]

In June 1862, Wesley too wrote to Marie, in order to tell her that he would not be going away from Winchester for any length of time, and that she would be very welcome to visit him at the end of the month. Further, if he could be of any assistance in finding suitable lodgings for her brother, she was to let him know. And he concluded, 'I think you will be pleased with the *Israel*.[79]

At 7 o'clock in the morning, the same month, Mrs Wesley wrote to tell Marie about the seaside accommodation on the Isle of Wight:

> Ventnor is certainly an extremely pretty place, but it has great drawbacks — there are scarcely any houses *near* the sea and the beach is *all shingle*. I thought them so great when I was there last autumn that I and one of my sons settled ourselves about four miles to the west of Ventnor, at Milton, in a house *on* the beach, where we could walk down a few steps out of the garden on to very good sands. It is equally sheltered with Ventnor. There are hot baths in the house and a bathing-machine on the sands and a charming little Cove, nearby, where gentlemen bathe.
>
> I can recommend the people for their *perfect honesty* and attention, and they promise anything one wants from the villages a little way off. The terms, in the season, are 2 guineas a week for apartments and *board,* which is *extremely good* and served in your own rooms, or you may merely take the lodgings and buy your own provisions. The name is Brown, Victoria Baths, Milton.
>
> A lady and gentleman are staying with me, besides another friend, and my younger boys [Charles and William] are at home, so I can with difficulty get a quiet moment *for writing*. So pray excuse this almost illegible scrawl. . . .
>
> P.S. There are nice little carriages and donkey chairs to be had at Milton.[80]

Writing from Salisbury in 1861, William Aylward requested that his son Theodore Edward,[81] might be considered as an articled pupil. And Wesley immediately replied:

> From the description you have given me of your Son, and from your being connected with musical affairs, I would receive your Son as a Pupil of mine at a reduced premium and make part of it payable on his leaving me and taking a situation.
>
> I never take Pupils gratuitously, and I view a Pupil's taking my duty at a Cathedral as an advantage *to him* which should be paid for liberally, rather than considered as a service to myself.
>
> You are, perhaps, aware that I have had the very highest advantages as to *Pianoforte* style and practice. My Father was the friend of Clementi, John Cramer, Kalkbrenner and Moscheles, etc., and their style I teach, although I have not played much in public myself. My hand is small and modern mechanism demands such incessant practice that, out of London, one is inclined to neglect the subject.
>
> Should your Son come here I think he might ease you in his expenses by taking a few young Pupils. [82]

Meanwhile, in September, the Cathedral authorities regretted that it was necessary to admonish Dr Wesley for neglecting his duties: first there had been a sudden cancellation of the Choristers' daily practices in the preceding July, owing to his absence without the Precentor's knowledge; secondly, his insistence on not attending the voice-trials and his subsequent blatant refusal, having decided to come, to give an opinion as to the candidates' comparative merits when requested to do so, all of which events had caused considerable friction.[83]

And another note was sent to Wesley, two years later, reminding him not to excuse himself from Sunday services prior to the Precentor's permission being granted.[84] Hence his opinion to Aylward senior, namely that 'a Pupil's taking his duty at a Cathedral was an advantage *to him,*' without mentioning how such an arrangement was equally beneficial to the organist, thus allowing for Wesley's frequent absences from *his* duties!

JAMES KENDRICK PYNE, JUNIOR

In 1863 Wesley made special arrangements with Aylward for a prospective pupil, who was travelling home to the West Country, to be met at a railway station:

> A Son of Mr Pyne of Bath leaves me by the 9.50 train tomorrow morning on his way home, and will have to stop about two hours in Salisbury. He is very young, and I am anxious about him and if you could, without much convenience, take him in charge and have him sent off by the next Bath train I should *feel extremely* obliged. Very *Fair.* If anyone meets him he could hardly be mistaken.[85]

The eleven year old Kendrick Pyne (1852-1938) had just been appointed organist of All Saints' Chapel, Bath. He belonged to a family of musicians of at least three generations: his father, a pupil of Samuel Wesley, was the organist of Bath Abbey for over fifty years; his grandfather was formerly a Director of Music at the famous Foundling Hospital in London; and his great-grandfather was a notable tenor, and another member of the family Madame Bodda Pyne (Miss Louisa Fanny Pyne) was an operatic singer in the mid-nineteenth century. She made a highly successful tour of the United States in 1854, and later received a pension from the Civil List.

'Kenny', the eldest son, was articled to Wesley in 1864, later moving with him to Gloucester where he was educated at the King's School and appointed assistant organist of the Cathedral, as well as choirmaster of the Gloucester Festival Society. His future appointments included St James's, Cheltenham (1871), Aylesbury Parish Church (1872), Christ Church Clifton; Chichester Cathedral (1873), and St Mark's, Philadelphia; but failing to obtain a professorship at Pennsylvania University, he returned to England in October, 1875, when he was appointed organist of Manchester Cathedral, remaining there until he retired in 1908. And he also held the organistships to the Manchester Town Hall (1877) and Victoria University (1903); a professorship of the organ at the Manchester Royal College of Music (1893) and a lectureship in Church Music at Victoria University, where he became Dean of the Faculty of Music (1908). Archbishop Temple made him an honorary Doctor of Music (Lambeth) in 1901.

Dr Kendrick Pyne was certainly the Marcel Dupré of his times, having an extensive knowledge of the organ music of the French School. His recitals were given on the fine Cavaillé-Coll organ in the Town Hall. And in 1927 the City Council recommended:

> That, having regard to Dr Pyne's distinguished service as City Organist extending over a period of fifty years, he be released from that portion of the terms of his appointment which provides that he shall give not less than forty recitals per season, and that in lieu thereof it be henceforth a condition of his appointment that he shall give an organ recital as and when required by the Town Hall Committee. That, in future, his salary shall be £200 per annum inclusive.[86]

He died in Ilford on 3 September, 1938, at the age of eighty-six, having achieved all that Wesley himself would have been truly proud to have done.[87] And of his great teacher and friend Pyne later wrote:

> When I was about ten years old, my Father went to open the organ at St Thomas's Church, Winchester. I remember his returning home with great delight saying that in the streets of Winchester he had met his old friend Wesley. The meeting led to a revived friendship, and from that moment, several times a year, visits were exchanged between Bath and Winchester, and, later on, Gloucester, that continued till the death of Wesley.
>
> It was at my Father's house that Wesley wrote for his little godson Ernest (who was afterwards a Magdalen boy, and died some three years ago in America),[88] his delightful hymn-tune [Eden][89] so well known to children, to the popular words 'There is a happy land'.
>
> I went on my first visit to Wesley at Winchester when I was twelve. The most apocryphal tales are told as to his eccentricities. I lived with him for sometime and do not share in the view. He was moody, often absent-minded, nervous and irritable; but not more than one would expect from an artist, who is not accustomed to hide his feelings. He had a keen sense of sly humour. He carried in very wet weather an enormous gig umbrella of a vivid green colour. Now after my being articled to him, when I was about thirteen, he used to go to the afternoon service at Winchester College, held on Sundays after the Cathedral service. We waited in the ante-chapel until Dr Moberly had finished his sermon, and then walked up between the boys to the organ, which hung over the sanctuary at the north-east end. He frequently used to make me carry this enormous green gingham through the rows of the boys to my great discomforture, and I can see the sly twinkle in his eye as he turned round to me when we arrived at our destination. . . .
>
> The Cathedral precentor was an unusually zealous officer. In a moment of musical enthusiasm he had written an anthem which interested us all very much. This gentleman had the temerity, in the presence of Wesley, to conduct

the rehearsals. It was indeed a wonderful sight to see him directing affairs, Wesley grimly standing by his side. I am bound to say the precentor was *not* a favourite with the Winchester choir. . . . I remember this precentor used to unearth music by composers like Porter, Vaughan, and other inane anthems, which he insisted upon having performed. When one considers that this kind of relationship existed for many years everywhere, and that Cathedral organists — professional musicians of high standing — were liable to be thwarted on every side by such people, one need not be surprised at reading some of Wesley's views on such matters. I think he took such an anachronism too seriously, instead of seeing the somewhat comical side of the relationship as he might well have done. Hence the tinge of bitterness in his remarks is not to be wondered at.[90]

VI.

In 1863 the novelist Florence Marryat came to stay in Winchester, where she was made much fuss of by the social circle of the Cathedral Close. Unfortunately, five years later, this circle found itself and its beloved city cruelly portrayed in the lightest of disguises in the second volume of her novel *Nelly Brooke;* for she described 'Hilstone' as one of those somnolent places which, going to sleep six days in the week, wake up on the seventh, namely, their market day, to make an extraordinary fuss over the most trivial topics and events of a commonplace existence. And she continued, 'Hilstone could boast of a cathedral! and the cathedral towns of our native country possess an individuality exclusively their own, for which all those who do not dwell therein, may be thankful.'

However, there were three special planets round which the lower satellites revolved: Mrs Filmer, the Dean's daughter, Dr Nesbitt, the Cathedral organist, and Mr Rumbell, 'a bachelor canon with a bass voice, which all the spinsters declared to be marvellous in its perfection.' Concerning the character of the organist, that is to say of Dr Wesley, she wrote:

> He was a man of powerful intellect, and great musical ability, but with an uncertain and violent temper, and a reserved disposition which forbid his opening his heart to anyone. He was very much courted and deferred to in Hilstone, but everybody was more or less afraid of him. On his part, he treated the townspeople with politeness because it was his good-will and pleasure to retain his appointment as organist amongst them; but there was ever a cynical look to be discerned lurking behind his readiest smile, and in his heart, he hated and despised them all. . . .
>
> He carried on a secret feud against all the musical canons, but especially against Mr Rumbell with his bass voice, and Mr Pratt with his tenor voice, who had both attempted to interfere with the instruction of the cathedral choir. Dr Nesbitt would laugh in his sleeve at the mere notion of either of these men knowing anything of music; a first rate musician himself, and with the capability of making the splendid organ under his charge sound in such a manner that all England would have been glad to crowd to hear him, he would

yet on occasions mount the loft stairs in so bad a humour, that neither choristers nor canons could by any possibility follow the chords struck by his wayward fingers. And then Dr Nesbitt would be delighted at the public failure, and before he had given the cathedral authorities time to reprimand him, would lull their anger by such exquisite music as is seldom heard upon this lower earth. He knew, too well, that however Mr Rumbell might puff with indignation, or Mr Pratt weep with chagrin, all Hilstone would vote against his dismissal. His fame was too wide spread for such a step to injure anybody but themselves; he would at once be gladly seized upon and engaged by some rival cathedral town, and they would have lost the glory of being able to boast that they had not only the finest organ, but the best organist in England.

Miss Marryat also informed her readers that the organist was a welcome participant in the private concerts of the deanery, and that his invalid wife never went into society; for she was 'stowed away somewhere in the recesses of his dark, damp house.'

In March, 1863, Wesley wrote to Miss Marie Parkes, a former pupil then living in Sheffield, as he believed that she could obtain a large list of subscribers for his new compositions there. And yet,

> The trouble is to get the subject noticed by the *hundreds* of persons who would give their names if *cleverly* consulted. Now — can you advise me as to the employment of one or more agents in Sheffield who would collect me names. Of course, I should remunerate them. . . . I assure you that were I to put these works into the music-sellers' hands in London, I should lose everything. By working myself through friends, I may make *something considerable* by the undertaking. It is *time I did* make something as from *leaving London* I have thrown my chance *away*. . . . Therefore I mean to work up the matter the *Cockles Pills* way. That is, my pupils here are doing it for me. I have asked for the Queen's patronage just to give a *name* to the work, the Anthems, but I hope the quality of the Books will not need such patronage. . . .
> P.S. I wrote an Anthem for our great marriage day here.[91]

Although nothing further came of this project, the anthem referred to in the postscript was 'Give the King Thy judgments, O God' (Novello),[92] which Wesley had composed at the request of a local committee, formed to organise patriotic rejoicings in celebration of the Prince of Wales' marriage on 10 March, 1863. Unfortunately, his commission of £70 was quietly spent on a meagre display of fireworks!

At the beginning of November, Wesley took part in a concert at the Agricultural Hall, Islington, to mark the inauguration of the Grand Organ built by Henry Willis for the International Exhibition (1862). He played his Fantasia 'Andante Cantabile' (1849) and an 'Extemporaneous Fugue', and afterwards his brother Glenn conducted the beginning of part II of the *Messiah*.[93]

In 1851 Wesley began compiling his *European Psalmist* and was able to report to a possible subscriber, three years later, that between four and five hundred pages had been engraved. This labour of love, however, was to take Wesley some twenty years to complete.

His earliest hymn-tunes first appeared in Hackett's *National Psalmist* (1839): *Hampton* (where he was once evening organist) and *Harewood* (named after Harewood Park, in Herefordshire, which Wesley once visited on horseback).

And it was because he desired to write better tunes to hymns of new unusual metres that Wesley accepted the musical editorship of *A Selection of Psalms and Hymns* (1864), which had been arranged for use in the Church of England by the Rev. Charles Kemble, Rector of Bath. This hymnal was 'a cut book', that is to say, each page was horizontally sliced leaving the tune above and the words below the cut page, thus allowing the half-pages to be turned separately to any hymn or any tune — a method which was later utilised in *The Scottish Psalter* (1929).

One of Wesley's most popular tunes *Aurelia* appeared in this book for the first time. Strangely enough the version of the music given in modern hymnals is incorrect in so far as the third and fourth lines are concerned. The following taken from *The European Psalmist* gives the correct and more effective version:

Aurelia became a firm favourite of English congregations, after it had been sung at the Thanksgiving Service for the Recovery of the Prince of Wales at St Paul's Cathedral in 1872, when it was set to the hymn, 'The Church's one foundation'. Kendrick Pyne has related the story of the tune's origin as follows:

> I was in his drawing-room in the Close, Winchester, as a lad of thirteen, with Mrs Wesley, my Mother and Mrs Stewart (the Mother of the distinguished General Stewart who fell in Egypt); we were all discussing a dish of strawberries when Wesley came rushing up from below with a scrap of MS. in his hand, a psalm-tune just that instant finished. Placing it on the instrument he said: 'I think this will be popular.' My Mother was the first ever to sing it to the words, 'Jerusalem the Golden'. The company liked it, and Mrs Wesley on the spot christened it 'Aurelia'.[94]

In February 1864, the Canon-in-Residence informed the Chapter that he had received through the Precentor several messages from Dr Wesley, followed by a letter, all expressing his unwillingness to attend the voice-trials except for the payment of a fee.[95] But Wesley reluctantly complied with their wishes. And in March, they requested him 'to play a voluntary before every service on Christmas Day, Easter Day, Ascension Day, Whitsunday and Trinity Sunday, to commence playing when the clock strikes, and to continue until the Clergy have taken their places in the choir.'[96]

On the one hand, we are told that no one could ever forget the wonderful effects that his organ-playing produced: 'His improvisations were masterpieces, and during them he would get lost in the atmosphere he created and quite oblivious of his surroundings. Thus, when he played the readers to the lectern he would often keep them standing, waiting there, while he poured forth his thoughts and feelings in wonderful strains.'[97] And on the other, after he had made an almighty hash of playing the anthem, he left his articled pupil Mr David Parkes to play the final voluntary and then made himself very visible — stalking about at the back of the Nave as the choir processed out, as if to give the impression that he was there only to *listen* to the service!

At the end of September, in the presence of both the Chapter and the Organist, the Precentor formally complained of Dr Wesley's irregularity of attendance at the weekly rehearsals of the full choir and his complete inattention if he did appear, and finally, of his leaving the choir-stalls too much during the services that was detrimental to the singing. Wesley immediately denied his absences from the choir-practices, although he promised to undertake the entire rehearsals himself and to be only occasionally in the organ-loft during services.[98]

AN UNWELCOME VISITOR

Samuel Tuckerman (1819-90), the son of an American merchant, was the organist of St Paul's Church, Boston, and afterwards of Holy Trinity Church, New York. He made several visits to England in the 1850s, having armed himself with letters of introduction, for the purpose of collecting church music and information on cathedrals, in general. He then stayed in each city for two or three months, taking copious notes about each choral establishment, and in due course returning to his native land, where he lectured on his subject. With the assistance of his great friend Dr George Elvey, a successful petition was signed by many eminent musicians requesting Archbishop Sumner to confer on Tuckerman the Lambeth Music Doctorate in 1851.

Naturally he wished to visit Winchester Cathedral, and Dr Elvey kindly gave him a letter of introduction which he duly presented to Wesley. If only he had been told beforehand of the organist of Winchester's unfriendly feelings towards his friend. (Dr Elvey had evidently defeated him in both the Gresham Prize competition and the Windsor organistship.) And it so happened that Wesley tore open the letter, read it, and hastilly committed it to the fire, exclaiming, 'Elvey! Who is Elvey?' He then rang the bell violently for his butler, who immediately rushed into the drawing-room to be told by his master: 'John, this man is an imposter. Show him the door!'

There was nothing else for Tuckerman to do, but to catch the next train to London, where, in no uncertain terms, he related his unhappy experiences. A fortnight later, however, Dr Elvey was handed a telegram with the following instructions: 'Send down your friend Tuckerman — I have put up "The Wilderness" for him to hear to-morrow.'

Having caught the afternoon train to Winchester, Tuckerman was welcomed at the railway station by Wesley personally, who then treated him as a special guest in his house. After dinner they walked over the lawns to the Cathedral, where Wesley extemporised magnificently for two hours, much to the enjoyment of his American visitor.[99]

THE FINALE

To celebrate the opening of the North London Working Men's Industrial Exhibition in the Agricultural Hall, Islington, on 17 October, 1864, Wesley had composed a short cantata, 'Ode to Labour' which was later published privately. Its fine bass song, 'When from the Creator's hand' was once sung by Hubert Parry at one of the Eton College concerts. He had come to know Wesley while he was at Twyford School, through the Luards who lived in the Close. And it seemed Wesley was amiably disposed towards the boy, for he allowed Parry to sit on the organ-stool with him during services in the Cathedral: 'There I used to sit,' he recalled, 'while old Wesley, with his eyebrows raised and his chin sticking out, ruminated on the organ. He was awfully kind to me.'[100]

Wesley was very much at the height of his musical powers when he came to Winchester, but they sadly began to wane in his fifties. And in 1865, when the opportunity came of exchanging the fishful waters of the Itchen for similar joys in the Upper Severn, near Gloucester, he welcomed it. Yet his friends have never forgotten 'this short thin man, with a decided limp, and wearing a dark-brown wig, who would be seen taking off his coat, turning up his shirt-sleeves and his trousers to his knees, and playing as no Winchester organist had ever played before.'[100]

GLOUCESTER CATHEDRAL CHOIR, LOOKING WEST

From a 19th-century drawing, by permission of the Dean and Chapter.

CHAPTER SEVEN

Gloucester Cathedral (1865-1876)

JOHN AMOTT'S death at the beginning of 1865 made a vacancy for an organist at the Cathedral. The articled assistant Mr. J. A. Matthews (1841-1925),[1] a former chorister and an unsuccessful candidate for the post, later recalled how Dr Wesley had been asked to act as an assessor and had surprised the Dean and Chapter by declaring: 'Gentlemen, I have decided to accept the post myself!' It seemed as if the Archbishop of Canterbury had just accepted a minor canonry.

A former lay clerk also recalled the day of the 'mock' trial, when the dean had told him of the *great* Dr Wesley's appointment: 'He came to judge those who were in for the trial, but he has accepted the post himself because he is fond of fishing, and he hears that some good fishing is to be had about here.'[2] And so *The Gloucester Journal* reported:

> We understand that there will be no competition, as it is universally allowed that Dr Wesley's pre-eminence entitled him at once to preference. We look forward to this appointment as the crowning point to raise our Cathedral Choir to rank among the most distinguished in the country.'[3]

Wesley was appointed on the 18th of February, 1865. His salary was fixed at £150 a year, and also included 'a house of residence to be kept in external but not internal repair, at the cost of the Dean and Chapter.'[4] The additional sum of £25 was made available in case Wesley required the services of a deputy for the daily instruction of the Choristers, which he declined, but accepted seven years later.[5]

The Wesleys had to move into temporary accommodation, since Amott's house in Palace Yard, which is still the official residence of the Cathedral organist (now No. 7 Miller's Green), was taking several months to have the necessary alterations made. On the first floor the ceiling of Wesley's music room was heightened to achieve better sound-effects; also a new upper storey and another music room for teaching purposes were later added at considerable expense. In July the same year, Wesley wrote to his third son Francis Gwynne, who was then a tutor at Winchester College:

> The day has been so fine that *everything* looks well. I think my house is really improved. I have been unable to find out when I might expect it to be finished but I think it may be more than a month just. The attics are made very good and having windows both front and back is very attractive, at least it was so to-day.
>
> I played the service. Called on the dean. He was napping. He came to the service and waited for me coming out to be the first to wish me all good.[6]

THREE CHOIRS FESTIVAL 1865

In April, Wesley was officially appointed the conductor of the Gloucester Festival by the Stewards, who requested him to draw up a suitable programme of oratorio music for the occasion in September. And yet, at almost fifty-five years old, Wesley was beginning to feel his age and to suffer from nervousness. Certainly all the planning for the Festival must have taxed his energies, especially the crescendo of clerical opposition that was mounting against the performance of oratorio music in the Cathedral:

> This year the Dean opens his door, but runs away, leaving the Earl of Ellenborough to do the honours at the Deanery; the Bishop seizes the opportunity to make a tour on the Continent, and some few others follow his example. No more powerful blow, short of closing the doors of the Cathedral, could have been given to the Festival by those in authority. Yet the undertaking proceeds, and tickets are bought as they were never bought before. In truth, the protest against interference is too marked to be mistaken, and we sincerely hope that it may have the effect of making the Dean and Bishop see that religious music can never desecrate a religious building, especially when given in the sacred cause of charity.[7]

The opening service was duly held on Tuesday, September 5, at ten o'clock in the morning. In the charity sermon, one of the canons eloquently defended the Festival Meetings and justified the singing of oratorios in the Cathedral itself. Dr Wesley's Cathedral Morning Service in E and his father's anthem 'Thou, O God, art praised in Zion,' were sung. And the newspapers noticed that Dr Wesley had played his favourite organ piece, Bach's 'St Anne' Fugue, 'in his well-known and artistic style.'

The only services in the Festival Week were Choral Matins at 8 o'clock and Evensong, which was said at 5 o'clock. It was significant that there were no daily services at all in the Cathedral on either Monday or Satruday, as the former day was spent in the necessary rehearsal of both the chorus and orchestra. The choral music of the services on Wednesday, Thursday and Friday, included the following canticles: Samuel Wesley's Morning Service in F, Mendelssohn in A, and S. S. Wesley's Chant Service; and the anthems were Palestrina's 'Out of the deep' and S. S. Wesley's 'Praise the Lord, my soul' and 'O Lord, my God.'[8]

If the music critics praised Wesley's conducting and William Done's organ-playing, they felt otherwise about the lay clerks' singing because they were uncertain of their 'leads', which were both out of time and tune. And they therefore trusted that more attention might be given to the choral services of future Festivals. The oratorios included Beethoven's 'Christ on the Mount of Olives' (1803), Mendelssohn's 'Elijah' (1846), 'Hymn of Praise' (1840) and Part II of 'St Paul' (1836), as well as Mozart's *Requiem* (1791), Spohr's 'Last Judgement' (1826), and the *Messiah*.

The first evening concert of secular music in the Shire Hall consisted of two Overtures: Rossini's 'William Tell' (1829) and Spohr's 'Faust' (1816). At the next concert, the music included 'Spring' from Haydn's 'Seasons' (1801), Mendelssohn's romantic setting of Goethe's *Die erste Walpurgisnacht* (1831) and also his Piano Concerto No. 1 in G minor (1831), with Madame Arabella Goddard as the soloist. And there followed other items, including Spohr's Overture to 'Jessonda' (1823), that 'linked sweetness too long drawn out according to present day notions.'[9] No wonder, for the concert finished at eleven-twenty!

Mr Joseph Bennett, a music critic, noticed that the most puzzling figure on the concert platform was that of the conductor Dr Wesley, whose beat was little regarded — a circumstance which appeared least to trouble him:

> Gradually Wesley's face lightened and beamed. The music having hold of him, presently took entire possession. He swayed from side to side; he put down the baton, treated himself to a pinch of snuff with an air of exquisite enjoyment, and then sat motionless, listening. Meanwhile [Henry] Blagrove conducted with his violin bow.[10]

And at the final evening concert, the audience heard Beethoven's Symphony No. 8 in F (1812), Spohr's Dramatic Concerto for Violin in A minor, and parts of Mozart's opera, 'The Magic Flute' (1791).

After some thirty years absence, Wesley had now returned to the public concert platfrom. One of his admirers was a seventeen year old schoolboy Hubert Parry, whose home was at Highnam Court, two miles outside Gloucester. He was quite overwhelmed by the excitement of the Festival, and fourteen pages in his personal diary were devoted to its events.

Although he criticised Wesley's rapid *tempi* in the oratorios, he was utterly ecstatic over Mendelssohn's music, and above all declared that the *Messiah* was 'the greatest music ever composed.' Moreover, Wesley's masterly improvisation of a fugue on the organ, the following Sunday, is described in detail:

He began the accompaniment in crotchets alone, and then gradually worked into quavers, then triplets and lastly semi-quavers. It was quite marvellous. The powerful old subject came stalking in right and left with the running accompaniment wonderfully entwined with it — all in the style of Old Bach.[11]

WESLEY'S ACCOUNT BOOK

It was necessary for the Festival conductor to keep a business-like record of all payments made to the musicians; and Wesley's *Gloucester Music Festival Accounts* (1865),[12] now in the possession of the Royal College of Music, make fascination reading.

Mademoiselle Tietjens, the principal soloist, was paid the great sum of £350, Madame Arabella Goddard, the pianist, the sum of £52 10s., and Mr Henry Blagrove, the leader of the orchestra, received £40. Both Mr William Done (piano accompanyist) and Mr George Townshend Smith (organist) were each given £21. Whereas the eight visiting choristers (from Worcester and Hereford) received £4 each, the local ones were given £1 each. All the ladies of the chorus received between £4 and £5 each. And the final statement ran as follows:

Principal Singers	£1,058 4
Organists and Pianists	£94 10
Band	£760 5
Chorus	£840 1
Hire of Music	£60
Hire of Organ from Mr Willis	£52 10

Total £2,865 10s.

THE MUSICAL ELLICOTTS

Constantia Ellicott, the wife of the Bishop of Gloucester and Bristol, was an amateur singer. Her private concerts in London enabled the members of the aristocracy to meet the famous actors and musicians of the day, though her more modest 'At Homes' in the Bishop's Palace were devoted to the singing of madrigals and modern songs.

Soon after his arrival in Gloucester, Wesley was invited to conduct her Ladies' Society. That fateful occasion must have been the shortest rehearsal he had ever taken; for having listened to their screechings for a few bars, Wesley immediately slammed down the piano lid and rushed out of the drawing-room, shouting 'Cats!'[13]

Bishop Charles Ellicott (1819-1905), a former Dean of Exeter and an eminent biblical scholar, had equally found his wife's musical *soirées* very irksome. On the other hand the late Sir Herbert Brewer recalled a Sunday afternoon, after Wesley's 'Wilderness' had been sung in the Cathedral, when the Bishop told him that he had disliked the anthem, not because of its music but because of its length, having also added: 'I don't know where Dr Wesley has gone; but all I can say is, that if he still composes anthems that length, they won't keep him in either place very long!'[14]

And yet, his daughter Miss Rosalind Ellicott (1857-1924) was very musical, having entered the Royal Academy of Music in 1874, and subsequently became a professional singer and a composer of some merit. Her cantatas and orchestral music were later performed at both the Cheltenham and Gloucester Festivals.

During Christmas of 1865, Hubert Parry noticed that the music of Herr Schachner, a German piano teacher in London, was very fashionable at the Bishop's Palace — much to his great boredom. And in January, he described his dinner party for the Wesleys, when he listened to the Doctor's curious views on Beethoven, Mendelssohn and Spohr, and most important of all, to the sensible advice: that if Hubert wanted to make any real progress in the art of orchestration, he would require lessons from a London master.[15]

Writing to his sister Eliza, in March of 1866, Wesley said: 'I am salubrious. I have not been to London for a long time — I suppose I must come soon. What about *them fowls?*' And then changing to his favourite subject of antiques, he added: 'I did not write about the Coffee Pot, being very poor. I hope it is still to be had. If you hear of anybody having a fine Harmonium to sell, let me know.'[16]

A CASE OF BAD MANNERS

At the Worcester Festival, Wesley's last minute message, that he was unable to play the organ in a performance of the *Messiah,* resulted in the following caustic report in a London newspaper:

> On inquiry it was found that, amidst the war of the Worcester elements, the musical Doctor had come into collision with the medical Honorary Secretary Dr Williams, a respected physician of this town. . . .
>
> Mr Done, the conductor, late on Saturday received a dispatch from Dr Wesley, stating that owing to peculiar circumstances he could not fulfil his engagement as organist, but offering to send Mr Hamilton Clark, of Queen's College, Oxford, as his substitute. Dr Williams did not want to feel the pulse of his Festival Committee. He at once, by telegram to Dr Wesley, prescribed for the patient by stating that his resignation was accepted, and as regard to a substitute the Committee would dispense with his nominee and select one for themselves. . . .

The Stewards are naturally very indignant at Dr Wesley's throwing them over at the eleventh hour, but there is no explanation as to his motives; but Dr Wesley's eccentricities were manifested so strongly during the last Gloucester Festival that no astonishment need to be expressed at a little Worcester vagary. . . .

It is said from Gloucester that Dr Wesley is so engaged on some forthcoming work that he could not spare the time to be here, but if so, why did he not give due notice to the conductor before he accepted the engagement?[17]

In his diary Hubert Parry has described a grand wedding on New Year's Day of 1867, when Gloucester Cathedral had been lavishly decorated in spite of the dean's prohibition of floral displays at Christmas, and how Wesley had composed a new anthem for the occasion — probably 'God be merciful unto us', and how the choir had been worked up to some efficiency for the first time since his arrival.[18]

II.

When the Wesleys moved to Gloucester, young Kendrick Pyne was invited to come and make his home with the family. He continued his musical studies under Wesley and his general education at the King's School, next to the Cathedral, where he was appointed an articled assistant.

On Speech Day of 1867, the fifteen year old lad distinguished himself by appearing in the School plays as 'Portia' and 'Whiskerandos' (from Sheridan's *Critic*), so that his Master was able to write afterwards to a friend:

I went to hear Kenny at the school-speaking to-day. He acted as the Advocate 'Portia' in a long scene from *The Merchant of Venice*. He was the *best* of the lot by very long odds. This, people seemed to know. Really, I am glad he got on so capitally well as I rather quaked at the thought of *my assistant* speaking amongst the schoolboys. I wish you had been there.[19]

Also in the same letter, Wesley sarcastically observed: 'That blind man can't see his way to pay me the 2s. 6d.' And on New Year's Day he received a magnificent scroll, thanking him for his kindness in conducting the Choral Service in Huddersfield Parish Church on 14 November, 1867.[20] It was signed by the choirmembers and also by the organist Henry Parratt, who was the eldest brother of (later) Sir Walter Parratt.

THREE CHOIRS FESTIVAL 1868

Wesley now faced the exacting rehearsals of both the chorus and orchestra, which were so exhausting, we are told, that several performers declared that they would be unfit for work the following day if they remained any longer. Here is a typical incident during one of the morning rehearsals, as related by Mr William Cummings:

Dr S. S. Wesley, the conductor, seemed to be more than usually absent-minded, and he wasted a considerable amount of time. At length Henry Blagrove, the leader of the violins, whispered to me, 'The orchestra are becoming very impatient, *do* try to get the doctor to go on.'

I immediately stepped up to the conductor's desk and said: 'Dr Wesley, will you kindly run through my music at once; I want to get away?'

'Why such haste?' he slowly replied.

Knowing his weakness for fishing, I thought to enlist his sympathy by saying: 'I want to make some arrangements for some grayling fishing.'

At the sound of the word 'fishing' Wesley instantly put down his baton and, folding his arms, said: 'Grayling fishing! *you* get grayling fishing, a young man like *you!* It is shameful. Here am I, an old fisherman, and never had a chance.'

More conversation — of a piscatorial rather than a musical nature — followed, with the result that Wesley forgot all about the rehearsal and the music.[21]

The programme of the opening service included Tallis's Responses, Rogers's Canticles in D, and Wagner's popular Motet, 'Blessing, honour and glory.' But a critic acidly commented that 'the music was scrambled through in evident haste; and had it not been for the excellent organ-playing of Mr J. K. Pyne, junior, there would have been little to interest the musical portion of the congregation.'[22]

On the Tuesday afternoon, the audience heard part of Haydn's 'Creation' (1798) and Samuel Wesley's *Confitebor* (1799) — a setting of Psalm 111, which the composer once considered to be his greatest work. And yet, its 365 pages in manuscript have never been published and only thrice performed: once in London (1826), once in part at the Gloucester Festival (1868), and finally in York Minster (1972) under the baton of Dr Francis Jackson.

Between these choral works came a short orchestral *Intermezzo Religioso* by Hubert Parry, which had been composed at Eton and completed while he was studying in Stuttgart, during the autumn of 1867. However, a former war correspondent unmercifully lampooned its first performance in a London newspaper:

If it had been a playing out of a congregation any *intermezzo* would suffice, and that Hubert Parry would have received as much attention as is ordinarily paid to voluntaries after long sermons. The movement of the *Intermezzo* itself has the character of a dirge . . . and the whole had the sin of being thrust in the programme where it was not wanted.[23]

Owing to the conductor's unsteady beat and utter nervousness, Beethoven's *Mass* in C (1807) collapsed at the beginning of the *Kyries*. Undoubtedly Wesley had every reason to be nervous, having had only one day's rehearsal for the entire Festival programme. And he had also to face those lions of Victorian musical criticism, ever ready to pounce upon an innocent victim from their den in the New Inn at Gloucester. In fact, he later informed Parry that the music critic, who had uttered vitriolic remarks against his *Intermezzo,* scarcely knew a note of music but had always managed to coerce his editor to allow him to write the critique of the Festival because of a personal grudge, and a desire to cause as much harm as he could muster.

On the Wednesday morning, Wesley began a performance of the 'Elijah' (1846) without a baritone soloist, and Kendrick Pyne had to deputise. Although the absence of Mademoiselle Drasdil ruined a quartet, she condescended to arrive on the platform in time for 'Woe unto them who forsake him'! Otherwise, we are told, the Baal choruses were given 'with capital precision, the trumpets being especially telling — and went far to atone for the misfortunes of the day before.'

And on the Thursday morning and afternoon, a programme of over five hours music included selections from Spohr's 'Calvary' (1835), Mendelssohn's 'Hymn of Praise' (1840), Handel's 'Samson' (1743) and the first performance of Schachner's oratorio, 'Israel's Return from Babylon'. However, during the last half-hour of the concert, Parry noticed that 'a complete lassitude took possession of everybody concerned. The principal singers gave up the ghost, the chorus was incapable of singing, and the audience got more incapable of listening.'[24]

On the one hand, it seemed that Wesley had little skill in devising programmes of a suitable length, though a Worcester newspaper had reported one important innovation in his management of the secular concerts, namely, 'the plan of setting down for each evening, if not a complete opera, as much as could be presentable under the circumstances.'[25] And on the other, it was untrue to say that Wesley lacked a breadth of vision, though his canvas was sometimes too large for a provincial festival to undertake, especially with less time for rehearsals. For example, at this particular Festival, he had included the *Messiah,* Beethoven's Symphony No. 5 (1808), a Haydn String Quartet, Mendelssohn's 'Reformation' Symphony No. 5 (1830) and *Die erste Walpurgisnacht* (1831), as well as music from both Carl Weber's *Der Freischütz* (1821) and Mozart's *Don Giovanni* (1787).

III.

Wesley was suspicious of publishers, preferring to get his compositions printed privately and financed by obtaining lists of subscribers. In 1868, however, after much preliminary haggling, he decided to sell the entire copyright of his music to the London publishers, Messrs. Novello, Ewer and Company.

One can imagine Wesley sitting in their office, afraid to commit himself lest he might name too small a sum, and also their well-known manager Henry Littleton, busily writing his letters while waiting for his client's final decision. That deadlock was apparently continued for sometime since both composer and publisher, having said their gentlemanly good-byes at the close of each day, would go their respective ways. A capitulation ultimately happened to the resounding tune of £750. And with the cheque placed safely in his waistcoat-pocket, Wesley is reported to have declared: 'When I get home they'll think that I have been robbing somebody!'[26]

In writing to his friend Miss Emett, Wesley expressed his delight at hearing that she had leased a residence in Torquay: 'This is a favoured part of England, truly. I should be glad if I could reside in Devon, again, but that is improbable.' Next, he inquired after the health of Bishop Phillpotts, of Exeter; for 'he was a clever man and his manners most fascinating,' and yet, 'he hated appointing.'[27]

Henry Phillpotts was one of the most interesting of Victorian prelates. He championed the revival of religious life within the Church of England, and endeavoured to raise the standard of public worship by ordering the wearing of the surplice throughout the Exeter diocese. In 1847 he became the central figure of controversy in the famous lawsuit of the times, 'The Gorham Case', concerning the doctrine of baptismal regeneration.

THE GLOUCESTER ORGAN

In June 1869, Wesley requested that the Cathedral authorities should spend some money on their organ because it was in a state of disrepair. Undaunted by a frustrating reply from the Chapter Clerk, he wrote again:

> We cannot go on playing the organ without some change. We are liable at any moment to get into trouble with the Choir, and this is most painful, for when a difference arises the members of the Chapter do not know who is right and who is wrong. My nerves are too feeble to bear this.[28]

The organ had apparently received no attention since its restoration in 1847 by the youthful Henry Willis, who in later life recalled that his work at Gloucester was his stepping-stone to fame: 'I received £400 for the job, and I was presumptuous enough to marry.'

Although his aspirations were not realised in his lifetime, Wesley gained an active supporter in Mrs Ellicott, whose interest in the subject and willingness to improve things made him write to her:

> Deplorable as things are I feel I ought to offer an opinion to the effect of not spending money in making any portion of the present mechanism better. . . . I think that the right course is for the Friends of Church Music to receive a circular containing a preliminary list of subscribers to the Organ Fund.
>
> My small beginning — 10 guineas — may be introduced! We soon got more than was wanted at Winchester, and I doubt not we should do so here.[29]

There is a contemporary photograph of the organ-console[30] in Wesley's time, which was in its traditional position on the Quire side of the screen, between the smaller and bigger cases. Moreover, its stop-jambs with their respective paper labels can still be seen to-day.

MISS ELIZA WESLEY

It appeared that Wesley liked to discuss both family and business matters with his devoted sister, Eliza Wesley (1819-95). She was the organist of the City Church of St Margaret Pattens for over forty years, and would have achieved some distinction as a performer had it not been for her inherited nervousness. Neverthless, she was instrumental in getting printed the *Letters of Samuel Wesley to Mr Jacobs* in 1875:

> I am impelled to publish them by a sense of duty to his memory, in order to show that it was to his discernment and zealous perseverence that Bach's transcendent genius was made known and appreciated (although tardily, and through much opposition) by the English musical world.

She later bequeathed much 'Wesleyana' to the British Library, including two volumes of letters and newspaper-cuttings and a lock of her brother's baby-hair.

While she was staying with a friend in Tewkesbury in 1869, Wesley found the time to inform her:

> I have been poorly and am getting worse for want of change, and I have for months been struggling to get away and just now it is 'now or never' as the weather may fail, and there is that Worcester Festival for me to attend. At present, I have much anxiety as my Sons [Charles and William] are not settled, and they are too old to be on my hands.[31]

Wesley immensely enjoyed his visit to Tewkesbury, in spite of catching a sudden chill:

> I was awfully ill next day, for I ate new bread and bacon and drank 4 glasses of Port. Gracious! It was all owing to that chill I got on the lawn. The lawn is very nice but it is *low ground,* of course, and much shut in by the Abbey.[32]

In September, he thanked her for having made inquiries as to whether an American publishing house would print his little Chant Service, but informed her that it would be pointless since they were then buying anything published in England, and he continued:

> My Chant Service is just the thing for rustics and those who make in their throats the noise your Francis calls *collywobbling.* You may safely recommend it to all such persons. Your cleric may do me much good if he will *puff* my Chant Service in the *John Bull* [magazine]. . . .
> I fear I cannot get away again, as I have to prepare for two organ-performances and I am out of it all, and so much is done now by organists. I

will, God-willing, come and eat eels. You speak of next year as though we lived for ever. Well, I hope we may all see next year, but I don't like my prospects. I am not what I was. I don't like this place at all, but don't say so. I was very wrong when I left Exeter.[33]

After the Worcester Festival, Wesley had family troubles to discuss with her, especially as he wanted a temporary organistship for his youngest son William Ken, in order 'to help out expenses during his stay in London' as a medical student. And there was, too, his fourth son Charles Alexander, aged twenty-six years old and lately returned from Australia, who was working at accounts with a teacher like a young boy to get qualified. 'He is very steady, indeed,' Wesley wrote, 'and very pleasing 6ft 2in in height.' Having suggested that Charles might be suited to a dry-salter's business, he then asked Eliza whether she would be kind enough to assist him in the matter, for she had many contacts in the City — also adding, 'I am so anxious to get quit of my Sons, and it kills me!' Finally, he wanted her to undertake an errand: 'If you are going by Whittingham's, the second-hand book- and music-shop, please ask the price of Handel's Organ Concertos in score, and tell me.'[34]

A few days later, he hurriedly wrote to Eliza:

> I hear you went, again, to Oxford Street for me. Well, I hope you had other business! I had bought a score of the Concertos and only wanted to know the price to test my price by. But I also wanted an arranged copy — I have two, one of them Mr Best's which I don't approve of at all, and I see there is one in Whittingham's Catalogue. I wish you had told me, or given the publisher's name and date, no matter. . . .
>
> My Son was ordained last Sunday, so we address him 'the Reverend'!![35]

He was Wesley's third son Francis Gwynne, a musician, who had been ordained by the Bishop of Manchester to serve his title at Walkden Moor, near Worsley, Lancashire.

Meanwhile, Wesley was very worried over the weekly payments that his sister had been making to his medical son:

> As my Sons and I never transact *any business,* and as William's letters and refusals to explain things doubtful cause great irritation here, and often give Mrs Wesley a serious illness, I shall be glad if you will pay him the 33s. which he says he *must have.* It is much for me to allow as I am earning very little here. I have, as it seems to me, paid him up to next Tuesday; but I wish you would seriously get from him his statements of his receipts of me, before you pay any more.[36]

And in November, after gastronomic delights with his sister in London, he reported:

> I *did* get late for the train, and worst still, you gave me too much to eat and drink. I assure you, it does not do to *press* me to feast as I am easily made ill; and I drank so much of the Bitter Ale that I had a *bitter* ailment afterwards. . . .

> I see that Haden, precentor of Westminster, is dead. He has been a thorn in
> Turle's side, but Turle does not deserve much better. He never ought to have
> been at the Abbey. I wish it were vacant. . . .
>
> I have had lots of mullet but no eels. What are they a pound in London? I
> always liked the London eels which are *Dutch*.[37]

John Clarke Haden (1805-69), the son of a Derby surgeon, had been a
Minor Canon of St Paul's (1834-49), Rector of Hutton, Essex (1839-69)
and a Minor Canon and Precentor of Westminster Abbey (1846-69).

IV.

Whenever Wesley wanted information on musical matters, he naturally
turned to Eliza, an experienced church organist; for in November, 1869, he
required:

> Can you give me a list of most of the new hymns, to which new tunes have
> had to be put during the last few years, or can you introduce someone who
> will make a list, sending me the words, and whom I would *refresh* with a
> consideration. I am very anxious to finish my *European Psalmist,* and *this* is
> in the way. I must get hold of someone.
>
> I have been ill and feel weak and anxious rather. I have to select a Cottage
> Piano at Broadwoods, and wish to get one *nearly* new. If only I could get a
> higher class one by not having a positively new one.[38]

So she sent him a copy of *Hymns Ancient and Modern* (1868 edition), of
which the Dykes tunes immediately caught his imagination. At the time of
his death Wesley possessed a small upright piano, with a range of six and a
half octaves, which had been made by Erard.

In 1870 Wesley also enquired whether she had finished copying out the
Confitebor (Samuel Wesley), because their brother Robert might make one
of his *strong* requests to have the manuscripts returned:

> I should not be overcome with surprise to learn that you have gone in for a
> copy for yourself. If so, your eyes are none the better for it. (*Eliza had to
> wear spectacles.*)
>
> I may be in your village before long. I forget whether the Public is called
> The Red Lion or The Spotted Dog? Did they ever answer you about the pike-
> fishing at Tewkesbury? No matter, I have but little time for such things.[39]

By March, the same year, Eliza had sent him her incomplete copy of the
manuscript, having been utterly defeated by the immense task. Then her
brother wrote another letter concerning a family relationship:

> In a hurry I write to ask whether you can recollect having said anything
> which could make Erasmus angry with me. He answers no letters of mine
> and this, of course, is *not* agreeable. I fear you may have said something
> which may have *carried*. I shall be *so* very sorry if it is so.

How I wish I could return the *Confitebor* to Rob. It is nearly done. Please tell me any musical news you hear, occasionally, especially the deaths of country organists!!![40]

Their brother Erasmus, a professional engineer and a music-lover, was later appointed the Honorary Treasurer of the Royal College of Organists (1875-94). And the music was eventually returned to Robert, for Wesley has carefully noted on a small piece of paper: 'Memo. finished copying *Confitebor* 20 to 7 p.m. March 5, 1870.'[41]

ELIZA, THE CONFIDANTE

In another letter to her, dated 14 March, 1870, Wesley appeared to be suffering from nervous depression because he was anxious about his son Charles, who had just entered Gloucester Theological College, and also because of his wife's visit to their eldest son John, then living in Tadcaster:

> I write under the oppression of having to go out to my first meeting of the Festival Choral Class for this year. I am badly depressed in spirits. No amusement of any kind and very many cares from the unsettled position of my Son [Charles]. The change of weather, too, has given me much pain in the knee belonging to my broken leg!
>
> I have been alone here for three weeks. Mrs Wesley in Yorkshire with my Medical Son, who is worried by having to make a new arrangement with his assistant — who is trying for a larger sum. Never mind. I should like you to be here and hear all my hymn-tunes. *The European Psalmist* is now all engraved, extending to 560 pages, a good thick book. I hope it will suit *thick* heads. . . .
>
> I should like to hear the Passion music at Barnby's. When is it? They are doing Beethoven's *Mass,* too. I should like to hear that.
>
> There is *no* business for me here. No gaiety. All mean grasping tradesmen who send in bills, and you had need keep receipts.[42]

Wesley's desire to hear Bach's Passion was due to his preparatory work on the programme for the next Gloucester Festival.

ST MATTHEW PASSION

Sir Joseph Barnby (1838-96), in his capacity as musical adviser to the publishing firm of Novello's, had been requested to form a special choir in 1867 for the purpose of performing new editions of their oratorio music. It was the sixth concert that Wesley had wished to attend, when the Exeter Hall saw some 500 voices, singing Beethoven's *Mass* in D. Furthermore, Novello's had recently published a cheap edition of the *St Matthew Passion,* arranged by Sterndale Bennett. And it was this edition that Barnby had used for the Holy Week Concert in St James's Hall. Hence Wesley's note to Eliza in April of 1870:

I had hoped to come up to hear Bach's music, tomorrow evening. I cannot. Novello sent me tickets. I have returned them, to-night, with a request that if he has no objection he will send them to you. I hope you can be at home in the afternoon in case they come to you by post.[43]

He also corresponded with Barnby in July, informing him:

I must cut the Passion down to a *one Part performance*. The same with *Jeptha*. As you have gone through both works, you may perhaps, without much trouble, be able to give me valuable advice, and it would be truly welcome as there is so much to *distract* a poor country man like myself in such a place of residence.[44]

And in another letter to him, Wesley said:

I thought you might be expecting to hear from me in reference to the accompaniment of the Recitatives in Bach. I did not venture to speak on them when I had the pleasure to see you, from knowing that I might cause trouble if I failed to consider some local claims . . . and as my position here is not the bed of roses we hear of, I feel compelled to use that discretion which is 'the better part of valour' and attend to the local claims. A free agent, I should know what way *best to do*.[45]

It so happened that Wesley was anxious to augment the Gloucester Festival Chorus with 'the best selection of Mr Barnby's Choir,' but he added, 'It is bold to attempt it *here* as we have only *one* rehearsal!'

ELIZA, THE SCHEMER

In hoping that Eliza may be influential in getting Mr James Davison interested in his *European Psalmist*, Wesley then writes about *The Times* music critic as follows: 'He hates me. He will do nothing at my request. The way to get at him would be through some intimate friend of his. Do you know anyone? I know Henry Smart. Keep *quiet*, but let me know what you think.'[46] The sequel to that request was later related by Mr Joseph Bennett in his autobiography:

One day when Davison and I were busily editing the forthcoming number of *The Musical World*, Dr Wesley presented himself with a copy of the new edition under his arm, and, upon his tongue, a request that Davison would kindly accept it. There was no difficulty on that point, but it was clear that our visitor had more to say. He moved restlessly in his chair, grimaced, looked in my direction, jerked his head towards the door, and at last made it evident to the critic of *The Times* that a private interview was desired. Whereupon the two men passed to another room. A little later I heard the front door close behind the visitor, and Davison reappeared laughing. He told me that Wesley, after remarking that a review of *The European Psalmist* in *The Times* was specially desirable, stated that he could not expect Davison to spend time and labour upon such an article without remuneration. Forthwith he took a bank-note from his pocket and placed it in Davison's hand. At once the critic replaced the note in the pocket whence it had been drawn and joked the whole transaction away, as he well knew how, presently dismissing his visitor with a promise to notice the new edition briefly as soon as opportunity offered.[47]

V.

In April, 1870, Wesley answered the kind invitation of Mr Vinnicombe, assistant organist of Exeter Cathedral, to participate in a concert in the city, and also thanked him for his welcome report on the fishing prospects in the locality:

> I assure you such a letter was very refreshing to me, tied as I have been by a troublesome knee. I loosened a cartilage in using a heavy Swell Pedal of Willis's organ at the Agricultural Hall (Islington) nearly five years ago, and although it has plagued me a little before now, I had hardly expected it would have made me feel the change of season now to the extent it has; but it is much better, and I think will *let me off* very soon.
>
> I would rather you fixed the time for the performance, you think best. Please let me know when that is. I shall be happy to make some other effort in the cause on a future occasion. I merely say this from feeling very much obliged by your allusions to *fishing*. You have humoured my feelings that way, and I begin to fear my fishing days are over, almost.[48]

Writing in the following June to Eliza, he warned her that anxious business might bring him to London, and that he would be very glad of a bed. And he continued:

> I would not bore you, but I am so out of spirits that I really need companionship. I will drop my portmanteau about 3.30 or 4, tomorrow. I shall have then to hurry to Novello's. I will dine before I come to you. Please don't offer me *drinks* of ale and eels. I am sure they *doctor* the ale in town. I got dreadfully ill when there last week.[49]

And in August, he wrote to Miss Emett in Torquay, lamenting that he was not so much the master of his own time, but instead was the slave of so many. He regretted, too, having left Devon because he had found Gloucester so objectionable, and had to be contented 'to rank with the low ones — and I wish I could be at Torquay.' Finally, he informed her that his son Charles was busily studying Spanish — 'a knowledge of that language is valuable property now.'[50]

SOMETHING FOR NOTHING

In writing to (later Sir) Walter Parratt, he bewailed the fact that so many people wanted to use his music for nothing, which made him very angry. So he enclosed a printed form of reply to all future applicants that ran as follows:

> Sir,
>   I can but be flattered by your wish to adopt my tune, but I must inform you that I do not compose music for pleasure solely.
>   My profession being that of a musician, I can no more *give away* my compositions than a painter his pictures or a merchant his merchandise.
>   For the privilege of printing one of my hymn-tunes, for this special occasion, I require . . .[51]

It was clear that Wesley would be requiring the services of a proof-reader, if the final text of his *European Psalmist* was to be reliably accurate. His business friend Mr Henry Littleton thereupon suggested the name of Mrs Ann Mounsey Bartholomew (1811-91), the composer and organist of St Vedast's, Foster Lane, London, who was married to William Bartholomew, the well-known librettist to Mendelssohn. And in April of 1871, Wesley inquired of her:

> I beg to ask you if you can consent thus to assist me, and what terms you approve of stating? I have gone through my work carefully and consider it *correct,* but I am not contented and wish for further examination.[52]

After having answered several of her difficult questions, he acidly remarked:

> Of course, I wish ungrammatical errors pointed out. They are the worst of all. I know there are two: the one in Bach, the other in Gibbons. *I leave these.*[53]

By the 21st of June, Wesley was showing the signs of complete exhaustion, and he therefore wrote: 'Longest day! Dear me, I did not think there was so much to do.'[54] And in August he declared: 'As soon as my little *Psalmist* is out, I am pledged to do organ pieces for the million!'[55]

THREE CHOIRS FESTIVAL 1871

On the opening day there was a blue sky with much sunshine; and the gay bunting in the streets, together with the ringing of the Cathedral bells, gave a festive atmosphere to the City of Gloucester. The Mayor and the Corporation attended Matins, when Wesley conducted the combined choirs in Gibbons's Short Morning Service in F and Boyce's verse-anthem, 'O where shall wisdom be found?' And we are told that Kendrick Pyne had played the organ for the service, having earned the praises of the editor of *The Musical Times* for his fine performance of 'Bach's Pedal Fugue in B minor'.

On the Tuesday afternoon, a small audience filled less than half of the Nave for Handel's Overture to 'Esther' (1720), but 'the effect of the opening passages was marred by the rustling of dresses and the tramping of feet', belonging to the late-comers. Afterwards there came the martial music of Handel's *Dettingen Te Deum* (1743), Mendelssohn's popular setting of 'Hear my prayer' (1845), and selections from Handel's 'Jeptha' (1751) — concerning the performance of which Wesley had already consulted with Barnby.

Following the innovation of an evening concert of oratorio music on the first day of the Festival at the Hereford Meeting the year before, Gloucester Cathedral now witnessed an impressive scene; for a large audience, 'glowing with brilliant colour beneath the soft light streaming down from the lines of gas-jets above the massive Norman columns on each side [of the Nave],' had generally observed the request of wearing morning dress in order 'to preserve as much as possible the devotional character of the per-formances.'[56]

The first part of the programme included selections from the music of Haydn's 'Creation' (1798), but there was unfortunately some difference of opinion between the soloists and the conductor as he had taken the move-ments, too slowly. However *The Gloucester Journal* generously observed:

> Dr Wesley has not made conducting a special part of his work, and can scarcely be expected to have the command over the forces under him as some others who are more popular and more frequently engaged in this difficult work.[56]

And the programme ended with extracts from Handel's 'Israel in Egypt' (1739).

On the Wednesday morning, there was a favourable account of the 'Elijah' (1846). In spite of incessant rain and occasional lightning, an enthusiastic audience later made their way in flys and other vehicles to the Shire Hall for the first of the secular concerts. The music began with selec-tions from Handel's pastoral opera 'Acis and Galatea' (1721), followed by Mr Stainton's 'Fantasie sur Faust' for solo violin, the Finale from Spohr's 'Azor and Zemira' (1819), and finished with extracts from Carl Weber's Gypsy operetta 'Preciosa' (1820).

Berlioz once remarked: 'There is but one God — Bach, and Mendelssohn is his prophet.' And it is certainly evident that the Musical Wesleys upheld the Bach cause in England, so that it was sad to find a poor audience in Gloucester Cathedral for Dr Wesley's triumphant performance of the *St Matthew Passion*. But this favourable review was printed in *The Times:*

> The execution of this sublime, elaborate, and very difficult music was the most part strikingly good. There were occasional short-comings, but the feeling generally was such as to render it not at all improbable that henceforth like Handel's *Messiah* and Mendelssohn's *Elijah*, the Passion of Bach may become a permanent feature at the Three Choirs Festivals.

The concert then continued with the first performance of (later Sir) William Cusin's 'Gideon', and finished with Spohr's 'Calvary' (1835) — 'but performed to a weary and vanishing audience.' On the other hand, Dr Wesley was received with friendly applause before the final evening concert, when he conducted music from Mozart's 'Marriage of Figaro' (1786) and his 'Jupiter' Symphony (1788).

On the Friday morning, there was a performance of the *Messiah*. And the success of the Festival Week, we are told, was due to the labours of Dr Wesley, and above all, to the excellent precautions taken by the deputy Chief Constable, who had placed his officers in plain clothes at the railway stations, so that 'no robberies were committed in spite of the great influx of visitors.'

VI.

In 1872 the Chapter Clerk instructed Wesley that his official approval would be required before an assistant organist was appointed. And in March, Wesley was allowed the services of an assistant on the condition that he fulfilled his own duties. It is evident that the Chapter Clerk was anxious in case Wesley's favourite hobbies of fishing and shooting might lure him away from the daily instruction of the Choristers. Yet his anxiety was groundless:

> I have had so many things to engage me [Wesley wrote to a friend] that I not only am ill, but have to finish the orchestral score of an 'Ode' that is going to be performed at the Industrial Exhibition *this week*. . . . I shall be very glad to see again my fishing companion of earlier days — I have had no fishing for years, I may say.[57]

THE EUROPEAN PSALMIST

Wesley's antiquarian collection of hymn-tunes, dedicated to Queen Victoria, was published in 1872. Its aim was to supply music for every metre in common use in our English churches, and was begun 'in compliance with a request made to the editor long ago.' Moreover the book had taken over two decades to produce, and even longer if that request had really come from Dr Hook, while Wesley was organist at Leeds Parish Church.

Financial backing for the ambitious project had been guaranteed by a list of almost seven hundred subscribers, which is printed at the end of the book and included the following names: Archbishop Thomson of York and Bishops Ellicott, Moberly, and Wilberforce; Deans Lake (Durham) and Garnier (Winchester); several organists — George Arnold, Robert Atkins, Joseph Barnby, William Bower, John Corfe, Francis Gladstone, John Hopkins, Henry Parratt, David Parkes, Varley Roberts, John Matthews, William Spark and William Trimnell; several clergymen — Sir Henry

Baker, Charles Kemble, Sir Frederick Gore Ouseley and (later Bishop) Walsham How; several Holsworthy friends — the Reverend George Thornton, Dr Linnington Ash and James Higg; several ladies — Mrs Ellicott (wife of the Bishop of Gloucester and Bristol), Miss Maria Hackett (the Choristers' friend) and Miss Pearce (an organ pupil from Launceston); several cathedrals — including St Asaph, Chichester, Hereford and Lincoln, as well as the Warden and Fellows of both New College (Oxford) and Winchester; and finally the Duke of Buccleuch, the Earl of Ellenborough, Viscount Eversley, Mr W. H. Gladstone M.P. and Mr. Henry Willis. Nevertheless two names of distinguished Church musicians were absent from this list, namely Dr J. B. Dykes and Mr W. H. Monk, both of whom had contributed many tunes to *Hymns Ancient and Modern.*

Wesley was a conscientious business man, spending much of his time in getting lapsed subscriptions paid. A few of the original subscribers had died, as for instance Viscount Palmerston and William Horsley, and Wesley had therefore to write to one of his agents:

> *Can* you favour me with information respecting the residence of one of the subscribers to my work, *viz.* Mr J. Richardson, of Manchester. This gentleman gave his name through the late Mr B. Hine, and it was many years ago. I do not like to forward his copy until I hear from you.[58]

And yet, in thanking his friend William Bower for his assistance, Wesley maintained:

> In no instance did I ever think of calling upon anyone, who had the kindness to send subscribers [names] to the work, to make good the shortcomings of those who did not take the work or who neglected to pay. I hope you have not thought I had any such idea for it never entered my head.... I really have a wish to screw that Mr Wawn![59]

A full account of the music of *The European Psalmist* appears in a later chapter.

THE PRAISE OF MUSIC

In March of 1872, Wesley received the following letter from Charles Gounod, during his visit to England (1870-75):

> Dear Sir,
>
> I am acquainted with some of your compositions of which I have formed a very high opinion. I should consider it very amicable on your part and most attractive to the public if you would write for the 4th Concert of the Royal Albert Hall Choral Society which will take place on the 10th July, a Chorus (for 4 or 8 voices) of as broad a style and easy in performance as possible.
>
> I have been forced to publish myself the books of music of the 4 Concerts: I propose therefore to offer you the 10th part of the *net* profits upon the sale of the 4th book which will contain 10 pieces of music.[60]

And in April, he thanked Wesley for his immediate answer and supplied further information as requested:

> 1st. The Royal Albert Choral Society is merely Choral, that is to say, *without orchestra*: but *Organ* may be used or not; several of the pieces in the Programmes of these Concerts are to be performed without accompaniment: as regard to the *Sacred* or *Secular* character, it is at your entire convenience — The words *Latin* or *English,* as you like — the capital point is the *breadth* and *simplicity* in the style, to secure as good, clear, and sonorous an effect as we can obtain with a few rehearsals.
>
> I must also tell you that I put the *Conductor's Stick* at the disposition of the composer, and that I will feel most flattered if you accept to conduct your own piece, whose performance will take place on the *Wednesday* 10th of July. . . .
>
> P.S. On account of *the printer,* I should like to know, as soon as possible, the length of your piece, the performance of which could last from 6 to 8 minutes at the most.[61]

In fact, he sent several letters reminding Wesley that his music should arrive no later than the 25th of May.[62] At the end of that month, however, Gounod thanked the composer for his beautiful piece (which he had read through four times), and also informed him that he had pencilled in several suggestions for further consideration.[63] It was an unaccompanied work 'The Praise of Music' (Novello, 1874),[64] which Wesley had made 'sufficiently simple for performance by small choirs.'

A CIVIL LIST PENSION

In recognition of Wesley's great contribution to English Cathedral Music, the Prime Minister Gladstone had recommended to the Queen that he should be given the choice between a knighthood and a Civil List pension. And on 14 January 1873, Wesley accepted the pension as it would be a 'nice little nest-egg'!

Writing to Miss Emett, in March the same year, Wesley informed her how glad he was to know that she had finally settled in so nice a place as Torquay, and he added: 'You must try and build a great church and engage me at the music.'[65] And in June, Wesley received 'the sum of three guineas for tuition' from one of his organ pupils.[66]

In answer to another invitation from Mr Vinnicombe, of Exeter, Wesley said that he would certainly like to give a recital if there was a concert room with a complete organ in it, for the one at Honiton had wanted a soft Stop on the Great Organ. He also declared that he liked Devon so much that if circumstances had allowed he would have come to live there. However, he accepted his friend's kindness of a bed for the night, 'as when I am alone, I often get very dismal.'[67]

Meanwhile he was anxious to invite Charles Gounod to compose a new choral work for the next Gloucester Festival. And in November, the composer replied:

> I have had the subject of a new Sacred Composition entitled *The Annunciation* whose text is taken from the Gospels and the Prophets. A substantial part of my work has already been composed. . . .
>
> May I take this opportunity of telling you how much I deplore the fatal custom which, in England, attaches so exclusive an importance to the first appearance of a work in a Festival programme. In my opinion, this is a prejudice with a harmful influence on Musical Art in that it encourages Authors to work hastily and tends with each day to diminish this piety of contemplation for lack of which works of lasting value are becoming increasingly rare. As soon as a composition has been performed at a Festival, it would seem that it is no longer worthy of attracting attention in other directions. The result is that compositions are written at full steam: 'Time does not spare that which is done without it'.[68]

Unfortunately, there is no means of knowing what came of Gounod's choral work because it was not performed at the next Festival; but it may have been either *La salutation angèlique,* or 'The Redemption' that received its first performance at the Birmingham Festival of 1882.

VII.

Wesley's attention was now devoted to family matters. At the end of 1872, he had written to Mrs Rance Phipps, seeking her assistance in the obtaining of a minor canonry at St Paul's Cathedral for his third son Francis Gwynne, who was then a curate at St Michael's, Gloucester:

> It was most kind of you to receive my Son and his affairs as you did. We should so much like him to succeed in this instance, and so I venture to mention that his friend, the Warden of All Souls [College, Oxford] has written to say that he gave my Son's application to the Dean. . . .
>
> The Dean, I believe, likes to appoint minor canons who will be useful to *him* and adopt his views; and my Son is as docile and attached as a dog, and that is for me saying a great deal. . . .
>
> Were the living vacant here, where he is a curate, there would be a general wish expressed that he should have it; but I am sure *I* don't wish that, nor does he. He covets the London office immensely and it would be the making of him as he could carry out his views there, exactly. . . .
>
> If you hear from Chichester, I should like to know what they intend about electing an organist. I am told they employ a clergyman at present. (My late pupil Pyne has £800 a year offered him at Philadelphia and so left.) That part of England must be very agreeable, and I know several grey men who would like to go there.[69]

Sadly enough, nothing came of the minor canonry, but Francis did accept the living of St John Baptist, Hamsteels, in the Durham diocese, where he remained for thirty-seven years, retiring at the age of seventy.

Wesley was a great friend of the Parratt family, of Huddersfield. It has already been mentioned that Henry Parratt, who was organist of the Parish Church, had invited him to conduct a choral service there in 1867. His younger brother Walter later asked Wesley's advice on the bad treatment of lay clerks, which produced this statement from him:

> The great fact is that *all* that has been done to uphold the repectability of Church Musicians has been done by our Sovereigns and this influence ceased with the coming of the Sailor King William the Fourth. All is of a lower and less cultivated grade now. Such low wretched singing, as I have now to play to, I never met in my boyhood. The clergy are resuming their pre-Reformation status and subjecting professional musicians to the same domination as the lower members of their own order were governed by.[70]

His last appearance as an organ recitalist was made with Walter, when they opened Hill's new instrument in the Victoria Rooms, Clifton, in April of 1874.

THREE CHOIRS FESTIVAL 1874

A week before the Gloucester Festival, a special conference of representatives from the Three Cathedrals had decided that important changes should be made in the arrangements of the next Worcester Meeting. It seemed that the Dean of Worcester had positively objected to the Meetings, having declared that he would prohibit them in his Cathedral. On the other hand, the Bishop of Worcester had intimated that he would continue to patronize them if they were continued. Furthermore, both the Dean of Gloucester and the President of the Stewards, the Duke of Beaufort, were absent from that year's Gloucester Festival — and Bishop Ellicott was blissfully touring the Swiss Alps!

Between the opening service and the afternoon concert, the streets leading to the Cathedral were packed with spectators, all of whom were anxious to catch a glimpse of the Festival celebrities. Of the many callers upon Mademoiselle Tietjens was the sister of the Poet Laureate, Lord Tennyson, who had travelled all the way from Trent in order to hear her singing.

At the Tuesday afternoon concert, Wesley conducted Spohr's 'Last Judgement' (1826) and Weber's 'Jubilee' Cantata (1818), originally composed in honour of a Saxon king. In spite of three Stewards complaining at such a work being performed in a sacred building, nothing came of their complaints. It was certainly a busy day for the Festival Conductor, having ended with an evening concert in the Cathedral when both the 'Creation' and Rossini's *Stabat Mater* (1832) were performed.

On the Wednesday morning the music was devoted to the *Elijah,* and the evening programme contained selections from Mozart's *Don Giovanni* (1787), the Adagio and Rondo movements from Beethoven's Fifth Piano

Concerto (1809), together with Mozart's 'Jupiter' Symphony (1788) and his Overture to *Idomeneo* (1780).

The morning programme on the next day included Mendelssohn's 'Hymn of Praise' (1840), and Rossini's *Petite Messe Solennelle* (1864) which was regarded as 'the novelty of the Festival.' And the evening concert featured Carl Weber's music to his fairy opera 'Oberon' (1826), Mendelssohn's Incidental Music to 'A Midsummer Night's Dream' (1843) and Wesley's Songs — 'Silently, silently' and 'The Butterfly', followed by 'Rule Britannia' and 'God save the Queen' with the solos sung 'with great fire and energy' by Mademoiselle Tietjens herself.

Concerning the performance of the *Messiah* on the Friday, *The Gloucester Journal* reported:

> Critics accustomed to hear larger masses at the Crystal Palace and Exeter Hall express admiring wonder at the startling crispness and clear-cut intonation of our choral body, and they cannot be praised too highly for their work of to-day.[71]

The Festival Week did not finish with the traditional Ball, but with a dignified Choral Service in the Cathedral, attended by an immense congregation. The canticles were set to King in F and the anthem was Wesley's 'Praise the Lord, my soul.' Sadly enough, the musical parts of the Service were badly sung. And in his sermon Dr Barry, a Canon of Worcester and Principal of King's College, London, said that it was excellent for the Service to have included the simple congregational chant or hymn, with its more scientific music. But he also warned against the oratorios being allowed to banish the music of the Choral Service from its central position. And as a practical comment on the theme of the sermon, Wesley afterwards played the Dead March from 'Saul'!

CATHEDRAL MUSIC LISTS

In 1875 Joseph Bennett, a native of Gloucestershire and music critic of *The Daily Telegraph*, was appointed the editor of the *Concordia*, which was a new musical journal. As he wanted to print the Cathedral music lists throughout the country, accordingly he wrote to many organists having requested that they should forward copies of their weekly lists to his London office. And Dr Wesley eventually replied as follows:

> I am opposed to the publication of the lists you ask for. They are made out by young clerical precentors. The music in question is chiefly trash, and there is no professional knowledge amongst the parties concerned. The selections inflict a martyrdom on true artists. I don't think any respectable paper would insert them without exposing their error and the system that brings them into existence. . . .[72]

Nonetheless Bennett insisted upon having the Gloucester lists, and some blank forms, with a place for the organist's signature or that of his deputy, were immediately despatched, so that Wesley had to sit down at his desk and write another letter:

> I return the card myself, as I do not allow my deputy to sign papers intended for publicity on cathedral *business* — in a cathedral, a man must move as cautiously as possible.

And he concluded the correspondence with a strident broadside:

> You are dealing with this subject, pardon me, as though it were a child's plaything. But the lists will be sent you punctually by one of my deputees, only I beg you not to give *our names*.[73]

VIII.

In advising Eliza against making so marked an effort at hiding things in her letters, Wesley gave the following characteristic illustration:

> Look at the carp. When he hides himself in the mud he so stirs it up that he is *known to be there*. Had your letter be opened it would at once have been seen that there was *something* to conceal. Then a guess or two would have hit the nail on the head. You are not deep enough for my people and only safe when just the least bit more than silent.[74]

And in another letter he informed her:

> I have been ill a long while and am thinking of going to the seaside. It is bad to be alone, and I want to know if you are going to the sea and would look me up a little. My *liver* is sluggish and a very serious thing it is. Don't talk of me. Do you ever meet Erasmus?[75]

THE MOCK FESTIVAL

Wesley's last appearance at the Three Choirs Meeting was at Worcester in 1875. It was called the 'Mock Festival' because the Cathedral authorities had decided that the three Cathedral choirs only should be asked to give 'a series of anthems with organ accompaniment' — thus dispensing with the orchestra and professional soloists.

Their reasons for banishing oratorio music from the Festival were threefold: the system of admittance by payment to concerts, the fear of irreverence by the audience and musicians, and the cessation of daily worship beforehand in order to allow the Cathedral building to be prepared for the Festival. And we are told that a sad atmosphere descended over Worcester, for even the streets had been decorated with black flags and the cabmen had tied crepe bows to their whips.[76]

Wesley's music was well represented in the Choral Services by his Morning Canticles in E and his extended anthems, 'Let us lift up our heart' and 'The Wilderness'. In fact, his splendid organ-playing was the best part of the Services:

Dr Wesley played an organ voluntary, which he prolonged sufficiently to show that under skilful hands the instrument, which is undoubtedly rough and coarse, and wanting mellowness in some of its stops, has a certain sweetness in it as well as power.[77]

It was indeed a personal triumph for the doyen of our Cathedral organists; for Mr W. H. Gladstone, M.P., afterwards conveyed his appreciation to Mrs Wesley:

At the expense of leaving you rather abruptly the other day, I gained an admirable place for following your husband's immortal anthem 'Let us lift up our heart,' which I did with intense interest and sympathy. I am truly glad that the reformed Festival which has proved so successful should owe its principle and excellence to his guiding hand and brain.

It was to me not only an edifying but a touching thing to listen to our Veteran Organist and Prince of Composers revealing himself to us with that perfect dignity and pathos that always clothes his thoughts, but which one so often looks for in vain. Great as he is now I cannot but think he will be greater still in the eyes of those that come after.[78]

A SPECIAL DIET

In November, 1875, Wesley wrote to his sister complaining of breath-lessness; and afterwards, changing the subject, he remembered having left his 'bacca and pipe' with her in Islington. He explained too his dislike of going to hotels, because his diet would very often give the false impression of meanness, besides subjecting him to the waiters' sneers! And here is Wesley's description of the above diet:

I don't eat solid meat or drink wine, ale or spirits, nor tea or coffee. I take milk and pastry-pudding and broth and perhaps White Fish. *Vegetables* are good for me. *Good* arrowroot I like but it is hard to get.[79]

Concerning the food for his forthcoming visit, he advised Eliza:

If you are able to get a little of the Bermuda arrowroot, you might do so. Don't get the Hall arrowroot. I used to find that only pretty good. If not, a cup of good broth would be welcome.[80]

On the other hand, in his report of another visit to London, he confessed:

I had 4 oysters in the City. I don't think they suited me, but I much enjoyed them. My mouth is dry, and I only drank cold tea and milk at dinner.[81]

And he sent the following note for Eliza to give her apothecary:

I am in want of the medicine Sir W. Gull prescribed and you made up. The sweet *Iron* stuff. It would be kind to send me a similar supply to-morrow morning. As it would make only a small parcel I should be glad if you would add a few things useful in a home, such as first-class Mustard, Peppers (not Cayenne), and a tin of Mustard plasters.[82]

129

Meanwhile he had invited Mr Joseph Bennett to dine at the Norfolk Hotel, near Paddington Station, for he had something important to discuss. The music critic readily accepted Wesley's invitation. After an excellent meal served in a private room, his host proceeded to the special business that involved co-operating in a radical plan: the abolishing of Cathedral Chapters and all Precentors by replacing them with a smaller staff of *working* clergymen; the founding of a College of Preachers in London, which would supply every Cathedral with a qualified orator for a period of one month; and the establishing of a Central Fund into which all capitular revenues were to be paid. Finally, every Cathedral organist was to become the absolute Master of the Music in his own establishment.[83]

It seemed that Wesley had wanted his friend to act as the publicity officer, who would be required to write the preliminary pamphlet for circulation among all members of both Houses of Parliament. Having realised that his host had left him with most of the donkey work to do and with no salary to go with it, Bennett had more rewarding tasks to do; so nothing came of his host's chicanery.

And in his last letter to Bennett, he wrote: 'I beg to return the Cathedral's book [of Statutes]. Pity that that subject is stagnant. We are working railways with the rolling-stock of Henry VIII's reign.'[84]

Dr S. S. WESLEY, Aged 60

From a contemporary photograph taken in Gloucester, by permission of Mr F. C. Morgan.

CHAPTER EIGHT

The Holsworthy Correspondence (1870-1876)

A COLLECTION of letters, now in the possession of Sir Thomas Armstrong, is of considerable interest because they were written by Wesley to his friends in the West Country market town of Holsworthy, and in particular to the local physician, Dr Thomas Linnington Ash (1837-1917).

Ash was an amateur musician and frequently attended the Three Choirs Festival in Hereford, where he was the guest of either Sir Edward Elgar or the Cathedral organist, Dr George Sinclair. The latter used to display among his treasures a fishing knife which once belonged to Wesley. It seemed that this friendship, between a physician and a musician, had grown through their fishing expeditions in Devon, and that Ash used his influence at home, as many another generous physician had done since then, to obtain his friend professional work and to assist him in other ways.

In his boyhood, Ash had acted as a 'boots' at The Tree Hotel in Stratton where he was born. A person of outstanding ability, he was an accomplished orator and possessed 'a sweet tenor voice'. He played both the oboe and church organ, and was also the bandmaster of the Town Band. He was later appointed Justice of the Peace and also County Councillor.

Other letters were addressed to the Rev. George Wright Thornton, Rector of Holsworthy between 1870 and 1894. His church possessed a noble 16th-century tower built of granite, and in 1884 he had the chancel re-built in memory of his parents.

As a mark of affection, Wesley dedicated two anthems to his friends in 1870: 'O God, whose nature and property' (to the Rector),[1] and 'I am Thine, O save me' (to the Doctor).[2] And his letters fall into three main categories.

First, those addressed to the Rector concerning an invitation to re-open the Parish Church organ:

February 8, 1870

My dear Sir,

It gives me much pleasure to hear from you and the business you write on I will endeavour to attend to. I mean, I will go to Holsworthy (God willing) at the time named. I am engaged at Brighton about the time, and I dare say Dr Ash is not particular to a day.

As to terms, from the way the subject of my attendance is named, I feel disinclined to fix any, and prefer leaving the fee to those who order the proceedings. My travelling expenses are usually considered apart from the terms. Perhaps, Dr Ash will be good enough to tell me what the organ is, and who the builder is?

I hope my saying this will not seem offensive for, I assure you, I am so fond of Devon that I should always be willing to take engagements *there*. I often think that if opportunity offered I should like to retire to some quiet village, where I could fish a little and roam about in the winter with a gun, provided it was fine scenery and in Devon.

The organ in Holsworthy Parish Church is thought to have been built by either Renatus Harris or his contemporary, 'Father' Bernhard Smith who was responsible for the instruments in Adlington Hall, St Paul's, and Durham Cathedral. It was first erected in All Saints' Church, Chelsea, and afterwards was sold to Bideford Church as worn out; and finally, its adventurous history ended at Holsworthy in 1865. The fine woodwork of the original organ-case can still be seen in the South-aisle.

HIS ARTISTIC FIRMNESS

In his next letter, Wesley reiterated his love of the Devon scenery and his interest in the fishing prospects; but notice his artistic firmness especially when 'good cheer' and professional work were mentioned:

February 17, 1870

My dear Sir,

I am glad of an opportunity of coming to Devon. I think if I could hear of a very good place for *me*, as a musician in Devon, I should be tempted to close with it. But people don't understand the differences as to *quality* amongst professional men; and the universal way of providing music for a church is first to fix upon some mean stipend, and then parties struggle about whose friend shall be appointed.

When you have nothing to prevent it, I should so much like a few lines to tell me where the good fishing is that I can go to. I have got the Ordinance Map. I have constantly referred to it wherever I have been; and I bought it in Exeter when I first went there as Cathedral organist.

I have never been nearer you than Hatherleigh, a dull place. The coastal scenery I know to some extent: I have been at Clovelly Coast and Westward

Ho! and Hartland — I did not go to the Point. I prefer *sands* by the seaside. The wild rocks almost frighten me now.

I am very fond of Dartmoor and the Streams. I have walked and fished down the Tamar about the Duke of Bedford's place, Sudeley, and some miles higher up. It is the only well-preserved fishing that is good now. So many people fish. Pray pardon this rambling letter and my fishing allusions. . . .

As to good cheer, excuse me, but quiet and abstinence are what I like when I have to *play*.

And to Dr Ash, the organist of Holsworthy, he wrote:

February 23, 1870

My dear Sir,

It may seem odd what I am going to say, but it strikes me that in case the mechanism should not be very sound and useful, you may do well in reserving some little thing for a London hand to do. But this is a delicate point and hard of accomplishment as no doubt your builder will be at work up to the very last moment. I regret to say, it is very rare to find an organ finished at the proper time.

As to equal tuning — as you speak so clearly about it — I will own that I do not like it. It is a long story to enter on, so I will only say that I can never *enjoy* playing on an organ where notning is in tune, where simple triads produce the effect on the ear that dissolving views do to the eye before the picture has reached its full focus. *All* the organ-builders were against it but have had to yield to fashion, and, having once taken the plunge, they are like the Fox in the Fable and recommend all foxes to give up their tails. . . .

Pray don't name *me* in the matter, but I think I could get Bryceson to over-haul your mechanism at a very moderate fee. I dare say you *know* what it is to play a large organ with imperfect movements, during great changes of weather and in a remote locality.[3]

The Holsworthy Church organ was rededicated and afterwards opened by Wesley, though his return journey was anything but dull:

Wednesday, Evening, 1870

Dear Dr Ash,

On getting into the train at Okehampton I found, when too late, the Coachman had not given my coat to the Railway Porter. I sent for it by the Guard, who returned to Okehampton by the next train, and he said he would send it to Exeter before my train left, which was not done. I guess the Coachman had taken it away to where the Coach stops, and if you could see him to-morrow afternoon and secure it, I should feel thankful.

The truth is the poor fellow had been exasperated by the Proprietor of the Coach at their meeting at Hatherleigh — and the Coachman was longing to 'knock his head off,' 'knock him down,' etc., etc., all through the journey and at the Station. I heard him telling the Station Master of his wrongs. Hence he paid not much attention to my baggage and the coat was not seen, and I forgot to ask. . . . I am quite knocked up with 12 hours journey!

135

THE PROBLEMS OF RAIL CARRIAGE

The second group of letters is addressed to Dr Ash, concerning the adventures of a parcel which Wesley had sent from Gloucester:

October 13, 1870

It was long since a Friday the 7th that I sent off a small parcel by Rail, Carriage paid. I feared it would not reach you free of cost as there might be other company's rails to be gone over, but I *did* think it *would* reach you.

To-day, I have been to our office and I learn the parcel left Gloster for you, via Salisbury, the same day, Friday 7th. Our Office people did not know where your healthful and nice little town was situated, but they sent to Salisbury as it is in connection with their railway line, and the Bristol-Exeter is not so. I am vexed about it, and have written to the Manager. . . .

I am busy with my book. I will print 3 or 4 tunes as specimens. I think they may be popular and help the work. Strange that Mr Thynne did not send his name. Hoping you are well and all your family.

The Rev. A. C. Thynne, Rector of Kilkhampton, had evidently not subscribed to Wesley's *European Psalmist*. He was a keen cricketer and enjoyed singing comic songs at charity concerts.

Attached to the foregoing letter is a note, addressed to Wesley, from the General Manager's Office of the Great Western Railway Company at Paddington:

October 17, 1870

With further reference to your letter, I beg to say that the parcel referred to was handed to Dr Ash on the 13th inst. by the Holsworthy Carrier from North Tawton. The parcel had been tendered to the Driver of the Stage Coach on the 10th inst., but he for some reason refused to take it on. The agent at North Tawton was, therefore, compelled to hold it over until the Holsworthy Carrier called, which he only does casually.

'Casually' seems the correct word, for that small parcel had taken a week to travel some 120 miles.

And after an interval of two years, the question of parcels is again mentioned in the following letter; for Wesley recalls North Tawton with equal suspicion, particularly as he wants to place copies of his *European Psalmist* with the subscribers:

June 20, 1872.

Dear Dr Ash,

At last I have the pleasure to send you my work. It leaves by Rail this evening. I sent it via Exeter and North Tawton and sincerely hope this is correct.

I enclose all the Holsworthy copies to you, as I think you said you would circulate them for me. Please receive the money and enclose it *en masse!* to me. I hope you are well and Mrs Ash and Mrs Bishop.

Unlike his father, Wesley had a flair for business affairs; and it is hoped that the promised subscriptions were returned to him *en masse*. He also told Dr Ash about his journey to Yorkshire and his plans to travel to Ireland for a change of scene, 'as the kind proprietors of all the fine things at Killarney have given orders to their stewards and keepers to show us the lions.' And he added, 'You can go, too, if you like?'

A NEW CARILLON

The third group of letters refers to Wesley's two tunes, composed for the Carillon that Dr Ash had kindly presented to Holsworthy Church in 1874. And to one of his friends, who had assisted in the delivery of the *European Psalmist* copies to local subscribers, Wesley wrote:

> Dear Mr Honey,
>
> I know Dr Ash is very busy just now, so I don't ask him to send me any account of the Bells. Please give me a line to say how the Tunes went off and whether they, mine I mean, were set *fast* enough.
>
> Is it true — it cannot be, I am sure — that Holsworthy has gone off, disappeared, through spontaneous combustion and that a small portion of it — about as much as remained of the Kilkenny Cats — was seen about 100 miles off in the Atlantic and was mistaken for the Sea Serpent!

Wesley certainly possessed a puckish sense of fun, although he had not realised that his second tune was almost too much for the Carillon machinery to cope with! And here is the victim:

Wesley later borrowed the first tune as the theme of a set of variations for the organ, called 'Holsworthy Church Bells' — the original manuscript can be seen in the British Library.[4] Here is the melody:

It is interesting to find a certain affinity of style between Wesley's music and the Allegretto movement in Mendelssohn's Organ Sonata No. 4:

In March of 1874, Wesley was anxious to return a crate of empty bottles to Dr Ash, and he therefore wanted to know the best method of transportation as it had come by water from Ifracombe to Bristol. And yet, there was something else to be explained to the donor:

> I hope you will excuse it if there is any irregularity in the number and quality of the bottles returned. A few bottles I had treated our thirsty vergers to. A few burst. All the rest, excepting a few still I am glad to say *full*, will come — and there are 3 dozen in all.
>
> I suppose your Uncle has been busy with the trout already. I have been shooting several times, but not fishing.

And a year later, concerning the endeavours of Mr Cunningham to get something for nothing, naturally Wesley was very vigorous on the subject:

> It had previously occurred to me that strangers might wish for the Holsworthy Tunes, and that a fee to me was not unreasonable. Perhaps, you ought to go halves as you paid for the Chimes. I don't see why strangers should not pay? I think Mr Cunningham will not know if *you* paid me or not, and that were you disposed to charge all applicants a five pound note, as you suggest, there could be no harm done. . . .
>
> I think we could have taken the church living you name. Dear me, that arrangement might have got me into *peace* and *quiet!* Well, I am unlucky. The Holsworthy living is quite beyond us and, even if it were not, *the house* is by no means tempting. I suppose you get Clovelly herrings now.
>
> I shall not go amongst the Masons. I know an immense man in the craft. I think he is 'past' everything — past *bearing*. Would you like him to do anything for you in town? I know he would. He is a musical professor, but chiefly literary. Matthew Cooke is his name. . . .
>
> I fear Durham won't do for my son. The thing is how to get him away. My sons have got little tact.

Nonetheless, Francis Gwynne Wesley (his third son) managed to survive the storms of parish life, for he continued as the vicar of Hamsteels until the age of seventy. Also the copyright matter was amicably settled, though the fees remained unpaid:

> Tuesday, March 23 [1875]
>
> Dear Dr Ash,
>
> I beg to decline taking to myself more than half of fees arriving from the *Tunes*. You will give the other half to any Charity you please. Perhaps, it is best just to get the money before we settle how it shall be dispensed of.
>
> Your account of the *living* near you was tantalising. I almost wish you had not named it, and yet, it has given me pleasure to see *myself* so near the possession of *quiet* and comfort. . . . I have been thinking it was Bridgerule you had mentioned, but I now have found West Pulford on the Map. Could you ask some clergy and others to tell you of vacancies? I should be so obliged.

I don't know your status as a Mason, but I hear they give the *Masters* only a squeeze up in the high gallery! There are some good Masons here and one of them told me this.

If you make any stay in London and would meet me, I should much like to see you. I go up to choose two pianos and see a church organ being built for me by Willis.

Now please let me again urge you to look up the Devon livings or 'Starvelings', as a friend calls all *'livings'*.

Wesley very much wanted to place one of his sons in a West Country living, so that Marianne and himself might retire there. For that reason he felt that he must congratulate his friend on displaying 'a feeling about the livings which quite raises hope in me.'

And in another letter, he was pleased to observe a better atmosphere in the Close at Gloucester:

I think our canons must have heard of some of my complaints. They have been most civil these last few days. Still, our crotchety dean has so alarmed me that I feel most anxious to suit his society and be quiet that I may attend to writing.

A new little hymn-book is just out, 'edited' by me for a friend. I will bore you with a copy. . . .

This dull book was *The Welburn Appendix of Original Hymns and Tunes* (1875), which had been compiled by the Rev. James Gabb and dedicated to Archbishop Thomson, of York, 'whose interest in all that concerns the public worship of God within the churches of his diocese is thankfully recognized by his clergy.' And it seemed that Wesley had been inveigled into supplying 18 tunes for the hymnal by his son Charles, who was then assistant curate to both the Bulmer and Welburn parishes, where James Gabb was the Rector. However, 42 tunes were by Gabb himself and 10 of Wesley's had already appeared in his *European Psalmist*.

His next letter to Dr Ash related his experiences with the Crown agent for the sale of Church livings in London:

I like him very much. He is about to send me his new list of sales. He told me, at my request, about East and West Nutford. It was sold by auction at an emergency for £1,200. It brings in £250 per annum. He said it was *two* years since this took place, so the information about its sale was long in reaching you. I don't quite see *my* way, but don't you think that with such interest as I have, however small, I might expect something better than my son has to be given him? I was told that if I wrote to the Lord Chancellor and expatiated on the things of Church Music as to my long service, he would give my son a living.

A CLEAN RIVER

In May Wesley asked his friend to let him have some information on the living of Meeth, about three miles from Hatherleigh, because its incumbent had been there for fifty years or so, and would be surely near retirement. 'To me,' Wesley continued, 'it looks like a case worth *immediately* looking into. It is a great thing to be near a *clean* river.' Further, he had sent Dr Ash one of his anthems for friendly criticism which was later published in Novello's Collegiate Series, with several others:

> I assure I feel your views to be *refreshing*. I never now, where I am, hear *a word* about Music and you know I have to succumb to audacious ignorance at a Cathedral. What a mercy it would be if anyone would free me!! I would long have been free but for family matters.
>
> I am thinking of a run down to the Lizard to get a breath of air with a friend. I am not quite well.
>
> These little anthems are written for the young men at Clifton College to sing.

Between 1874 and 1875, Novello's published his anthems: 'Wherewithal shall a young man cleanse his way' (having a fine organ introduction and treble solo movement), 'O how amiable are Thy dwellings' and 'Let us now praise famous men'. This last anthem had been, in fact, composed for the Commemoration Day at Clifton College in 1873, but had to be revised by the composer for it was too difficult for the boys to sing.

The first director of music at Clifton was one of Wesley's former pupils. And in the British Library there is an anthem in manuscript, 'The Lord will give grace and worship,' on the back of which Wesley has inscribed his pupil's name in thick blue pencil — 'W. F. Trimnell, Walton Lodge, Clifton'.[5]

At the end of May 1875, he informed Dr Ash of his forthcoming visit to London, for the purpose of lobbying M.P.s against the Minor Canons' Bill then before the House, and he waspishly added: 'I am glad to know we are not yet to see the restoration of musical priests: Clergy merely musical and without any Cure of Souls. This idea was worthy of the Chapter of St Paul's!'[6]

THE LAST LETTER TO DR ASH

Gloster, Feb. 17 [1876]

> I got your letter. You named only one weekday in which your coach journeyed — Fridays. I fear, therefore, that you may expect me the day this letter reaches you. Sad it is I am worse. I think the cold of Sandown *may* be the cause but, then, I have been decaying for years. I see it now. I could not walk latterly, and now I stay in the house and hardly walk *there*....

Sir William Gull said my mind had much to do with it. So said my son and my doctor here. This comes of my getting out in the world when young, and remaining out from my love of the country. Worry, worry, worry. *No delight* anywhere.

This panting for breath is most dreadful! I eat very sparingly, only small quantities of light things. Gull told me to live on the cow but I find milk stuffs me up. What I prefer is tea, but they would not let me have more than a very little. *What* can be the real cause of this suffocation? They say there is a wrong pressure on the heart. . . . I write all through my panting and difficult it is.

I find from your letter that the Milker at Diptford fishes *himself.* This explains the paucity of fish, and also the ill-nature I experienced there with my son. Nice water if preserved, but not otherwise. I have been handling the woodcocks, and very fine heavy birds they are. Too kind of you to send them to me, as I never send you anything! I wonder if I may be permitted to taste the birds.

I do hope your Mother is well. How I should like to see her! Glad shall I be if God permits to visit you again.

Yours,

S. S. WESLEY.

P.S. A long letter for *me.*

CHAPTER NINE

The Final Cadence of a Musical Martyr

> And now for the flood-gate difficulties. I have moved from cathedral to cathedral because I found *musical troubles* at each. Until Parliament interferes to put cathedrals on a totally different footing as to music, I affirm that any man of eminence will find obstacles to doing himself and his music justice which will render his life a prolonged martyrdom.[1]

NOTWITHSTANDING such mordant feelings, Wesley's last years at Gloucester were years of gradual contentment, because he had indeed 'fought the good fight' against all the authorities he had ever worked with. He was now semi-retired, having more time for piscatorial pleasures and for the occasional visits to his sister in London. Whether or not this quiet provincial existence was good for his musical creativity is certainly questionable.

His nephew, Mr Wesley Martin, has maintained that he was a disheartened man, very eccentric (being the owner of 53 razors), and totally absorbed in his musical world. For his uncle would descend from the organ-loft, and, upon finding a crowd of visitors in the nave, would walk through them and afterwards ask the verger at the entrance what they were waiting for. In hot weather he would wander about, dressed in a linen suit and carrying a large green and buff carriage-umbrella. Nonetheless, he was regarded with great respect and Mrs Ellicott, the bishop's wife, was a frequent guest at his Sunday dinners.

The Wesley's were well-equipped for entertaining at table, since they possessed a fine old Wedgewood dinner-service, cut-glass tumblers and decanters, champagne and hock glasses, as well as several candlesticks and an engraved coffee-percolator. According to Kendrick Pyne, the Doctor was a *bon vivant:*

> Everything in the way of food and drink had to be of the very best. He always chose the eatables himself, and if owing to business this personal choice was not possible, woe betide the luckless purveyor if the viands were not quite up to the mark. He was an inordinate tea-drinker — morning, noon, and night — especially in the later years of his life. He possessed a wonderful recipe for a salad, the virtues of which were incontestable. It was said to have been by the celebrated 'Soyer'.[2]

HIS FIELD-SPORTS

Wesley was an accomplished angler and a skilled shot, whose greatest wish in life was to retire to a quiet village in Devon, where he could fish a little and roam about in winter with a gun. And in the fascinating Catalogue of the Sale of his possessions, which was held in College Green in July of 1876, the following books are mentioned: Bewick's *History of Quadrupeds* (1792), Walton and Cotton's *Compleat Angler* (1836 edition), Daniel's *Rural Sports* (1801-13), the Rev. H. Newland's *The Erne, Its Legends, and Fly-fishing* and also his *Angler in Ireland,* as well as nine volumes of *The Field* (1859-63). In addition, there are listed Wesley's fishing-tackle and numerous guns by eminent names, like Egg, Ladmore and Squires, together with his 'pruning-knife, shot-pouch and powder-flask.'[3]

Moreover *The Musical Times* later published an interesting photograph of a fishing-knife bearing the inscription, 'Dr S. S. Wesley: Winchester'. And Charles Wesley was bequeathed the silver-mounted flask that his father had used on his fishing expeditions until 'it took to leaking at the mouth.'

Wesley had a wonderful way with animals. Sometimes he would be seen going up to the dean's two big mastiffs, seizing them by their forelegs, turning them over and over, and playing with them as with children; and they would enter into the fun as much as he did. He passionately loved his handsome bull-terrier 'Rob', who was always served with the first slice of the Sunday-joint under the dinner-table. If his master played a particular melody, he would utter the most terrible of howls that could only be silenced by another melody.

'Rob' unfortunately died of a sudden fit, and his funeral was a very sad occasion. He was buried at night under a yew tree at the bottom of 'Wesley's Wilderness' as the organist's garden was called. The master himself carried the remains of his devoted companion, followed by his sons Francis and Charles, and by his assistant organist Kendrick Pyne. Wesley was so broken-hearted on the following Sunday that when the time came for the voluntary, he could only express his grief by a mighty wail upon the organ.

HIS FINAL VOLUNTARY

On Christmas Day of 1875, Wesley played the Cathedral organ for his last Choral Evensong, when he asked his assistant (Mr C. E. Clarke) to fetch his old score of the *Messiah,* for he wanted to play the Hallelujah Chorus after the Blessing. It was an unexpected request as he normally played one of Bach's organ fugues from memory or extemporised, and it was indeed his *Nunc Dimittis.*

Confined now to his house in College Green and suffering from Bright's disease, Wesley wrote his last letter to Miss Emett in Torquay:

> It is kind to express so much sympathy towards me. I am very ill, and worse lately, but the weather has been much against me. . . .
>
> If you are writing to Eliza, I would ask you to enquire of her whether Erasmus, our brother, expressed my wish to her to be allowed a loan of her invalid's chair. It could be sent by parcel's delivery company, I think, and by Great Western Rail. I would pay for all damage, if any, and it should be duly returned to her.
>
> I am glad you reside in so favoured a part of England. I hope you may be able to remain there always. I have so much regretted leaving Devon. Please excuse brevity.[4]

IN PERFECT PEACE

Dr Samuel Sebastian Wesley died on the morning of April 19th. His last words, 'Let me see the sky!' were addressed to his beloved sister Eliza; and their significance can be found in the letter that Mrs Alan Haig had written on the day before his death, in which were quoted the following lines from Philip Doddridge's hymn, 'God of my life, through all my days':

> But O, when that last conflict's o'er,
>   And I am chained to earth no more,
> With what glad accents shall I rise
>   To join the music of the skies.

And too, having realised Wesley's great love of his grandfather's hymns, it would have been natural for him to recall Charles Wesley's Morning Hymn, 'Christ, whose glory fills the sky.'

In describing the manner of her brother's death to Sarah Wesley, Eliza wrote:

> To you, my dearest Sarah, I owe one sad satisfaction of being with my dear brother in his last moments. He died this morning at 11 o'clock.
>
> Last night, those around him did not anticipate this change. I *did* and begged to be called in the night, if he was at all worse. One servant came to my door about 7 o'clock, saying he was not too well. I felt no surprise. Mrs Wesley, Willis, and myself were with him. I went to breakfast and in a few moments was told he had called for me. My name was the last he mentioned.
>
> His death was calm and peaceful, it was only ceasing to breathe. . . . Poor Mrs Wesley really feels her loss — it is a very trying scene.[5]

It was to be as simple as possible in keeping with Wesley's last wishes. The 'Great Bell' of the Cathedral was tolled for an hour on the Thursday morning, while the coffin was taken to Gloucester Station. With so little notice the Cathedral authorities were unable to arrange a special service. The family mourners were Wesley's sons: John, Francis, Charles, and William (his second son, Samuel Annesley was abroad); his brother Erasmus, and his brother-in-law the Rev. Francis Merewether (Vicar of Woolhope, near Hereford), who later read the prayers at the graveside.

And from St David's Station, Exeter, at half-past two, the cortège moved slowly up the hill towards the higher gate of the Old Cemetery, next to the ancient city walls overlooking St Michael's Church on Mount Dinham. The pall-bearers included three of Wesley's former pupils: Dr George Arnold (Winchester), Dr Francis Gladstone (formerly of Chichester), and Dr James Russell (Topsham).

On reaching the Cemetery, the coffin was placed on a bier beside the grave of Wesley's only infant daughter. And the inscription on the tombstone now runs:

In Memory of
Mary Daughter of
Samuel Sebastian Wesley
Of This City
She died February 13th 1840
Aged 9 weeks

Also Of The Above Named
Samuel Sebastian Wesley
Who Died At Gloucester
April 19th 1876
Aged 65 Years
Doctor of Music Oxon

— — —

Organist and Succentor
Of Exeter Cathedral
1835-1841

At the graveside were many local clergymen and musicians, including the organist of Exeter Cathedral with the members of his choir. And among the floral tributes was a cross with a wreath of white camellias from Sir Herbert Oakeley, of Edinburgh University, with the simple message 'From Scotland'.[6]

The Organist in Heaven

WHEN Wesley died, the Angelic orders,
    To see him at the state,
Press'd so incontinent that the warders
    Forgot to shut the gate.
So I, that hitherto had follow'd
    As one with grief o'ercast,
Where for the doors a space was hollow'd,
    Crept in, and heard what pass'd.
And God said:— 'Seeing thou hast given
    Thy life to my great sounds,
Choose thou through all the cirque of Heaven
    What most of bliss redounds.'
Then Wesley said:— 'I hear the thunder
    Low growling from Thy seat —
Grant me that I may bind it under
    The trampling of my feet.'
And Wesley said:— 'See, lightning quivers
    Upon the presence walls —
Lord, give me of it four great rivers,
    To be my manuals.'
And then I saw the thunder chidden
    As slave to his desire;
And then I saw the space bestridden
    With four great bands of fire;
And stage by stage, stop stop subtending,
    Each lever strong and true,
One shape inextricable blending,
    The awful organ grew.
Then certain angels clad the Master
    In very marvellous wise,
Till clouds of rose and alabaster
    Conceal'd him from mine eyes.
And likest to a dove soft brooding,
    The innocent figure ran;
So breathed the breath of his preluding,
    And then the fugue began —
Began; but, to his office turning,
    The porter swung his key;
Wherefore, although my heart was yearning,
    I had to go; but he
Play'd on; and, as I downward clomb
    I heard the mighty bars
Of thunder-gusts, that shook heaven's dome,
    And moved the balanced stars.

Thomas Edward Brown (1830-97)[7]

POSTSCRIPT

After her husband's death, Marianne Wesley moved to London where the rest of the family lived. On Tuesday, 23 May 1876, it was reported in *The Daily News* that 'the Queen, acting on the advice of the Prime Minister, has been pleased to continue to Mrs Wesley the pension of £100 per annum from the Civil List, granted to the late Dr Wesley in consideration of his service to musical art.'

She lived at No. 57 Finborough Road, South Kensington, where she died on 28 February 1888, in her eightieth year. Here is an outline of her children's very chequered careers:

MARY (December 1839—13 February 1840) died at the age of nine weeks and is buried in the Old Cemetery, Exeter.

JOHN SEBASTIAN (1836/37—20 July 1924) was educated at Winchester College, where he was a Commoner (September 1850 — after October 1854, but before October 1855). He subsequently trained as a surgeon at King's College and Westminster Hospitals, London, and gained his M.R.C.S. (1862), L.S.A. (1863), and M.B. (1864). Although he was registered as a general practitioner in 1867, he was removed from the Register of the General Medical Council, fifteen years later. His appointments included House Surgeon at St Pancras and Norton Dispensary, Assistant House Surgeon at King's College Hospital, and finally Medical Practitioner at Wetherby, near Tadcaster, Yorks. He died at Wonford House Asylum, Exeter and is buried in St Michael's churchyard, Heavitree.

SAMUEL ANNESLEY (28 December 1837—1925) was educated at Lancing College (April-December 1853). He emigrated to Australia but returned, at his father's request, in 1869. He became a farmer and married a Miss Mason, who had nine sons and three daughters.

FRANCIS GWYNNE (29 January 1841—21 November 1920) was educated at Twyford School and Winchester, where he was a Commoner (January 1855—December 1859). He proceeded to All Souls' College, Oxford, where he was Bible Clerk (1861-65), taking the degrees of B.A. (1865) and M.A. (1880). He was appointed a Tutor at Winchester (1865-68), afterwards ordained deacon by the Bishop of Manchester and served his title at Walkden Moor, Lancs. (1869-71). Ordained to the priesthood by the Bishop of Gloucester and Bristol in 1871, he served a second curacy at St Michael's, Gloucester (1871-74). Lastly, he was appointed Vicar of St John Baptist's, Hamsteels (1874-1911), a mining village in County Durham — eventually retiring to his beloved Winchester, where he lived at 'Aurelia', No. 10 Christ Church Road.

Although his father had dissuaded him from entering the musical profession, he was an accomplished musician and later founded a scholarship at the Royal College of Music in collective memory of his grandfather, great uncle and father (i.e. Samuel, Charles junior, and Samuel Sebastian), which was to be awarded on a competitive examination in organ extemporization.[8] A gifted conversationalist and connoisseur of antiques, he was a member of the Hampshire County Club.[9] And his valuable music library, including several manuscripts in his father's authograph, was bequeathed in his will to the Royal College of Music.

CHARLES ALEXANDER (4 February 1843—18 March 1914) was not educated at Winchester. It seems he spent a few years with his brother Samuel in Australia, but returned to England where he entered Gloucester Theological College in 1870. He was ordained deacon by the Bishop of Gloucester and Bristol to serve his title at Holy Trinity, Bristol (1872), and then priest, having been appointed Chaplain to the Clifton Union and the Barton Regis Workhouse (1873). His numerous curacies included St Martin's, Bulmer (1875), St Thomas's, Pendleton (1877), St Helen's, Darley Dale (1879), and St Saviour's, Bamber Bridge (1882). Finally, he was appointed Rector of Grosmont, in Monmouthshire (1884-1914).

WILLIAM KEN (8 July 1845—5 April 1879) was educated at Winchester, where he became a Commoner (September 1861—December 1863), and also at Trinity College, Cambridge. His medical studies began in 1869, when he gained his M.R.C.S. and was appointed a surgeon at St Bartholomew's Hospital, London. By 1877 he was working at Pusilawa, in Ceylon. However, having contracted tuberculosis, he returned to England and died in Chichester, two years later.

CHAPTER TEN

PANDORA'S BOX:
Services, Anthems and
The European Psalmist (1872)

> But while we are bound to recognize that [Wesley's] music, even at its best, lacks the full measure of that indefinable universal appeal beyond the bounds of race and creed that we find in the work of the great men, and in his father's best things, yet there is not the least doubt that he is one of the very foremost names in English artistic history in the nineteenth century.[1]

THIS OPINION of the late Dr Ernest Walker is certainly valid. Although the musical world may judge Wesley's church compositions by his well-known anthems, like 'Ascribe unto the Lord,' 'Blessed be the God,' and 'The Wilderness,' it must be remembered that his sacred and secular music included two fine Cathedral services, forty anthems, over twenty organ works, Anglican chants, countless hymn-tunes, almost thirty songs, quadrilles for the piano, orchestral versions of two anthems, and his effective Symphonic Overture in C major.

In a letter to his friend Dr J. B. Dykes, Sir Frederick Ouseley maintained: 'We can, even in this vile nineteenth century, emulate those great lights who have gone before us, and shown us how to adorn with sacred song the heart-stirring service of our beloved Prayer Book.' And he then continued: 'I do not think we ought to be *theatrical* for the sake of effect, nor do I like the Spohrishness of Wesley's style.'[2]

What truth is there behind this labelling of Wesley's idiom of writing? Certainly he had submitted several compositions for Spohr himself to comment upon, and it is not facile to suggest that he was subconsciously influenced by Spohr's love of chromaticism and remote keys. In fact, in his youthful works, he freely borrowed ideas from Spohr's opera, *Jessonda* (1823). Compare, for example, the following bars with Wesley's music set to the words — 'And the ransomed of the Lord' (*The Wilderness*):

Also compare this extract from *Jessonda* (No. 28) with his setting of the words — 'Called you is holy, so be ye holy' (*Blessed be the God and Father*):

Again returning to *Jessonda,* the following Recitatives (Nos. 6, 16, 22) immediately gained Wesley's attention:

For they later inspired the opening bars of both his popular anthem *Wash me throughly* (1853) and unfamiliar organ work, his *Andante in E minor* that was posthumously published in 1877:

In this organ work, there can be seen both his love of chromaticism and constant use of octaves in the right hand, as well as the Spohrish chords of the diminished sixth. It seems that, whenever in need of further inspiration, Wesley would unashamedly borrow from *Jessonda*. But his Pandora's Box of musical ideas has quotations from other composers.

For example, the passage 'Bring me forth beside the waters of comfort, (*The Lord is my shepherd*) is derived from Attwood's setting of *Come, Holy Ghost* (bars 19-24):

Furthermore, the subject of the Fugue after his *Choral Song* (1842) comes from the fugato section, 'Tell it out among the heathen that the Lord is King,' which appears in John Travers's verse anthem *Ascribe unto the Lord*:

One of Wesley's last organ pieces, *Andante in A major* was indeed composed as a paraphrase of the Larghetto movement in Beethoven's Symphony No. 2. And the influence of Mozart, some of whose songs he edited in 1861, is apparent when one compares Mozart's last movement to his *Divertimento No. 4* (K.4396) with the opening bars of Wesley's *Andante in E flat* (4/4):

Wesley's finest organ work is the extended *Andante in F major,* published in his *First Set of Three Pieces for a Chamber Organ* (1842), which the late G. M. Garrett considered to be a complete illustration of the composer's extraordinary technical skill as a player. 'It demands,' he says, 'clear, crisp, part-playing; the power of changing the position of the hand instantaneously and with certainty; and a touch of the closest and smoothest character. These were among Wesley's most notable qualities as a performer.'[3] It is written in the Romantic and pianistic style of Mendelssohn, whose influence has been seen elsewhere in Wesley's organ variations, *Holsworthy Church Bells* (1874).

Samuel Wesley's devotion to Bach's music certainly influenced the taste of his son Samuel Sebastian, who liked to include one of Bach's *Forty-eight Preludes and Fugues* in his organ recital programmes. And his pedantic *Introduction and Fugue in C sharp minor* (1836) is reminiscent of the Master, as also the final bars of the majestic *Andante in E flat* (2/4) with their strong affinity with the conclusion of Bach's *Prelude in E flat*:

Nor must be forgotten his interesting organ reharmonisations of hymn-tunes with interludes between the verses, entitled *A Selection of Psalm Tunes No. 1* (1838). A second volume was announced but never published. In his Preface to the second edition, dated July 1842, Wesley maintained:

> Whether an organ be a good one of its kind, or otherwise, we all feel how important it is, that, in playing chords, the hands should not be crowded with notes. In writing for the organ, as for the orchestra, there appears a like necessity for attaining clearness and distinctness in the division of the harmonies, of not doubling certain notes, and of spreading out the sounds which compose a chord at distant intervals. Perhaps it may not be too much to assert, that some of the most beautiful effects in the organ music of Bach, as in the orchestral writings of Spohr, arise from the clear and distinct mode of writing of these exquisite composers, who, though no doubt very different *men* in this respect, seem to advance a somewhat similar claim on our admiration. . . .
>
> To write in four or five *real parts* has not been the composer's present object. The counterpoint of English Psalmody is more simple than that of the German; it is indeed strictly simple; and real part-writing appears less essential in simple than in florid counterpoint. In this work, the object has rather been to put down each chord in a somewhat clear and orchestral position, and in a manner suited to the character of our smaller English instruments.

And in a footnote, Wesley draws attention to the freshness of Maurice Greene's church music, and particularly to the boldness of William Boyce's subjects — comparable to the best specimens of Handel, e.g. his anthem *Turn thee unto me*. And he also mentions the slow Fugue in E major, printed in Bach's *Forty-eight Preludes and Fugues*. Here is part of Wesley's interlude, based upon the well-known 'St Anne' tune and written in the best style of the Master:

THE CATHEDRAL SERVICE IN E

Written for the choir of Leeds Parish Church and published in 1845, this work is a masterpiece. For it marks the watershed in English church music between the settings of Henry Purcell and those of Stanford. Wesley's setting of the *Te Deum* is very much ceremonial music for a civic occasion. Both remote keys and exciting modulations were his basic tools in writing creative music for the liturgy, where cohesion is achieved through the utilisation of similar themes. And yet, this caustic review appeared in a London newspaper:

> Whatever in this composition is new is not good, and whatever is good has been heard before in a better form and in better company.... We rather think the composition was originally written in *E flat*, and transposed into *E natural*, which makes the harmonies somewhat fresher and more novel.[4]

Whether the music had been heard before or not, there is no means of knowing. But Wesley did use the music of 'The Father of an infinite Majesty' for the final section of his anthem, *Praise the Lord, my soul.* Notice how the fine slow movement in the key of A flat has been composed in the stately style of Boyce.

In the *Jubilate* Wesley has double-pedalling, unusual for his times; and a vivacious *Gloria* in the style of Spohr extends to some forty bars of music. However, his true greatness as a church composer is to be seen in the *Credo,* where the flowing and independent accompaniment might have been written by Stanford himself! There are sumptuous chords for the words, 'God of God, Light of Light', a chromatic pedal part symbolizing Christ's sufferings and voices in monotone, emphasizing the mood of the doctrinal statements.

Certainly the tonal structure of the Evening Canticles has heightened the expressiveness of the text, where 'Abraham and his seed for ever' is one of the finest pasages that Wesley has ever written. And the musical phrase of 'world without end' is later borrowed for the words — 'Ye are the blessed of the Lord,' in the last part of his anthem *Ascribe unto the Lord*. Also J. W. Elliott (1833-1915) has plagiarised a few bars of the *Gloria* in his hymn-tune *Day of Rest* (bars 13-15).

His *Short Full Cathedral Service in F* (1869) remains a very useful setting for unaccompanied services. Its melodic lines have been judiciously moulded, so that both the chordal and contrapuntal sections are equally balanced. But it is not a parody of Samuel Wesley's one in the same key with its English cadences — much in evidence in his son's earliest published anthem, *O God whose nature* (revised in 1870).

THE ANTHEMS

Wesley comes very much into his own when composing verse-anthems for a special occasion, demanding professional singers and the acoustics of a large building. If his father liked to commence a choral work with a few bars of unison singing (*In Exitu Israel*), he similarly copied him in the youthful full anthem *Glory to God on high*:

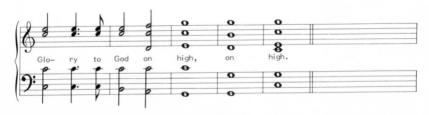

Wesley's wisdom in leaving the secular musical world of London for the more restrictive life of a provincial cathedral organist is questionable, to say the least. He very much disliked the musical isolation of Hereford, where he was coerced into playing the piano at local concerts: 'We got on tolerably well,' he once reported, 'but I hate playing the mountebank on these occasions.' One wonders, too, whether he had nursed second thoughts and had really wanted to return home where he would have been among professional musicians again.

It is significant that some of his finest music was composed in his early twenties, when the influences of his early musical life were still in his sub-conscious mind, thus producing such notable anthems as *The Wilderness* and *Blessed be the God*. And the Hereford congregation must have been stunned by the organ accompaniment of the former work, with its running pedal passages (revised in later editions) and its impressive chords (e.g. 'And a highway shall be there . . . the unclean shall not pass over it'). No wonder, with his feet so busily occupied, Wesley later added this note to an edition issued privately at Winchester: 'In places where the Pedals require two feet, it may be well to get an assistant to open and shut the Swell-box'! In both anthems, he has carefully selected the texts, having no doubt inherited his father's literary interests.

Blessed be the God and Father begins with a solemn unaccompanied choral passage, and the organ is only introduced during the last three bars to enhance the intensity of the phrase, 'Christ from the dead'. After the effective recitative sung by only the men's voices, the treble soloist takes over and leads into a mellifluous aria 'Love one another,' which is written in the romantic style of Spohr, but with the additional interest of a chromatic pedal accompaniment. Then a dramatic recitative ends with a sumptuous organ chord, 'But the word of the Lord'. Again the organ punctuates, but this time with six massive chords before the entry of the chorus that repeats the preceding music — followed by a lively fugato section with two stately Amens.

The Wilderness is one of Wesley's finest verse-anthems, portraying the telling message of the Prophet Isaiah. The first movement consists of a verse-section, sensitively written, describing a desert's being brought to life with joy and singing. The second movement begins with a magnificent bass aria, which has one of the most effective organ parts ever written. It is a *tour de force!* And it finishes on the bright chord of A major. Afterwards a short tenor recitative, portraying the miracle of a lame man's leaping as an hart, is followed by another verse-section culminating in the entry of the full choir with the words, 'For in the wilderness shall waters break out,' in which much use is made of sequential phrases and dischords in close texture — reminiscent of Bach's polyphony. Another dramatic recitative, 'And a highway shall be there,' is punctuated by massive enharmonic chords played by the organist, followed by a short verse-ensemble in a remote key. The third movement forms a spirited fugue in the classical style of his father's music, but culminating in a catenae of adventurous modulations in the Spohrish style at the close:

Finally, opinions differ as to the merits of the last section 'And sorrow, and sighing shall flee away,' although the composer intended the 'turns' in the treble part to be performed differently each time.

Before completing the Hereford period, we must look at Wesley's outstanding sacred song, *I have been young and now am old*, composed for the celebrated baritone Mr Henry Phillips (1801-76), which was first performed at the Three Choirs Festival of 1834. Its symphonic style of orchestral accompaniment is full of dramatic intensity, and yet, there are sensitive passages of a pastoral nature for the woodwind. Here is the theme of the first movement (Moderato) that is first given to the oboes and then taken up by the opening bars of the song:

The second movement is reflective, forming an instruction on Christian conduct. Here is a typical passage:

And the final movement is exuberant, especially its punctuating solo cornet — proclaiming the joy of God's salvation:

O Lord, Thou art my God is Wesley's longest verse-anthem, which he submitted for his doctorate exercise at Oxford in 1839. As Dannreuther says, 'The sheer musical invention is that of a virile genius who knows his J. S. Bach not only contrapuntally but emotionally, and loves him,'[5] but it is my belief that Samuel Wesley's massive contrapuntal music was the greater influence.

It is interesting to find sixteen bars of organ introduction, unusual for Wesley, as he normally improvised leads into his anthems. The first movement is written in the broadly eighteenth-century style of Battishill, with sections for *cantoris* and *decani* singers, and with an impressive passage where both choirs sing fortissimo 'Thou art my God'. The second movement contains a flowing bass aria, with a florid passage at the words 'Holy Name', and the third movement has a robust double chorus, 'He will swallow up death in victory.' The organ part is particularly interesting, for there is a quotation from *The Wilderness* at the entry — 'the rebuke of his people,' as well as clusters of semiquavers giving additional brilliance to the words — 'for the Lord hath spoken it.'

The fourth movement 'For this immortal must put on immortality' takes the form of a minuet with its dotted rhythm reminiscent of Maurice Greene's *Thou visitest the earth,* and it is sometimes sung separately. And the final double chorus might have been composed by William Croft, with its scintillating treble part proclaiming God's forgiveness. Moreover the music is coloured by Wesley's great love of diatonic dissonance, especially in the repeated phrases, 'He will save us.' No wonder Dannreuther declared that this anthem 'should be studied and recognized as masterly wherever the English language is spoken.'

Wesley regarded the publication of his *Twelve Anthems* (1853) as an important event, since he maintained: 'I think they may claim notice for the manner in which the words are expressed and for the new use made of broad massive harmony combined with serious devotional effects.' In the latter remark it is worthwhile stating Dannreuther's opinion, that 'Wesley's way of expressing religious emotion appears more individual than either Spohr's or Mendelssohn's, and it is for that very reason better worth hearing.'[6]

Ascribe unto the Lord was written for a missionary service in Winchester Cathedral, between 1849 and 1853. It is a *tour de force,* even more so if one hears the orchestral version that Wesley made for the Gloucester Festival of 1865. An impressive drum-roll introduces the entry of the recitative sung by the men's voices, in which great care has been taken over the accentuation of the text. And towards the end of the first section, a climax is achieved in 'O worship the Lord' by the use of a remote key, but the music eventually returns to a G major chord at the close. A mocking fugato section 'As for the gods of the heathen' follows, ending with a chromatic scale in the bass part. The composer obviously intended the first five bars of the passage 'Their idols are silver and gold' to be unaccompanied. The dramatic entry of the chorale 'As for our God' is fortissimo, and in many ways it is similar to Bach's harmonization of 'Break forth, O beauteous heavenly light' in his *Christmas Oratorio.* The final movement 'The Lord hath been mindful' begins with the warm tone of the 'cellos in the accompaniment and finishes with the sumptuous sound of both the brass and drums!

O give thanks has the appearance of three separate choral works put together to form an extended verse-anthem. In fact the last movement was set to a Latin text (*Ave Maria*) in 1880. After an exciting first movement there is a flowing treble aria, 'Who can express' with its bold melodic phrases often based upon rising arpeggios, like 'All nations whom Thou hast made . . . and glorify Thy name'. This Wesleyan trait is similarly found at the beginning of *Blessed be the God,* as well as in a later phrase 'But the word of the Lord'. Also identical phrases are repeated from other works; here are two instances:

Man that is born of a woman is a full anthem. It is a setting of some words from the Anglican Burial Service and intended to be sung before Purcell's anthem, *Thou knowest, Lord, the secrets of our hearts.* Wesley's masterly skill of conveying intense pathos by means of sequential phrases is evident in his setting of the phrase, 'full of misery' that is similar to the phrase, 'never shall die' in Croft's anthem, *I am the Resurrection.* Also compare the suspensions in the passage, 'deliver us not into' with Purcell's setting of the words, 'for any pains of death.'

In one of his essays, the late H. C. Colles maintained that Wesley saw in the cathedral service the means of contemplating in terms of art the deepest emotions and the highest aspirations of humanity. Certainly all the powers of Wesley's creative mind and artistic skill were focused in his penitential, if not self-reflective, anthems: *Cast me not away* (1848), written in the *cappella* style with its poignant discords at the end; and also *Wash me throughly* (1853) with its arched sequences and bold fugato passage, 'for I acknowledge my faults.' Here is one example of how Wesley achieves tension in the section, 'And forgive me all my sin':

Also appearing in his volume of *Twelve Anthems* are *Thou wilt keep him in perfect peace* and *Let us lift up our heart*. The former anthem was intended to be sung after the Third Collect at Evensong and contains many examples of the use of suspensions; and notice how Wesley has borrowed bars 18-20 from *Ascribe unto the Lord* for the musical phrase, 'Whose mind is stayed on Thee.'

Let us lift up our heart is written in the cantata style. Its extended first movement begins with a chorus for double choir — particularly notice the accentuation of 'doubtless Thou art our Father' that ends in the bright key of A major. The next section has a beautiful melodic phrase, 'be not very sore, O Lord' followed by detached chords in 'Behold, see, see, we beseech Thee'. It continues with a flowing fugato passage, 'Oh that Thou would'st rend the heavens' — unfortunately interrupted by too many Spohrish chords. And the movement ends with a chorus, where there is used chromatic writing in the accompaniment and strident melodic phrases in the choral parts of 'Thy Name is from everlasting.'

The second movement has one of Wesley's finest bass arias, 'Thou, O Lord God'. The emotional intensity of its text is enhanced by the enharmonic texture of the organ part, as well as by the opening theme in B minor being finally repeated in C major. The short third movement forms a chorale which is set to words from Charles Wesley's hymn, 'Thou Judge of quick and dead.' And the last movement consists of a fugato chorus that ends quietly with the words 'everlasting rest.'

All go unto one place was 'composed on the lamented death of the Prince Consort' in 1861. Notice the majestic introduction, the flowing crotchets in the extensive tenor passage, and the dramatic rhythm of 'an house not made with hands,' ending on the chord of C major.

Another anthem, *Praise the Lord, my soul* was written in the same year to celebrate the opening of the new organ in Holy Trinity Church, Winchester. As usual, Wesley begins with the men's voices in unison which is followed by ensemble sections in the verse-anthem style. Notice how the immense power of 'the Lord sustained me' quickly diminishes to a pianissimo in the sequential passages 'O hearken Thou' and 'My King and my God', in order to introduce the reflective verse 'Early in the morning will I direct my prayer unto Thee.' And the movement finishes with the repetition of the bold introductory theme of 'Praise the Lord, my soul.'

The second movement has the lyrical treble solo, 'My voice shalt Thou hear betimes, O Lord,' which is taken over by the other voices. After a section for double choir, there comes the emphatic plea of 'give ear, hearken Thou' that is followed by a diminuendo and the reticent affirmation of 'my King, my God'. And the third movement takes the form of a chorale, thus preparing for the transition to the well-known music of 'Lead me, Lord.'

In celebration of the Prince of Wales's Wedding in 1863, Wesley composed his finest extended anthem, *Give the King Thy judgments*. If its contrapuntal brilliance was due to his father's earlier influence, then its chromatic expressiveness was truly original. Nowhere else, apart from *The Wilderness,* has the organ been given such an important part in emphasizing the changing moods of the text. And in his frequent use of punctuating organ flourishes, Wesley had become a true forerunner of Parry who once sat next to the composer on the organ-stool, during his schooldays in Winchester. Here is a quotation showing the lyrical nature of the treble part with its sequential phrases:

The European Psalmist (1872)

In many ways this Collection of some 600 hymn-tunes was a complete failure on account of its pedestrianism and unsuitability for parish use; and yet it remains a treasure house of tunes for the hymnologist.

Since Wesley has given many incorrect names to the tunes that are derived from either places he visited or from his gazetteer (e.g. Ath, Bromberg, Fürth, Passau, Plock, Prum, Thorn, St Trond and Usedom), it is necessary to undertake considerable detective work. And besides, there is the mysterious composer 'Andreas Cnophius', who is named as the creator of the pseudo-tunes *Belfont* (133) and *Goldberg* (154); whereas, in fact, they are derived from the chorale *Herr Christ der ein'ge Gottes-Sohn* (Bach's Cantata No. 96). If the source of the tune *Penitence* (176) is indeed the sixteenth-century anthem, 'Lord, for thy tender mercy's sake,' Wesley's tune *Sparsholt* (161) unashamedly borrows several bars of music from *Abridge* (151).

Furthermore, there is the curious sub-section of anonymous tunes (461-487) having Swiss place-names, like Basel, Berne, Büren, Elgg, Giornico, Lucerne, Lugano, Martigny, Steckborn, Schwyz, St Bernard, Thun, Zug and the gastronomic Gruyere! On the one hand there is a suspicion that these unsingable tunes may have been composed by either Wesley's wife or his sister Eliza. And on the other, such a theory is immediately discounted if the following remarks in a letter to his proof-reader were true: 'There is *one* tune by a living writer. I don't care for such stuff as I see nowadays. *Nothing great now.*'[7] That tune is *Lucknow* (450), composed in 1856 by Kendrick Pyne's father, who was organist of Bath Abbey. *The European Psalmist* is divided into four sections.

The first section (1-269) contains music set to familiar psalm-tune metres: Long Metre (1-84), Common Metre (85-240), and Short Metre (241-269). These tunes are almost all derived from Scottish, English and Welsh sources, e.g. *Abridge, Bristol, Caithness, Cheshire, Darwall's 148th, Dundee, Egham* (a magnificent discovery), *Martyrdom, Old 100th, Rockingham, St Bride, St James, St Mary, Song 67, Surrey, Tallis's Ordinal, Wareham, Windsor, Winchester Old* and *York.* There are also three tunes by his father Samuel Wesley (*Bethlehem, Bristol* and *Gilgal*), a tune by his uncle Charles Wesley (*Berkshire*), and some twenty tunes by the editor himself, including *Dinmore* (set to 'O God, unseen, yet ever near'), *Hampton* (on which Sir Hubert Parry later based an organ prelude), *Hereford* (set to the metrical version of Psalm 103, 'The Lord abounds with tender love' — Hymns Ancient and Modern (1904 edition) was the first hymnal to marry this tune to Charles Wesley's well-known ordination hymn, 'O Thou, who camest from above,' but the last line must read — 'And make my sacrifice complete'), *Holsworthy, Morning Hymn* (set to 'New every morning is the love'), and *Wensley* (set to Bishop Ken's Evening Hymn for the boys of Winchester College in 1674).

The second section (270-414) has many chorales from Lutheran sources, together with tunes from other traditions to give further interest. Wesley's preoccupation with the former tunes was stimulated by his examination of Miss Catherine Winkworth's *Chorale Book for England* (1863). Unfortunately the chorales in *The European Psalmist* have been given spurious names, again selected from Wesley's gazetteer, e.g. *Augsburg* (Allein Gott in der Höh sei Ehr), *Coburg* (Ein' feste Burg), *Hamburg* (Vater unser im Himmelreich), *Luther's Hymn* (Nun freut euch), *Marck* (Nun danket alle Gott), *Varel* (Watchet auf!), and *Weimar* (Schmücke dich).

Wesley's love of Bach harmonizations is truly evident in his accurate reproduction of the chorales from Bach's 371 Harmonized Chorales, St Matthew Passion and Christmas Oratorio, e.g. the three versions of *Herzliebster Jesu* (325, 330, 394), *Innsbruck* (312), *Passion Chorale* (393), *Wir Christenleut* (334), and *Ermuntre dich* (360).

The tunes in the second section from other sources include the *Old 104th*, *Adeste Fideles* ('Portuguese Tune'), *Sicilian Mariners* (306), Arne's florid *St Martin* (316), Spohr's stately *Berlin* (414), Boyce's *Chapel Royal* (346) and *Halton Holgate* (281), set to 'Bright the vision' and similar in style to Wesley's *Hereford*. And the editor's contribution — an arrangement of *Reliance* (356), set to his favourite hymn, 'Abide with me'; and his ten tunes including *Alleluia* (392), *Harewood* (410), set to his grandfather's 'Rejoice, the Lord is King!, *Leintwardine* (270), and his striking tune *Wrestling Jacob* (401), also set to his grandfather's 'Come, O Thou Traveller unknown'.

The third section (415-615) has over a hundred tunes by the editor, undoubtedly inspired or more likely aggravated by the new tunes of his contemporaries, J. B. Dykes and W. H. Monk, which had been published in Hymns Ancient and Modern (1868 edition). Here is a list of Wesley's better tunes, in which can be noticed the powerful harmonic pattern of *Bath New* (460), the influence of the chorale tune *Vater unser im Himmelreich* in *Brecknock* (517), set to John Wesley's superb translation, 'Thou hidden love of God'; the powerful texture of *Cornwall* (441), set to Charles Wesley's 'O love divine'; the intense chromaticism of *Dies Irae* (547); the part-song idiom of *Epiphany* (528), set to Bishop Heber's popular words, 'Brightest and best'; the fascinating cadences of *Gweedore* (530), now happily set to Charles Wesley's 'Author of life divine'; the chromatic bass-line of *Kerry* (500), set to 'Sun of my soul'; the sequential phrases in the third line of *Mara* (554), still requiring suitable words; the orchestral idiom of the second version of *Orisons* (540), set to 'Abide with me'; the anthem-style of *Triumph* (573); and the effective pictorialism of *Wigan* (430), set to Matthew Bridges's 'Behold the Lamb of God!', as well as *Whitby* (610), set to the stirring words, 'Fierced raged the tempest'.

In this third section, Wesley has frequently borrowed ideas from other composer's tunes, whenever inspiration failed him. For example, the third and fourth phrases of *Aurelia* (451) — Wesley's only tune to have been published in Hymns Ancient and Modern in 1868, are derived from J. M. Haydn's *Calcutta* (435):

Compare the ending of *Bury* (424) with that of Monk's *Nutfield*, particularly as both tunes are set to the hymn, 'God that madest earth and heaven' —

And *Bedminster* (432) is similar to Bishop Jenner's *Quam dilecta*, for both tunes are set to the hymn, 'We love the place, O God' —

Also compare *Dover* (423) with the ending of Dykes's *St Cuthbert* (both set to 'Our blest Redeemer'); and likewise the last line of Smart's *Pilgrims* with *Eden* (527), the tune that Wesley wrote for his godson Ernest Wesley Pyne —

167

Not only has Wesley borrowed the fourth line of his tune *Harewood* (410) in the second line of *Arran* (532), but he has also quoted from his anthem, 'Lead me, Lord' in the tune *Epworth* (558) —

Finally, compare the following phrases of Stainer's *Sebaste* with the ending of *Gilboa* (574) —

The fourth section (616-733) contains useful music for parish church choirs by the editor and his father. There are four settings of the *Kyrie* and the *Sanctus,* countless Anglican single and double chants, an introit and six short anthems, besides S. S. Wesley's *Benedicite* and Chant Service in G.

Dr Wesley's compositions are rightly placed in the Romantic period of English music. As a composer, when Victorian church music was abysmally dull, his anthems set a standard for the professional giants who followed in the English Renaissance. His clarion call for definite reforms within the Cathedral system has at last come to fruition in the founding of both the Royal School of Church Music and the College of Preachers in London, but sadly all too late for him to see. And he would have rejoiced to find so many eminent musicians in the organ-lofts of our cathedrals and city churches. Wesley, indeed, bestrode the insular world of Victorian church music like a Colossus, and it is sad to recall that his great crusade was so misunderstood by the ecclesiastics he had come to serve.

CHAPTER ELEVEN

List of Compositions, Musical Sources and Printed Editions

Key: B.L. = British Library, R.C.M. = Royal College of Music.

ANTHEMS

All go unto one place
> 'composed on the deeply lamented death of His Royal Highness the Prince Consort' in 1861. Published by Hall, Virtue & Co. (1861) and Novello, Ewer & Co. (before May 1868). Modern edition edited by Sir Walter Alcock (Novello, 1908).

Ascribe unto the Lord
> composed for a Missionary Service in Winchester Cathedral, between 1849 and 1853. MSS. *R.C.M. 4034*, ff.1-54 (including the full orchestral score made for the Gloucester Festival of 1865). Published in 1853.† Another edition by Novello, Ewer & Co. (1874).

At Thy right hand
> a short chorus, published in *The European Psalmist* (1872), No. 725.

Ave Maria
> published in *Cantica Sion,* or English Anthems set to Latin words, No. 5 (Novello, 1880). This music also forms the final section of the anthem, 'O give thanks'.

Blessed be the God and Father
> composed by request of the Dean for Easter Day, 1834, in Hereford Cathedral, 'on which occasion only Trebles and a single Bass voice were available.' Incomplete MS. can be seen in the Hereford Cathedral Muniment Room (dated 1834). Published in 1853.† Further editions by Hall, Virtue & Co., and Novello, Ewer & Co.

Blessed be the Lord God of Israel
> composed for Christmas Day (1868) and published by Novello, Ewer & Co.(1868). Also see *The Musical Times Supplement* No. 310 (1884).

Blessed is the man
> Introit for Men's Voices, published in *The European Psalmist*, No. 729. MS. *B.L. Add. 40636*, ff.1-2.

By the waters of Babylon
> two versions, either for Soprano or Alto Voices, MS. *B.L. Add. 40636*, ff.70-72.

By the word of the Lord
> composed for the opening of the organ in Winchester Cathedral in 1854. MS. (voice parts only) *R.C.M. 4030*, ff.81-95.

Cast me not away from Thy presence
> composed at The Black Swan, Helmsley, in 1848. Published in 1853.† Another edition by Novello, Ewer & Co. (March 1870).

Give the King Thy judgments, O God
> 'composed for the occasion of the Marriage of H.R.H. The Prince of Wales' (1863). MS. *R.C.M. 4032*, ff.12-23. Published by Novello, Ewer & Co. (March 1870).

Glory to God on high
> MS. *R.C.M. 4030*, ff.95-101. Two versions for eight or four voices.

Gloria in excelsis
> incomplete version for four parts with orchestral accompaniment. MS. *R.C.M. 4030*, ff.78-80. Also a different setting, dedicated to Willingham Fowler Esq., and published as an anthem by Novello, Ewer & Co. Dr Garrett later included it in his edition of Wesley's Communion Service in E (Novello, 1896).

God be merciful unto us
> composed for a Marriage Service in 1867. MS. *B.L. Add. 40636*, ff.58-64. Published by Novello, Ewer & Co. (January 1872).

I am Thine, O save me
> composed for the first issue of a monthly magazine, *The Musical Remembrancer* (March, 1857) and a revised edition (Novello, Ewer & Co., 1870) was dedicated to Linnington Ash, Esq., M.D. Modern edition by Watkins Shaw, published by Novello (1976).

I will arise

composed in 1869 and published in *The European Psalmist,* No. 724. MS. *B.L. Add. 40636,* ff.5-7. Novello, Ewer & Co. (1874).

Let us lift up our heart

published in 1853.† The organ accompaniment was scored for orchestra by Sir Edward Elgar and had its first performance at the Worcester Festival (September 6, 1923). Modern edition by Sir Edward Bairstow was published in 1914 by Bayley & Ferguson (*Choral Album* No. 1181).

Let us now praise famous men

composed in 1873 for Commemoration Day, at the request of Mr. W. F. Trimnell, who was the first Director of Music at Clifton College. It was thought too difficult, and therefore Wesley was asked to submit a simpler version which was published in Novello's *Collegiate Series* No. 14 (1874), and first performed in 1877. The first version was published by Novello, Ewer & Co. (1876).

Lord of all power and might

composed in 1873. MS. *B.L. Add. 40636,* ff.12-13. Modern edition: *Four Short Anthems* No. 3, published by Bayley & Ferguson (1928).

Man that is born of a woman

published in 1853.† Another edition by Novello, Ewer & Co. (1870).

My soul hath waited

composed after 1874 and dedicated to his son, 'F. G. Wesley, Durham.' MS. *B.L. Add. 40636,* ff.24-32.

O give thanks

published in 1853 (see note on *Ave Maria*).† Also see Novello's *Collection of Anthems* Vol. III, No. 66 (1872).

O God, whose nature

published about 1831. MS. can be seen in the Hereford Cathedral Muniment Room (dated 1834). In 1870 the composer made a final revision (Novello, Ewer & Co.) which he dedicated 'to the Rev. G. W. Thornton, M.A., Rector of Holsworthy, Devon.' Modern edition: *The Musical Times Supplement,* No. 770 (April, 1907).

O how amiable

published in Novello's *Collegiate Series* No. 18 (1874). Modern edition by J. E. West, published by H. W. Gray: New York (1929).

O Lord, my God (Solomon's Prayer)

published in 1853.† Also by Hall, Virtue & Co., and Novello & Co. *Musical Times Supplement* No. 314 (April, 1869).

O Lord, Thou art my God
>composed about 1836, later submitted for his doctorate exercise at Oxford and sung in Magdalen Chapel (June, 1839). Published in 1853.† Another edition by Novello, Ewer & Co. (1870).

Peace, troubled soul
>short chorus composed in 1869 and published in *The European Psalmist*, No. 727.

Praise the Lord, my soul
>composed for the opening of the organ in Holy Trinity Church, Winchester, on September 10, 1861. See Novello's *Collection of Anthems* Vol. III, No. 59 (1872). Modern edition by C. Hylton Stewart, published by Bayley & Ferguson (1926).

Sacred Songs: The Collects in Verse for the First Three Sundays in Advent:
>Almighty God, O give us grace (Treble)
>Most blessed Lord (Treble)
>Lord Jesu Christ (Bass)
>published in 1851. Modern edition by Sir Frederick Bridge (Novello, 1908).

The Face of the Lord
>published in 1853.† Another edition by Novello, Ewer & Co. (1870).

The Hundredth Psalm
>'Arranged for, and sung at the Ceremony of Laying the Foundation Stone of Netley Hospital, Hants, by Her Most Gracious Majesty, The Queen' (May 19, 1856). Published by Novello & Co. *R.C.M. LXXI.E.13(22).*

The Lord is my shepherd
>published in Novello's *Collegiate Series* No. 40 (1875). Also modern edition issued by Novello & Co. (1934).

The Lord will give grace
>composed for W. F. Trimnell, Walton Lodge, Clifton, who was one of Wesley's former pupils. MS. *B.L. Add. 40636*. ff.34-36.

The Wilderness and the Solitary Place
>composed for the re-opening of the organ in Hereford Cathedral on November 6, 1832. Complete organ score MS. can be seen in the Cathedral Muniment Room (dated 1834). Other MSS. *R.C.M. 1065*, ff.174-96, as well as full orchestral versions made for the Birmingham Festival (1852): *R.C.M. 4030*, ff.1-21 and *4120*. The first printed edition was advertised in *The Musical World* (October 15, 1840). Another edition was published in Wesley's *Twelve Anthems* (1853).†

And the final edition was dated 'Gloster, May 14, 71'. Novello, Ewer & Co. (1874).

Thou, O Lord God
A sketch for a solo. MS. *R.C.M. 4030,* ff.105-06.

Thou wilt keep him in perfect peace
published in 1853.† Second edition published by Hall, Virtue & Co. Also see Novello's *Collection of Anthems* Vol. V, No. 107 (1874).

Tho' round Thy radiant throne on high
for solo, duet, and chorus in unison. MS. *B.L. Add. 35039,* ff.68-9.

Three Introits
   i.   I will wash my hands in innocency, O Lord
   ii. Blessed is the man that feareth the Lord
   iii. Hear Thou in heaven Thy dwelling-place
composed about 1842. Modern edition published by Novello & Co. (1906).

To my request and earnest cry
composed in 1844. MS. *B.L. Add. 40636,* ff.14-17. Modern edition by Sir Edward Bairstow, printed in *The Musical Times Supplement* No. 758 (April, 1906).

Trust ye in the Lord
a sketch for chorus with organ accompaniment. MS. *R.C.M. 4030,* ff.102-04.

Wash me throughly from my wickedness
published in 1853.† Also see Novello's *Collection of Anthems* Vol. IX, No. 186 (1876).

Wherewithal shall a young man cleanse his way
MS. *B.L. Add. 40636,* ff.18-23. Published in Novello's *Collegiate Series* No. 19 (1875).

---

†*Anthems* by Samuel Sebastian Wesley
Vol. 1. Published in London: Addison & Hollier, 210 Regent Street, and Novello, Dean Street, Soho, & Broadway, New York (1853).

Also the following

Agnus Dei
composed in 1837 for soprano solo with organ, or orchestral, accompaniment. MS. *B.L. Add. 40636,* ff.44-57.

Benedictus qui venit
>composed in 1832 for solo voices with orchestral, or piano, accompaniment. MSS. *R.C.M. 4030,* ff.67-77 and ff.55-65.

He is coming
>a Carol, composed in 1874. MS. *B.L. Add. 40636,* f.43.

Rock of ages
>composed in 1832, for chorus with organ accompaniment. MS. *B.L. Add. 40636,* f.39.

Sanctus
>composed for the Hereford Festival (1834). MS. *B.L. Add. 40636,* ff.65-66.

ANGLICAN CHANTS, PSALTERS, AND HYMN TUNES

A Collection of Chants
>arranged for the Psalter throughout the Month, with some additional Chants. Incomplete, probably arranged by S. S. Wesley. MS. *R.C.M. 4035,* ff.1-36.

Chants for Four Voices
>by S. S. Wesley. MS. *R.C.M. 674.*

The European Psalmist
>Single and Double Chants, see pp.500-28.

The Psalter, with Chants
>First edition published in Leeds by T. W. Green (1843); and a second edition published in Leeds by T. W. Green and also in London by Rivington, Hamilton, Adams & Co. (1846).

A Selection of Psalms and Hymns
>arranged by the Reverend Charles Kemble, M.A., Rector of Bath. Musical editor: S. S. Wesley. Published in London by John F. Shaw & Co. (1864 and 1866).

The European Psalmist
>A Collection of Hymn Tunes, Chants. An Easy Service, Short Anthems, etc. edited and revised, and much of the music composed by Samuel Sebastian Wesley, Mus. Doc. Dedicated by permission to Her Majesty The Queen. Published in London: Novello & Co.; Boosey & Co.; Hamilton, Adams & Co. (1872).

The Welburn Appendix
>of Original Hymns and Tunes by the Reverend James Gabb. Musical editor: S. S. Wesley, Esq., Mus. Doc. Published by Novello & Co. (1875).

Collection of Hymn Tunes
> compiled by Mrs Marianne Wesley in 1879, 'to the loved memory of one whose preferences have chiefly guided this collection from his father's hymn tunes,' S.S.W. MS. *R.C.M. 4036*, ff.1-54.

Hymn for Christmas
> set to words, 'O come, loud anthems let us sing,' and composed in 1870. MS. *B.L.Add. 40636*, f.42.

Hymn for all Nations
> set to words by M. F. Tupper, with music specially commissioned for the Great Exhibition (1851). MS. *R.C.M. 4038*, f.127. Published in London by T. Hatchard (1851).

SERVICES

A Morning [Communion] and Evening Cathedral Service in E
> composed at Leeds and published, together with Wesley's Preface, by Chappell, Music-seller to Her Majesty (1845). Price 15s. Modern edition by Dr G. M. Garrett was published by Novello, Ewer & Co. (1896). Also of the Evening Service: Church Music Society (1975).

A Short Full Cathedral Service in F
> first published in 1869. MS. can be seen in the Hereford Cathedral Muniment Room. A modern edition was issued by Novello, Ewer & Co. (1900).

A Short Chant Service in F
> first published by Arthur Hall, Virtue & Co., London (1855), who issued a second edition in 1860. An arrangement of the Evening Service for Treble voices by Dr H. G. Ley was published by Oxford University Press (1932). [Another *Chant Service in F* was published by Novello, Ewer & Co. in 1869].

A Short Chant Service in G
> first published in *The European Psalmist* (1872), Nos. 730-733.

Benedicite, omnia opera
> A Chant setting composed for *The European Psalmist*, No. 728. Reprinted by Novello, Ewer & Co. (1887).

OTHER CHORAL WORKS

The Ode to Labour
> composed for the opening of the North London Working Men's Industrial Exhibition in the Agricultural Hall, Islington, on October

17, 1864. MS. *R.C.M. 4039*, ff.29-81. Published by the composer in 1875. Price 7s. 6d. The words are by W. H. Bellamy. *B.L. H.1779*.

The Praise of Music
> an unaccompanied double chorus composed for the 4th Concert of the Royal Albert Hall Choral Society on July 10, 1872, at the request of the conductor, Charles Gounod. It is set to an Ode by Thomas Oliphant (*d.* 1879). MS. *R.C.M. 4039*, ff.82-110. Published by Goddard & Co., London. Second edition printed by Novello in *The Collegiate Series* No. 2 (1874), and a third one by Stainton de B. Taylor. See Hinrichsen Edition: No. 623 (1961).

SACRED and SECULAR SONGS

Abraham's Offering
> a sacred song, with orchestral accompaniment, composed for the baritone Mr Henry Phillips, which was first performed at the Hereford Festival (1834). Full Score: MS. *R.C.M. 4030*, ff.42-51.

Arising from the deep
> a part-song published in Novello's *Collegiate Series,* No. 6 (1874).

At that dread hour (Faith)
> a glee set to words by William Linley, which was composed in 1832 and awarded a prize by the Gentlemen's Glee Club of Manchester. Published by D'Almaine & Co., London (1834) and also in Novello's *The Orpheus* (New Series) No. 284 (1879).

Blessed are the dead
> a song set to Lord Byron's poem 'Heaven and Earth', and published by Mori & Lavenu before 1839.

By the rivers of Babylon
> a song set to words by Lord Byron, and published by Novello & Co.

Did I possess the magic art
> a song set to a ballad by Rogers, and published by Mori & Lavenu before 1839.

For Charity's sake
> a song composed for fêtes in aid of the Liverpool Hospitals, with words by M. F. Tupper, and published by James Smith of Liverpool (1860).

I have been young and now am old
> a sacred song, with orchestral accompaniment, composed for Mr Henry Phillips who gave the first performance at the Hereford Festival (1834). Full Score: MS. *R.C.M. 4030*, ff.22-41.

I wish to tune my quiv'ring lyre

a glee set to words by Lord Byron, which was awarded a prize by the Gentlemen's Glee Club of Manchester in 1833. Published by D'Almaine & Co. (*c.* 1840), and also in Novello's *The Orpheus* (New Series) Vol. VI, No. 168 (1879).

Millions of spiritual creatures

a work for solo voices and chorus, with orchestral accompaniment, which is a setting of part of Milton's 'Paradise Lost'. The first performance was given at the Gloucester Festival (1835). Full Score: MS. *R.C.M. 4030*, ff.52-66.

O when do I wish for thee

a song composed in 1835. Also arranged for piano solo by H. J. Bertini, and published by J. Dean & Co.

Ophan hours the year is dead

a song set to a poem by Shelley. MS. *B.L. Add. 40636*, ff.78-79. First published by Cramer & Co., and also by Novello, Ewer & Co. between 1867 and 1872.

Shall I tell you whom I love?

a part-song set to words by Browne, with 'cello and piano accompaniment, and published by Chappell & Co., etc., after 1861. See also Novello's *Part-Song Book* (Second Series) Vol. XV, No. 421 (1869).

Silently, silently

a song for soprano solo and set to words by W. H. Bellamy. It forms part of Wesley's *Ode to Labour* (1864). Instrumental version: MS. *B.L. Add. 40636*, ff.83-84. Published for the composer by Cramer & Co., between 1864 and 1872.

Strong in hand and strong in heart

a song for tenor solo from Wesley's *Ode to Labour* (1864).

The Bruised Reed

a sacred song for soprano solo, with piano or organ accompaniment, and set to words by W. H. Bellamy. It was composed on March 6, 1834, and first performed at the Hereford Festival of that year. MS. *R.C.M. 4038*, ff.73-74. Published in C.D.Hackett's *National Psalmist* (1839). Modern edition issued by Stainer & Bell: Galaxy (1974).

The Butterfly

a song set to words by Lady Flora Hastings, and published by J. B. Cramer & Co. between 1872 and 1876.

The Mermaid

a part-song composed in 1873, set to words by C. A. Burroughs, and published in Novello's *Collegiate Series* No. 3 (1874).

The Smiling Spring
> a song set to Monsieur De Beranger's ballad 'Maudit Printemps', and dedicated to Henry Mullinex, Esq. MS. *B.L. Add. 40636*, ff.80-82. Published by J. Dean & Co. between 1831 and 1837.

There be none of beauty's daughters
> a song set to words by Lord Byron, with orchestral accompaniment, and dedicated to William Knyvett before 1856. Full Score: MS. *R.C.M. 4032*, ff.1-11. First published by Addison, Hollier & Lucas, and also by Novello, Ewer & Co.

There breathes a living fragrance
> a song for soprano solo with piano accompaniment, composed in 1833. MS. *B.L. Add. 40636*, ff.73-75.

Young Bacchus in his lusty prime
> composed for solo voice and chorus with orchestral accompaniment. 'A very young production. S.S.W.' Full Score: MS. *R.C.M. 4031*, ff.10-19.

Wert thou like me in life's low vale
> set to Sir Walter Scott's poem, 'The Legend of Montrose', with piano accompaniment (dated December 29, 1832). MSS. *B.L. Add. 40636*, ff.85-86; and *R.C.M. 4031*, ff.6-7. Published by Novello, Ewer & Co.

When fierce conflicting passions rend the breast
> a glee set to words by Lord Byron, and published in Novello's *The Orpheus* (New Series) No. 275 (1879).

When from the Great Creator's hand
> composed for bass solo from Wesley's *Ode to Labour* (1864).

When we two parted
> set to words by Lord Byron. MS. *B.L. Add. 40636*, ff.87-88.

You told me once
> a ballad set to music by 'S. Wesley, Junior' and published by William Hawes, about 1830.

PIANO WORKS

Air with variations, in E
> composed about 1830 and dedicated to his piano teacher, J. B. Cramer.

Dances
> MS. *R.C.M. 4031*, ff.5, 32.

Introduction and Rondo

    based on an Air from Spohr's opera 'Azor and Zemira', dedicated to Mrs Hawes and published by W. Hawes, about 1830.

Jeux d'esprit: Quadrilles

    composed in the style of Heinrich Herz (*d.* 1888) and dedicated to Mrs Martin Cawood, who lived in Leeds. Published by Chappell & Co.(1846).

March and Rondo

    composed in 1842, and published by J. B. Cramer & Co.

Piano Solo and Presto

    composed in 1834. MS. *R.C.M. 4038*, f.72.

Rondo in G

    published by Mori & Lavenu, before 1839.

Waltz

    published in a musical journal *The Harmonicon* (September, 1830) Vol. 8, Pt. 2, pp.366-67. Modern edition arranged by Jack Werner, and published by J. B. Cramer & Co. in *Newly Discovered Classics for Piano* No. 5 (1942).

ORGAN WORKS

A Studio for the Organ

    Dedicated to Vincent Novello, Esq. (London: J. Dean, 148 New Bond Street, 1836). Another edition was issued in 1869.

    No. 1 *Introduction and Fugue in C sharp minor*. No further pieces were published in this series.

    Modern editions:

    (a)   edited by Dr G. M. Garrett, who gives two versions of the *Introduction*: Novello, Ewer & Co. (1893-1900).

    (b)   edited by Henry G. Ley, published in Novello's *Original Compositions* (New Series) No. 231 (1952).

A First Set of Three Pieces for a Chamber organ:

    i.   *Andante in E flat (4/4).*

    ii.   *Andante in F.*

    iii.   *Choral Song [and Fugue].*

followed by

A Second Set of Three Pieces

    i.   *Andante in G (3/4).*

    ii.   *Larghetto, with variations, in F sharp minor.*

    iii.   *Andante in E flat (2/4).*

These Six Pieces are respectfully dedicated to Wesley's former organ pupil Lady Acland (*d.* 1856), of Killerton Park, near Exeter. They were originally published in two small oblong books in 1842. A second edition was issued by Novello, Ewer & Co., between 1867 and 1876.

Modern editions:
(a)   edited by Dr G. M. Garrett: Novello, Ewer & Co. (1893-1900).
(b)   edited by E. H. Thorne, *S. S. Wesley Six Organ Pieces*: Bayley & Ferguson, Glasgow.

A Selection of Psalm Tunes
'adapted expressly to the English Organ with Pedals,' and published in two books (1838). A second edition, with a Preface, printed and sold by R. Cocks & Co., London (1842).
Modern edition by Dr G. M. Garrett was issued by Novello, Ewer & Co., between 1893-1900. There are also fascinating interludes.

A Voluntary: Grave and Andante
published in the *Organist's Quarterly Journal*. Also modern edition by Dr G. M. Garrett — *Original Compositions for the Organ* No. 97: Novello, Ewer & Co. (1887).

An Air, with variations, composed for Holsworthy Church Bells
composed about 1874. MS. *B.L. Add. 40636*, ff.110-113.
Modern editions:
(a)   edited by Dr. G. M. Garrett: Novello, Ewer & Co. (1893-1900).
(b)   edited by H. A. Chambers: Novello & Co. (1947).

Andante in A major
published posthumously by Novello, Ewer & Co., 1877. 'Dr Wesley wrote it as an intentioned paraphrase of the Second Movement (Larghetto) of Beethoven's Symphony No. 2 in D major' (*The Musical Times* Vol. XIX, January 1878, p.36). MSS. *B.L. Add. 40636*, ff.90-96 (Full Score), and ff.97-102 (Manuals only).

Andante in C major
MS. *B.L. Add. 40636*, ff.123-124. Modern edition by John E. West — *Original Compositions for the Organ* No. 15: Novello, Ewer & Co. (1893-1900).

Andante in E minor
published posthumously by Novello, Ewer & Co. (1877). It contains a direct quotation from Wesley's anthem 'Wash me thoroughly.' MSS. *B.L. Add. 40636*, ff.103-106 (Complete Full Score), and ff.107-109 (Rough draft).
Modern editions:
(a)   edited by Dr G. M. Garrett: Novello, Ewer & Co. (1893-1900).
(b)   edited by Stainton de B. Taylor: Hinrichsen Edition No. 541b (1958).

Fantasia: Andante Cantabile in G major (4/4)

'as performed by the composer at the Agricultural Hall,' Islington, on November 3, 1863, 'to mark the inauguration of the Grand Organ built by Willis for the International Exhibition' (*B.L. Add. 35020*, f.75). But the first performance was given during the Birmingham Festival (1849); and it was also included in Wesley's programme for his opening recital on the new Willis instrument in St George's Hall, Liverpool, on September 18, 1855. Published by Virtue & Co., London. Modern editions:

(a)   edited by Dr G. M. Garrett: Novello, Ewer & Co. (1893-1900).
(b)   edited by Stainton de B. Taylor: Hinrichsen, Edition No. 541c (1957).

Larghetto in F minor

composed between 1835 and 1845. See MS. *B.L. Add. 40636*, ff.121-122. An edition, edited by the Rev. F. G. Wesley, was published by Novello, Ewer & Co., in 1893.

Meditation: Andante in C major

Modern edition edited by J. E. West: *Musical News* Office, London (1909).
See *Royal Academy of Music Library No. 065424.*

The National Anthem, with variations

first performance by the youthful composer took place in St Mary Redcliffe, Bristol, in October 1829. Modern edition edited by Dr G. M. Garrett, published in *Original Compositions for the Organ by S. S. Wesley*: Novello, Ewer & Co. (1893-1900).

ORCHESTRAL WORKS

March

Full Score: MS. *R.C.M. 4031*, ff.8-9.

Orchestral Piece

not in autograph, but discovered among the composer's papers. Full Score: MS. *R.C.M. 4031*, ff.20-31.

Symphony in C major

in autograph. Full Score: MSS. *R.C.M. 4033*, ff.1-61; also see *4039*, ff.1-28.

ARRANGEMENTS

Air and variations by L. A. Kozeluch
    arranged for the organ by S. S. Wesley, who played the work on the new Willis instrument in St George's-in-the-East, on June 26, 1852. MS. *R.C.M. 4031*, ff.33-34.

Ten Songs by Mozart
    arranged for the piano by S. S. Wesley, Mus. Doc., and published in *Chappell's Musical Magazine* No. 4 (London, 1861).

Thou, O God, art praised in Sion
    an anthem by Samuel Wesley arranged by Samuel Sebastian Wesley. First published by Novello and Virtue (1861-67). Also see Novello's *Collection of Anthems* Vol. III, No. 62 (1876).

Additional Notes

In view of the comprehensiveness of the following notes it seems unnecessary to compile a separate bibliography. What may be useful, however, is a brief description of the manuscript sources and particular articles on which this biography has been based.

Bliss Corespondence Vol. VII (1839-40), in the British Library (Add. 34573).

Dr S. S. Wesley Compositions, bequeathed in 1920 by his son, the Reverend F. G. Wesley, to the Royal College of Music (MSS. 4025-4120).

Edwards Papers Vol. XIII, presented to the British Library (Egerton 3097).

Gloucestershire Collection (Gloucester Public Library).

Letters and Musical Sketches of Musicians Vols. 2 and 3 (The Royal College of Music Library).

Letters from Samuel Wesley to Vincent Novello (1811-25), presented to the British Library (Add. 11729,11730).

Minutes from the Chapter Act Books and Archives (Exeter, Gloucester, Hereford and Winchester Cathedrals).

Miscellany (1939), including the Letters to the Reverend W. E. Dickson, Precentor of Ely Cathedral (1860-62), presented to the British Library (Add. 45498).

Musical Remains of Dr Wesley, presented by William Barclay Squire, Esq., to the British Library (Add. 40636).

Private Correspondence, in the possession of Sir Thomas Armstrong, Sir John Dykes Bower, and the Reverend A. D. Parkes.

S. S. Wesley Letters (1824-76) and *Collections relating to S. S. Wesley,* bequeathed in 1895 by his sister Eliza Wesley to the British Library (Add. 35019, 35020).

Sowerbutts Collection (The Royal College of Organists).

SPECIAL ARTICLES

'Samuel Wesley, 1766-1837' by Gerald W. Spink (*The Musical Times,* October, 1937).

'S. S. Wesley's Organ Compositions' by Dr G. M. Garrett (*The Musical Times,* July, 1894).

'Wesleyana' by J. Kendrick Pyne (*The Musical Times,* June, 1899).

'Samuel Sebastian Wesley' by F. G. Edwards (*The Musical Times,* May-July, 1900).

'Samuel Sebastian Wesley. Sketch of the Life of the Great Composer: Winchester Memories' by an anonymous writer (*Hampshire Observer,* 5 February, 1910).

'Samuel Sebastian Wesley: A Biography' by Gerald W. Spink (*The Musical Times,* January-June, 1937).

'Samuel Sebastian Wesley and the European Psalmist (1872)' by Erik Routley (*The Hymn Society Bulletin* Vol. VII, No. 126, January, 1973).

'Samuel Sebastian Wesley' by Watkins Shaw (*English Church Music,* 1976).

'The achievement of S. S. Wesley' by Watkins Shaw (*The Musical Times,* April, 1976).

Notes to Pages 1-4

NOTES TO CHAPTER ONE

1. John Wesley's Preface to *The Sunday Service of the Methodists of North America* (1784).
2. *The Letters of the Reverend John Wesley,* edited by John Telford (The Epworth Press, 1931) Vol. 3, pp.226-228.
3. Frederick Gill, *Charles Wesley: The First Methodist* (Lutterworth Press, 1964), p.100.
4. *Ibid.* p.48.

5. *Ibid.* p.71.
6. *B.L. Add. 27593,* f.6.
7. *Ibid.* ff.6, 33.
8. *B.L. Add. 35012,* ff.63-64.
9. *B.L. Add. 11729,* f.86.
10. *Ibid.* f.59.
11. *The Bach Letters to Benjamin Jacobs,* edited by Eliza Wesley (1875). Letter XIII (Hinrichsen Edition, Peters Edition Limited, 1957), pp.33-34.
12. *B.L. Add. 11729,* f.79.
13. *Ibid.* f.41.
14. *Ibid.* f.283.
15. *B.L. Add. 27593.*
16. Consult Hans F. Redlich's article, 'The Bach Revival in England: 1750-1850' (*Hinrichsen Music Book* Vol. VII, 1952).
17. *The Bach Letters* No. XI, p.29.
18. Further information on Samuel Wesley can be found in the following books:
James T. Lightwood, *Samuel Wesley, Musician* (The Epworth Press, 1937).
Erik Routley, *The Musical Wesleys* (Herbert Jenkins, 1968).
Francis Routh, *Early English Organ Music From The Middle Ages To 1837* (Barrie & Jenkins, 1973).

NOTES TO CHAPTER TWO

1. James Lightwood, *Samuel Wesley,* p.90.
2. *B.L. Add. 35012,* f.44r. 'July 6, 1813'.
3. *Ibid.* f.46.
4. *Ibid.* f.49.
5. *B.L. Add. 11729,* f.146.
6. *Robert Glenn Wesley* (d. 1844) was the Music Master at Christ's Hospital. Although there is no evidence in the records of that Charity to prove Sammy's attendance, it seems likely he went to the Bluecoat School, without wearing the uniform, at the age of six years (*Exeter and Plymouth Gazette,* April 28, 1876).
7. John S. Bumpus, *A History of English Cathedral Music: 1549-1889* (T. Werner Laurie, 1908) Vol. 2, pp.478-479.
8. *The Musical Times,* February, 1898, p.82.
9. *The Morning Post,* March 17, 1823.
10. *B.L. Add. 35019,* f.8.
11. *The Morning Post,* December 30, 1823.
12. *B.L. Add. 35019,* f.187.
13. *Ibid.* ff.4-5.
14. *B.L. Add. 35012,* ff.109-110, Underneath 'Old Sam' has drawn a characteristic sketch of 'Fishy and his Kite'.
15. Maria Hackett, *Correspondence and Evidence respecting the Ancient Collegiate School attached to Saint Paul's Cathedral* (1832), p.2.
16. *B.L. Add. 11729.*
17. *Ibid.* f.235.
18. *B.L. Add. 11729,* f.277.

19. *B.L. Add.* 35020, f.6.
20. *B.L. Add. 35019*, f.130.
21. *Ibid.* f.131.
22. Modern hymn books have renamed them: *Cannons, Fitzwilliam,* and *Gopsal.*
23. *B.L. Add. 35012*, ff.63-64.
24. *Dorset Archive Office.*
25. *B.L. Add. 35012*, f.69.
26. *B.L. Add. 35019*, f.133.
27. *B.L. Add. 35012*, f.77.
28. *Ibid.* f.79.
29. James Lightwood, *Samuel Wesley*, p.213.
30. *B.L. Add. 35012*, f.78.
31. *Bristol Gazette*, October 8, 1829.
32. A modern edition was edited by G. M. Garrett (Novello, 1893-1900). 'Old Sam' also wrote a set of Eight Variations on a similar theme in December, 1817. *B.L. Add. 34089.*
33. *B.L. Add. 35007.*
34. *B.L. Add. 14344*, ff.39r-52r. A modern edition of the former work has been edited by Walter Emery (Novello, 1964).
35. *B.L. Add. 35012*, ff.87r-88.
36. *Ibid.* f.73r.
37. *B.L. Add. 35019*, f.183.
38. *Ibid.* f.185.
39. *The Musical Times*, May, 1900, p.298.
40. *Ibid.* p.299.
41. *B.L. Add. 35012*, f.106r.
42. *R.C.M. MS. 4030.*
43. *R.C.M. MS. 4031.*
44. William Hawes's *Anthems and other Sacred Music, as performed in the Chapel Royal* (1831).

NOTES TO CHAPTER THREE

1. *Chapter Act Book: 1814-1834*, pp.355-356.
2. *Ibid.* p.365.
3. The earliest-known organ at Hereford Cathedral was built by Renatus Harris in 1686, from which instrument some pipes remain to-day. Also in the same year, George Dallam added the 'Chaire Organ'. Additional work was later done by Snetzler, Green, Avery and Lincoln. In 1806 Elliott added pedals and pedal-pipes (*viz.* Henry Willis's article in *The Rotunda*, Vol. 5, 1933-34, pp.1-9).
4. *Chapter Act Book*: 1814-1834, p.372.
5. *Ibid.* p.383.
6. *Ibid.* pp.381-382.
7. *The Parish Choir*, Vol. 3, p.31.
8. *B.L. Add. 35019*, ff.6-7.
9. *Hereford Cathedral Muniment Room.*
10. *Hereford Journal*, November 7, 1832.
11. William Crotch, *Lectures on Music* (Longman, 1831), p.73.
12. *B.L. Add. 35019*, ff.12-13.

13. A copy of the organ part of Samuel Wesley's Morning and Evening Service in F, which is in his son's autograph and dated 1835, can be seen in the Hereford Cathedral Muniment Room.
14. *B.L. Add. 35019*, ff.10-11.
15. *Ibid.* ff.14-15.
16. *Ibid.* f.176.
17. John Bumpus, *A History of English Cathedral Music: 1549-1889* Vol. 2, p.370.
18. *Ibid.*
19. *The Musical Times*, October, 1907, p.799.
20. *English Church Music* Vol. 5 No. 1, 1935, p.4.
21. John Bumpus, *A History of English Cathedral Music: 1549-1889* Vol. 2, pp.374-75.
22. *The Musical Times*, June, 1895, p.407.
23. *Chapter Act Book: 1814-1834*, p.394.
24. *Ibid.* p.454.
25. *Cathedral Archives.*
26. *B.L. Add. 35019*, ff.16-17.
27. *Ibid.* ff.18-19.
28. *Hereford Times*, Saturday, September 13, 1834.
29. *B.L. Add. 40636*, ff.7, 65-66.
30. *R.C.M. MS. 4030*, ff.42-51.
31. *Hereford Times.*
32. Daniel Lysons, *Origin and Progress of the Meeting of the Three Choirs* (Revised edition, 1895), p.124.
33. *B.L. Add. 35019*, f.20.
34. 'Old Sam' took part in concerts there, in 1811, when he played the organ in St Philip's Church and the piano in the King's theatre for performances of the *Creation* and *Messiah*. 'Mr Wesley presided at the organ with very distinguished ability; his concerto and antiphona evinced alike his genius and his science.'
35. *B.L. Add. 35019*, ff.22-23.
36. He was the great-grandson of John Merewether (1655-1724), who lived in Devizes and attended Bishop Ken during his last illness. His daughter later married a grandson of Izaak Walton.
37. *R.C.M. MS. 4038*, ff.1-71.
38. *R.C.M. MS. 4036*, ff.1-54.
39. *Chapter Act Book: 1834-1844*, p.32.

NOTES TO CHAPTER FOUR

1. *Cathedral Archives 7061.*
2. *Ibid.*
3. *Chapter Act Book: 1832-1838.*
4. *Cathedral Archives 7061.*
5. Betty Matthews, *The Organs and Organists of Exeter Cathedral* gives the specification.
6. *The Musical Times.* June, 1899, p.379.

7. *B.L. Add. 31764*, f.32.
8. *B.L. Add. 34573*, f.25.
9. *Ibid.* f.35.
10. *Ibid.* f.41.
11. *Oxford University City and County Herald,* June 22, 1839.
12. *R.C.M. MS. 3052.*
13. *B.L. Add. 11730*, ff.225-226.
14. *Clara Anastasia Novello* (1818-1908) was the daughter of Vincent Novello and a celebrated soprano.
15. *B.L. Add. 11730*, f.227.
16. *The Musical World,* May 13, 1836, pp.143-144; also consult W. T. Best's letter published in *The Musical Times,* October 14, 1892, p.374.
17. Dr William Spark, *Musical Memories* (Swan Sonnenschein, 1888), p.36.
18. *B.L.* f.345: Dr S. S. Wesley: *Original Compositions for the Organ,* edited by Dr G. M. Garrett (Novello, Ewer & Co., 1893-1900).
19. *A Selection of Psalm Tunes* (R. Cocks & Co., London, 1842).
20. *B.L. Add. 35019*, f.24.
21. *Chapter Act Book: 1838-42.* (Item 3582.)
22. *Cathedral Archives 7061.*
23. Consult *Memoir & Letters of the Rt Hon Sir Thomas Dyke Acland,* edited by his son Arthur H. D. Acland (London, 1902).
24. R.C.M. MS. 2141: 'Memoranda, accounts, etc. S.S.W.' (1836).
25. *The Sowerbutts Collection.*
26. *Chapter Act Book: 1838-1842* (Item 3582).
27. *Cathedral Archives 7061.*
28. *Ibid.*
29. *Ibid.*
30. *Ibid.*
31. *Ibid.*
32. *Ibid.*
33. *R.C.M. MS. 3053.*
34. *Ecclesiastical Law* (1957), p.177, footnote.
35. *Chapter Act Book: 1838-1842* (Item 3582).
36. William Spark, *Musical Memories,* pp.83-86.
37. *B.L. Add. 35020.*
38. *The Leeds Intelligencer,* October 23, 1841.
39. William Spark, *Musical Reminiscences: Past and Present* (Simpkin, Marshall, Hamilton, Kent & Co. Ltd., 1892), p.166.
40. W. R. W. Stephens, *Life and Letters of Walter Farquhar Hook* (London: Richard Bentley & Son, 1878) Vol. 2, p.135.
41. *Chapter Act Book: 1838-42.*
42. B.L. Add. 35020, f.3r.
43. *Ibid.* f.4r.
44. *Cathedral Archives 7061.*
45. *Ibid.*
46. *Ibid.*
47. *Ibid.*

NOTES TO CHAPTER FIVE

1. W. R. W. Stephens, *Life and Letters of Dean Hook* (1878), Vol. 1, pp.369-370.
2. *Ibid.* Vol. 2, p.172.
3. From an anonymous report, signed 'Anglicus' and dated 1849, which was published in *The Parish Choir* Vol. 3, pp.148-149.
4. *The Choral Service* (John Parker, 1843), p.513.
5. *Life and Letters of Dean Hook* Vol. 2, pp.132-133.
6. *Ibid.* p.124.
7. *Ibid.* p.334.
8. *Ibid.* p.93.
9. *Ibid.* p.137.
10. Dr William Spark, *Musical Reminiscences*, p.64.
11. *Ibid.* p.166-167.
12. *The Parish Choir* Vol. 1, p.26 (The monthly magazine of the Society for Promoting Church Music: February 1846—March 1851).
13. *The Ecclesiologist* Vol. 5, p.173 (The journal of the Cambridge Camden Society: 1841-68).
14. *The Parish Choir* Vol. 3, p.149.
15. *The Musical Examiner*, September 30, 1843.
16. *The Choral Service*, p.305.
17. *B.L. 1220.*
18. *B.L. 1236.*
19. *R.C.M. MS. 4001.*
20. *B.L. Add. 35020,* f.3.
21. *Ibid.* f.3.
22. *Ibid.* f.5.
23. Dr William Spark, *Musical Memories*, p.91.
24. London: Chappell, Music Seller to Her Majesty, 50 New Bond Street. Price 15s.
25. *B.L. Add. 11730,* f.227.
26. The Preface to Wesley's *Morning and Evening Cathedral Service*, p.iii.
27. *Ibid.* p.iv.
28. *Ibid.* pp.iv-v.
29. *Leeds Parish Church Records.*
30. *Leeds Public Library F784.*
31. *Heinrich Herz* (1803-88) was a popular composer and pianist, who later established a piano factory in Paris.
32. *Viz.* Frank Kidson's article, 'Homes of Past Leeds Celebrities': No. 4 'Genteel Districts of An Earlier Day' (*The Yorkshire Evening Post*, October 2, 1919).
33. *Kellow John Pye* (1812-1901) was born in Exeter and entered the Royal Academy of Music in 1823, when he received the first piano lesson there and studied composition under Dr William Crotch. In 1832 he gained the Gresham Prize medal for his anthem, 'Turn Thee again, O Lord' (Novello). He later gave up his musical career and entered the wine merchant's business of Plasket & Company.
34. *The Plymouth Weekly Journal*, June 25, 1846.

35. *Ibid.* July 2, 1846.
36. *The Leeds Mercury and Intelligencer,* July 17, 1852.
37. *The Times,* July 16, 1852.
38. *R.C.M. MS. 3066.*
39. Dr John Bishop's lecture, 'A frustrated revolutionary: H. J. Gauntlett and the Victorian Organ', given at the R.C.O. in November, 1971.
40. *B.L. Add. 35019,* f.137 [1847].
41. *B.L. Add. 35020,* f.4.
42. *B.L. Add. 35019,* f.189-191.
43. *Ibid.* ff.139-140.
44. *Ibid.* ff.192-194.
45. *Ibid.* ff.202-205.
46. *Ibid.* f.26.
47. *Ibid.* f.195.
48. *Ibid.* f.198.
49. *B.L. Add. 35020,* f.5.
50. *Ibid.* f.4.
51. *Ibid.* f.4.
52. *B.L. Add. 35019,* f.27.
53. *The Dykes Bower Collection.*
54. Published simultaneously in London and Leeds. A modern facsimile edition is published by Hinrichsen Edition, Peters Edition Ltd., No. 1961b (1965).
55. Dean Stanley's *Life and Correspondence of Dr Arnold* (London, 1844), p.182.
56. *A Few Words on Cathedral Music,* p.12.
57. *The Choral Service of the United Church of England and Ireland* (London: John W. Parker, 1843), pp.131-132.
58. Dr G. L. Prestige, *St Paul's In All Its Glory* (S.P.C.K., 1955), p.20.
59. The Cathedrals' Measure abolished freeholds in 1931.
60. F. E. Gretton, *Memory's Harkback: 1808-1858* (London, 1889), p.4.
61. *Ibid.* p.8.
62. *Chapter Act Book*: January 2, 1847.
63. *A Few Words on Cathedral Music,* p.9.
64. *Ibid.* pp.10-11.
65. *Ibid.* pp.11-12.
66. *Ibid.* pp.33-34.
67. Frederick Helmore, *Memoir of the Reverend T. Helmore* (Masters, 1891), p.88.
68. *A Few Words on Cathedral Music,* p.49.
69. *Ibid.* p.52.
70. *Ibid.* p.41.
71. *The Musical World,* September 8, 1849, p.567.
72. William Spark, *Musical Memories,* p.89.
73. *Ibid.* pp.93-95.
74. *Ibid.* pp.100-101.
75. *Royal School of Church Music MS.*
76. *R.C.M. MS. 4040.*
77. *The Leeds Intelligencer,* February 16, 1850.

NOTES TO CHAPTER SIX

1. *R.C.M. MS. 3063.*
2. *Chapter Act Book: 1824-50,* pp.430-431.
3. *Ibid.* p.432.
4. *The Musical Times,* February, 1850.
5. *B.L. Add. 35019,* ff.142-143.
6. *The Minutes of the Committee of Management* (The Royal Academy of Music Library).
7. Alan Rannie, *The Story of Music at Winchester College: 1394-1969* (P. & G. Wells Ltd.), p.29.
8. *Ibid.* p.30.
9. *Ibid.* p.26.
10. Dr W. A. Fearon, *The Passing of Old Winchester* (Warren & Son Ltd., Winchester 1924), pp.81-83.
11. C. A. E. Moberly, *Dulce Domum* (John Murray, 1911), p.119.
12. *Ibid.* pp.134-135.
13. *Chapter Act Book: 1824-50,* p.442.
14. *Ibid.* p.446.
15. *Chapter Act Book: 1850-76,* p.20.
16. *Ibid.* p.34.
17. *B.L. Add. 35019,* ff.145-146.
18. *The Musical Times,* May, 1898, pp.299-300.
19. *Ibid.*
20. *R.C.M. MS. 4031.*
21. *Modern edition,* edited by H. A. Chambers (Novello, 1947).
22. *Modern edition,* edited by P. F. Williams (Hinrichsen, 1961).
23. *R.C.M. MS. 4120.*
24. *The Musical World,* September 1852, p.620.
25. *Ibid.* October, 1852, p.680.
26. *Exeter Cathedral Library MS. 7061.*
27. *Ibid.*
28. *Ibid.*
29. *B.L. Add. 35019,* ff.177-178.
30. *B.L. H 900.*
31. *The Musical Times,* June, 1899, p.378.
32. *Ibid.* June, 1900, p.374.
33. *B.L. Add. 35019,* ff.124-125.
34. *Chapter Act Book: 1850-76,* p.52.
35. *Ibid.* p.55.
36. *Ibid.* p.58.
37. *The Musical Times,* July, 1900, pp.452-453.
38. *B.L. 3477.*
39. *Ibid.* p.5.
40. *Ibid.* p.6.
41. *Ibid.* p.7.
42. *Ibid.* pp.7-8.
43. *Ibid.* pp.15-16.

44. *Leeds Mercury,* November 15, 1856. Wesley's answer is printed in *The Leeds Intelligencer,* February 7, 1857.

45. *Sir John Dykes Bower Collection.*

46. *The Musical Times,* September, 1907, p.596.

47. *Modern edition,* edition by Stainton de B. Taylor (Hinrichsen, 1957).

48. *Chapter Act Book: 1850-1876,* p.61.

49. *Ibid.* p.70.

50. *Ibid.* p.132.

51. *R.C.M. MS. 3074.*

52. J. N. Dalton, *Manuscripts of St George's Chapel* (1957), p.462.

53. *Durham Chapter Act Book: 1847-1856,* dated November 20, 1855.

54. *B.L. Add. 45498,* f.102.

55. *Ibid.* f.105.

56. *Ibid.* f.101.

57. *B.L. Add. 35019,* ff.208-209, dated February 22, 1856.

58. *Ibid.* f.149.

59. J. R. Sterndale Bennett, *The Life of William Sterndale Bennett* (Cambridge University Press, 1907), pp.254-255.

60. *B.L. Add. 35019,* f.211.

61. *Sir John Dykes Bower Collection.*

62. *B.L. Add. 35019,* f.152. William Knyvett (b. 1779) died in Ryde on November 2, 1856. He was principal alto at the London concerts for some forty years. He was a Lay Vicar of Westminster Abbey, and was appointed one of the Composers to the Chapel Royal in 1802.

63. *Sir John Dykes Bower Collection.*

64. *Ibid.*

65. *Chapter Act Book: 1850-1876,* pp.147-148.

66. *Ibid.*

67. *Ibid.* p.151.

68. *Née* Maria Billington Hawes (1816-1886) sang the Aria, 'O rest in the Lord' in the first performance of the *Elijah* at the Birmingham Festival of 1846.

69. *Sowerbutts Collection.*

70. *Ibid.*

71. *Henry Wray* was the author of an interesting, unpublished diary which describes the contemporary events of the Choir. See Winchester Cathedral MS. *De Precentore* (1863).

72. *Chapter Act Book: 1850-1876,* pp.169-170.

73. *Ibid.* p.187.

74. *Modern edition,* edited by C. Hylton Stewart (Bayley & Ferguson, 1926).

75. *The Hampshire Chronicle,* September 14, 1861.

76. Kendrick Pyne's article, 'Wesleyana' (*The Musical Times,* June, 1899, p.380).

77. *B.L. Add. 35019,* ff.159-160.

78. *The Rev. David Parkes Collection.*

79. *Ibid.*

80. *Ibid.*

81. *Theodore Edward Aylward* (1844-1933) held several organist appointments, including Llandaff Cathedral (1870), Chichester Cathedral (1876), St Andrew's Church and the Public Hall, Cardiff (1886). He was the musical editor of the *Sarum Hymnal* (1870).

82. *The Musical Times*, May, 1937, p.432.
83. *Chapter Act Book: 1850-1876*, pp.196-197.
84. *Ibid.* p.216.
85. *The Musical Times*, May, 1937, p.438.
86. *The Manchester Guardian*, September 8, 1927.
87. *The Musical Times*, October, 1908, pp.636-641.
88. *Ernest Wesley Pyne* became an organist and orchestral conductor. He died on June 17, 1895.
89. *European Psalmist* No. 527.
90. *The Musical Times, June, 1899, pp.377-378.*
91. *The Rev. David Parkes Collection.*
92. *R.C.M. MS. 4032* (Autograph).
93. *B.L. Add. 35020*, f.75.
94. *English Church Music* Vol. V, No. 1 (1935), pp.5-6.
95. *Chapter Act Book: 1850-1876*, p.233.
96. *Ibid.* p.235.
97. *Hampshire Observer*, February 5, 1910, p.7.
98. *Chapter Act Book: 1850-1876*, p.243.
99. Lady Elvey, *Life and Reminiscences of George J. Elvey (London: Sampson Low, Marston & Co., 1894), pp.100-104.*
100. *The Musical Times*, July, 1898, pp.441-42.

NOTES TO CHAPTER SEVEN

1. *John Alexander Matthews* (1841-1925) was the organist of Cheltenham Parish Church (1866), and also the founder of the local Choral and Orchestral Society (1870).
2. *The Musical Times*, July, 1900, p.456.
3. *Gloucester Journal*, February 18, 1865.
4. *Chapter Act Book No. 7*, pp.84-85.
5. *Ibid.* p.170.
6. *R.C.M. MS.3076.*
7. *The Musical Times*, October, 1865.
8. *Gloucester Journal*, September 9, 1865, p.8.
9. *Annals of the Three Choirs* (1895), pp.231-233.
10. Joseph Bennett, *Forty Years of Music: 1865-1905* (Methuen, 1908), p.35.
11. Charles Graves, *Hubert Parry* (Macmillan, 1926) Vol. 1, pp.56-57.
12. *R.C.M. MS. 2141.*
13. Sir Herbert Brewer, *Memories of Choirs and Cloisters* (The Bodley Head Press, 1931), pp.84-86.
14. *Ibid.* p.86.
15. Charles Graves, *Hubert Parry* Vol. 1, pp.59-60.
16. *B.L. Add. 35019*, f.38.
17. *B.L. Add. 35020*, f.13 (possibly *The Morning Post*).
18. Charles Graves, *Hubert Parry* Vol. 1, p.73.
19. *The Musical Times*, October, 1908, p.637.
20. *R.C.M. MS. 4041.*
21. *The Musical Times*, February, 1898, pp.83-84.
22. *Ibid.* October, 1908, p.638.

23. Charles Graves, *Hubert Parry* Vol. 1, pp.102-103.
24. *Ibid.* p.104.
25. *Berrows' Worcester Journal*, September 12, 1868.
26. *The Musical Times*, July, 1900, p.456.
27. *B.L. Add. 35019*, f.165.
28. Joseph Bennett, *Forty Years of Music*, pp.43-44.
29. Sir Herbert Brewer, *Memories of Choirs and Cloisters*, pp.19-20.
30. *The Musical Times*, October, 1901, p.675.
31. *B.L. Add. 35019*, f.40-41.
32. *Ibid.* ff.43-44.
33. *Ibid.* ff.45-46.
34. *Ibid.* ff.49-52.
35. *Ibid.* f.53.
36. *Ibid.* ff.74-75.
37. *Ibid.* f.59.
38. *Ibid.* f.61.
39. *Ibid.* ff.77-78.
40. *Ibid.* f.79.
41. *Ibid.* f.81.
42. *Ibid.* f.85.
43. *Ibid.* f.91.
44. *The Musical Times*, May, 1937, pp.438-439.
45. *Ibid.*
46. *B.L. Add. 35019*, f.87.
47. Joseph Bennett, *Forty Years of Music*, pp.126-127.
48. *Gloucester City Library Archives.*
49. *B.L. Add. 35019*, ff.95-98.
50. *Ibid.* ff.167-168.
51. Sir Donald Tovey and Geoffrey Parratt, *Walter Parratt, Master of Music* (Oxford University Press, 1941), p.159.
52. *R.C.M. MS. 3077.*
53. *Ibid.* 3078.
54. *Ibid.* 3092.
55. *Ibid.* 3097.
56. *Gloucester Journal*, Saturday, September 8, 1871, p.7.
57. *Royal Academy of Music Archives.*
58. *Gloucester City Library Archives.*
59. *Sir John Dykes Bower Collection.*
60. *R.C.M. MS. 3055.*
61. *Ibid.* 3056.
62. *Ibid.* 3057, 3058.
63. *Ibid.* 3059.
64. *Modern edition*, edited by Stainton de B. Taylor (Hinrichsen Edition No. 623, 1960).
65. *B.L. Add. 35019*, f.172.
66. *Gloucester City Library Archives.*
67. *Devon and Exeter Gazette* (1910), quoted also in John Telford *Sayings and Portraits of Charles Wesley* (Epworth Press, 1927), p.195.

68. *R.C.M. MS. 3060* (translated).
69. *Gloucester City Library Archives.*
70. Quoted from Sir Donald Tovey and Geoffrey Parratt, *Walter Parratt*, p.158.
71. *Gloucester Journal*, September 12, 1874, p.8.
72. *The Lute* Vol. 3, No. 5, May, 1885.
73. Joseph Bennett, *Forty Years of Music*, pp. 36-39.
74. *B.L. Add. 35019*, f.107.
75. *Ibid.* f.109.
76. *The Annals of the Meeting of the Three Choirs* (1895) p.263.
77. *Berrows' Worcester Journal*, September 25, 1875, p.3.
78. *B.L. Add. 35020*, f.59 (transcript).
79. *B.L. Add. 35019*, ff.114-115.
80. *Ibid.* f.117.
81. *Ibid.* f.121.
82. *Ibid.* f.128.
83. *The Lute* Vol. 3, No. 5, May, 1885, p.98.
84. Joseph Bennett, *Forty Years of Music*, p.128.

NOTES TO CHAPTER EIGHT

1. *First edition* published in 1831, but revised in 1870 (consult *The Musical Times*, April, 1907).
2. *Modern edition*, edited by Watkins Shaw (Novello, 1976).
3. *Hereford Cathedral Archives.*
4. *B.L. Add. 40636*, ff.110-113.
5. *Ibid.* f.37.
6. *Royal College of Organists' Archives.*
All other quotations are from letters, now in the private possession of Sir Thomas Armstrong.

NOTES TO CHAPTER NINE

1. *B.L. Add. 35020*, f.32 (November 25, 1874).
2. *The Musical Musical Times*, June, 1899, p.380.
3. *B.L. Add. 35020, ff.53-54.*
4. *B.L. Add. 35019*, f.174.
5. *B.L. Add. 35020*, ff.25-26.
6. *Gloucester Journal*, April 29, 1876.
7. *The Oxford Book of Victorian Verse*, edited by Arthur Quiller-Couch (The Clarendon Press, 1919), pp.492-493.
8. *Sir Thomas Armstrong*, formerly organist of Exeter Cathedral and Principal of the Royal Academy of Music, won the competition in 1924, when he had to extemporize music to a film in the Strand Cinema. See Percy Scholes, *Mirror of Music* (Oxford University Press, 1947), Vol. 2, p.802.
9. *Hampshire Chronicle*, November 27, 1920.

NOTES TO CHAPTER TEN

1. Ernest Walker, *A History of Music in England* (Oxford University Press: Third edition, revised by Sir Jack Westrup, 1952), p.298.
2. *Sir John Dykes Bower's Collection.*
3. *The Musical Times* (July, 1894), p.448.
4. *The Morning Post,* February 26, 1844.
5. *The Oxford History of Music* (Clarendon Press, 1905), Vol. VI, p.290.
6. *Ibid.*
7. *R.C.M. MS. 3083.*

Index